EVERDARK CURSED

Published by Fairies and Fantasy Pty Ltd 2022
ISBN: 978-1-922390-47-9 (paperback)
ISBN: 978-1-922390-48-6 (hardcover)
Everdark Cursed (Beshadowed Book 4) copyright © 2022 Selina Fenech.
All rights reserved. www.selinafenech.com

www.selinafenech.com

EVERDARK CURSED

SELINA A. FENECH

BOOK FOUR OF

BESHADOWED

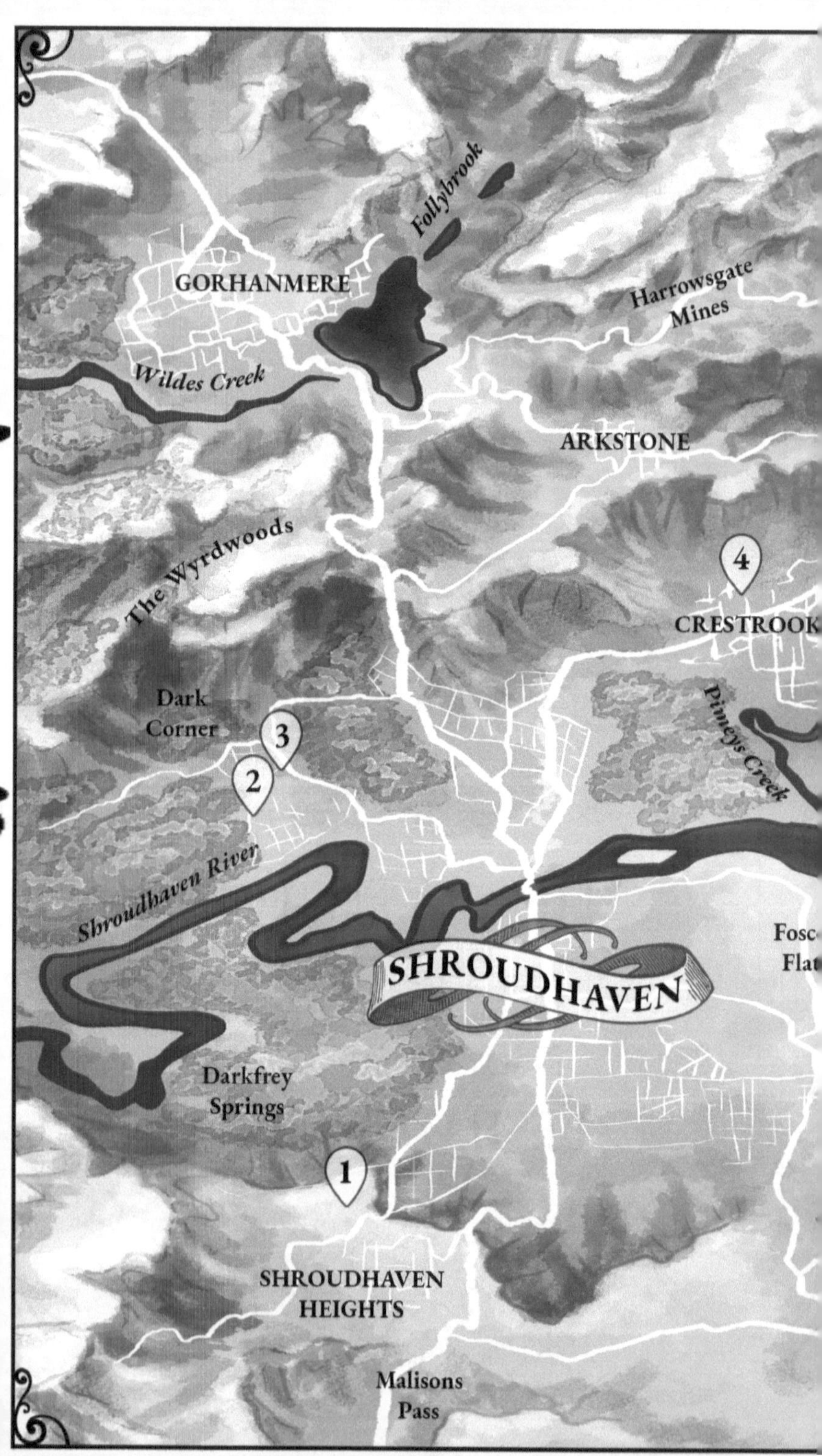

Follybrook
GORHANMERE
Harrowsgate
Mines
Wildes Creek
ARKSTONE
The Wyrdwoods
4
CRESTROOK
Dark
Corner
3
2
Pinney's Creek
Shroudhaven River
SHROUDHAVEN
Fosc
Flat
Darkfrey
Springs
1
SHROUDHAVEN
HEIGHTS
Malisons
Pass

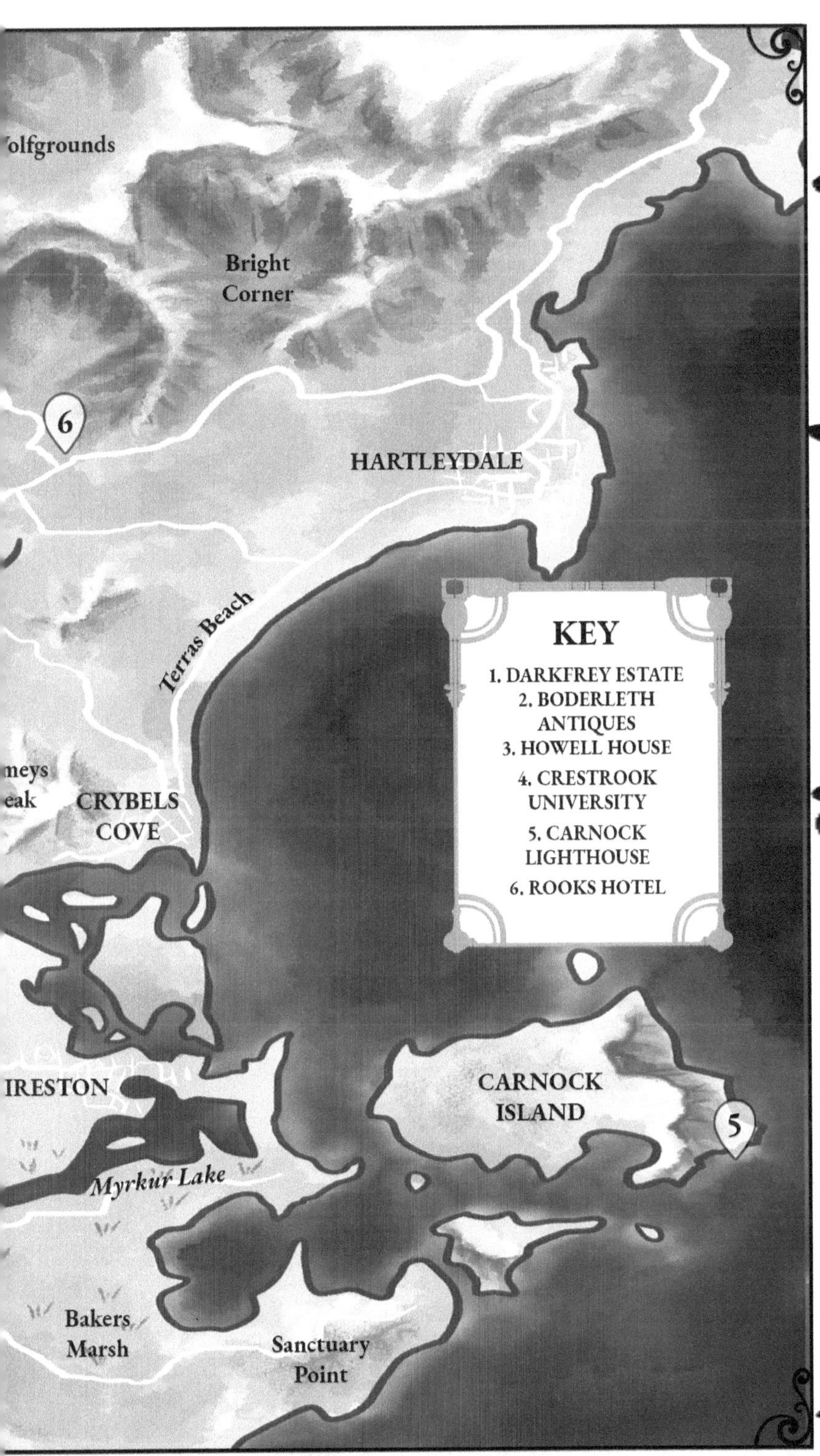

olfgrounds
Bright Corner
6
HARTLEYDALE
Terras Beach
meys
eak
CRYBELS COVE
KEY
1. DARKFREY ESTATE
2. BODERLETH ANTIQUES
3. HOWELL HOUSE
4. CRESTROOK UNIVERSITY
5. CARNOCK LIGHTHOUSE
6. ROOKS HOTEL
IRESTON
CARNOCK ISLAND
5
Myrkur Lake
Bakers Marsh
Sanctuary Point

CHAPTER ONE

How do you tell somebody that you enslaved their soul for the better part of fourteen years?

Everly had been mulling over that since she'd taken in the second piece of the Coruscare and learned more about the ancient god-like being inside her. About what it had done to Rylan. How it had influenced his feelings for her.

Dragging a bloodied and beaten-up man into Rylan's home probably wasn't the best way to lead into that discussion.

Everly had been making excuses all week, but this one felt legitimate. She adjusted her grip under Jasper's shoulder as she helped support him toward Howell House.

"Can we get some help out here?" Lian called from Jasper's other side.

The screen door swung open, and Rylan burst through.

His gaze went straight to Everly, passing over her body then up to her face.

His gravelly voice sounded dangerous. "What's happened?"

Cherry followed quickly after him, attention drawn straight to Jasper. His mouth dropped open, then his face closed into a cool glare.

He flicked his bright-red hair away from his eyes. "Did you guys do this for me ... because he betrayed me for the Bane? I mean, you didn't have to go to this extreme on my behalf, but I appreciate the gesture."

"It wasn't us," Tammy said from a couple steps back. "If it was, we'd have done a more thorough job. Maybe taken an ear as payback for stealing our property."

"She's just joking." Harper turned around to reassure Neri, who trailed at the back of the group. "We all know Tams is a sweetheart under all that black and nihilism."

Lian tsked. "We found him like this just down the lane."

She beckoned to Rylan, and he came over to take her place supporting Jasper. His arm brushed against Everly's where it looped around the injured man's back, and awkward emotions settled like bad yogurt in Everly's belly.

She wanted to tell him it was fine, that she could manage Jasper on her own. She wasn't the weakling she'd been when the Bane's influence had her cracking to pieces.

Rylan had only seen that side of her since he woke up, and he hadn't known her before that for years. She hated the idea that he thought her weak, or that he still needed to protect her—the way the Coruscare forced him to feel.

She felt strong now. Powerful. More energized than ever with twice as much of the Coruscare within her. It was a new kind of strength, in body and mind. As though she'd finally wrestled her dragon into submission.

But the words wouldn't come. As though she'd taken so long to work out how to talk to Rylan again that she'd forgotten how, and even simple words couldn't be forced through her lips. So they supported Jasper up the front steps together in silence.

Cherry's forehead creased as he held the door open and stepped out of their way.

The combined scents of lamb roast and childhood memories hit Everly as she stepped inside, covering the faint odor of blood and old sweat wafting from Jasper.

Birdie yapped madly up ahead. The old dog was nearly blind and deaf, but clearly had a good enough sense of smell to sniff out a stranger.

Rushelle's voice came from the kitchen. "What's going on, do we have a guest for dinner?"

"Med kit first, then we'll see about another plate," Lian replied, taking the lead.

Everly and Rylan helped Jasper to the kitchen, with

Harper, Neri, and Tammy following. Cherry closed the front door after them, then hovered at a distance.

Jasper hissed in a sharp breath as Everly and Rylan lowered him into a chair at the long dinner table. The action brought their faces close together.

Everly turned away from Rylan's gaze and the hint of vulnerability there that jabbed at her heart. Avoiding him wasn't fair. She had to talk to him and explain, but that couldn't be now.

Birdie skittered around on tappy paws, growling near Jasper's feet until Lian scooped her up and shooshed her. The table had been laid out in preparation for their arrival, and Rushelle hovered in the kitchen, holding a full baking tray with bright-yellow oven mitts.

"Oh dear, we got a little lost duck? We'll sort you out." She put the dish onto the counter and strode over to dig around in a large drawer.

Neri, who clung to Harper's back as though she were a human shield, poked her head around to take a wide-eyed look at Jasper. "Do you want me to—"

"Nah-uh," Everly hushed her gently.

She stepped closer and spoke softly, smiling to comfort Neri. "I think he just needs a bit of a cleanup. He'll be okay. Better if we keep your *talents* for later, just in case."

Everly directed the last bit to Harper, who replied with a knowing nod.

Harper took Birdie from Lian and transferred the tiny dog into Neri's arms. "Come on, let's go to the loungeroom, give them all some space."

Neri's eyes remained round as Birdie licked her chin and cheeks.

The mermaid girl had met the dog previously but her sheer awe of the creature remained. "Am I holding her right? Are all dogs so small? I just want to bundle her up and squeeze her. I won't. I won't squeeze her. But I want to."

Harper chuckled as they wandered away. "If you like little puppers so much, just wait until you see your first cat."

Rushelle strutted over with a first aid kit. She held her cleavage into her tank top as she bent over to inspect Jasper.

"Boy, someone did a number on you! Hold still, love, this might sting."

She tore open packets of gauze, tipped liberal amounts of antiseptic onto them, and cleaned the split skin on his curved nose.

Denny and Callan arrived, and Tammy kept throwing Callan confused looks until she hissed, "With all the drama going on, I'm shocked you haven't asked yet if I'm okay."

Callan shrugged, and his lips pulled into a half-smile. "I mean, clearly you're fine. I know you don't like me treating you like a kid and checking up all the time. See? I can learn."

"She sure is fine," Denny added with a leer, scratching

at his blond beard.

"For ghast's sake, dude, she's half your age! And also, no, just no," Callan growled. "Go and sit in your corner until *you* can learn something for once."

"Mo mand mit min mour morner," Denny mocked back, but slouched away to a chair across the room.

Rylan remained standing, looming over Jasper as he cast questioning glances between him and Everly. "Anyone going to explain what happened?"

"We found him on our way here. He said it was the Mesmans who did this." Everly grabbed some gauze as well and wiped at a spot of blood on her jacket.

Jasper's normally neat, dark hair hung bedraggled over his bruised face. "No, I said they ... they're doing worse. This was Nilson's handiwork. He caught me acting suspicious, which I suppose I was, but he took it the wrong way. He confronted me, and I provoked him."

Rushelle gasped. "Why in the Everdark would you provoke that badly stuffed sausage?"

"I needed an out because the Mesmans were beginning to suspect my espionage. Fleeing Nilson's wrath was the excuse I needed to get out of the estate with these." Jasper leaned away from Rushelle's wound cleaning and reached into his cardigan.

He pulled out a few sheets of crumpled paper and aged parchment, covered in notes and sketches.

Rylan took them, leafing through. "I've seen stuff like this before. I found notes like this when I was looking into the missing bodies—before someone took me out."

"And you think it's Vonny and Kole? I mean, they are fanatical nutjobs, but would they really have attacked their own?" Lian said as she reached for the papers to check them over.

"I can believe it." Tammy folded her arms tightly, tucking her shroudpool-stained hands out of sight.

Everly still felt chills when she remembered the madness in Kole's voice when he'd confronted her and Lian at the estate.

I can believe it too.

Jasper winced as Rushelle wiped around his blackened eye. "After they used me to get that Bane artifact, I realized something more was going on. So I've been watching them all week, trying to ascertain what they are doing. They've taken over a whole ballroom in the old part of the estate, plus a couple of other smaller rooms here and there, all kept secret, locked up."

"And you managed to get a look?" Rylan asked.

Jasper nodded. "I was lucky one day when Mordan called them away on short notice and I got in to see what they were working on. I had planned to simply retrieve some evidence. But after seeing what they were doing, I was worried about going to Mordan on my own, so I came here. I'm sorry to burden you all with this."

"Formal little chap, aren't you?" Rushelle beamed from him to Cherry. "I can see why you liked him."

Everly's eyes widened.

I thought Harper and I were the only ones in on that secret? Cherry flashed a hard look at Rushelle.

I guess not.

"Oops, sorry. Sorry. Don't know what came over me. I know *nothing*." She winked dramatically, then patted Jasper on the shoulder. "But don't worry about us, we're used to being on the Darkfreys' bad side."

"And what exactly are the Mesmans doing?" Rylan asked.

"Trying to open a shroudpool." Jasper pointed at where Lian had pushed aside the dinnerware and spread out the pages. "There are mentions of it here and here, mostly to do with the original crossing of shadyrs from the Everdark to this dimension, and Kole's notes all around that for his own plans. And see this sketch here? They are building that, now, in that ballroom."

"That's feels like a really bad idea," Everly said, leaning in to get a look at the notes. "A shroudpool at the estate? It sounds like a recipe for a nasty monster infestation. Why would they do that?"

"They want to go after Blaise. They want to get their son back." Tammy's voice was quiet and rough.

Her body flickered, like lights in a brownout. She wrinkled her nose and squeezed her eyes shut but didn't vanish entirely.

Silence fell over the room.

Callan broke it, murmuring softly to Tammy, "It wasn't your fault."

"Ugh!" She dodged away from his comforting hand.

"Couldn't they go through one of the other shroudpools around town if that's what they wanted to do?" Everly asked.

Callan still had his eyes on Tammy as he replied, "I'm guessing the Everdark isn't exactly a small place. A random shroudpool could take them who knows where in relation to where Blaise could be, and the Dark Corner shroudpool has been dormant since then, so it's not an option. If getting Blaise back is their goal, they would have to do ... *something* more. Ghast knows what though."

"No one actually thinks the kid could still be alive but, right?" Denny pitched in from over in the corner. "No one comes back from the Everdark alive."

With a sigh, Lian shook her head and lowered herself into her chair. "The Mesmans are in denial. They still talk about Blaise as though he's alive and waiting for them. But there's no chance. I'm sorry, Tammy."

"You think I don't know that already?" the goth-girl hissed.

Everly focused back on the papers, shifting them for a clearer view of another sketch that caught her eye. "I've seen these before. This is the sculpture thing that was at my house on my first night back."

That weird, skeletal effigy made of pitch-black bones had been destroyed and removed before anyone else could see it, but it wasn't the only time she'd seen something like it.

"There was one at the theater too," she added.

Callan nodded. "I think they are lures. Eidolghast lures. Set them up, and the ghasts are drawn to them. It was too strange, having a vasmire then a weroth show up at the theater so quickly after each other. And I'm sure I've seen one of these before. The night Dad died."

Lian inhaled audibly from across the table, and Rylan straightened, tense as a tightrope.

Callan cleared his throat. "I was so young then, and it was all so ... I never really thought much of it until I saw it again at the theater."

"So, the Mesmans are making these too? How? Why?" Lian's tone was icy cold.

"I'm guessing they set the one at the theater to get me out of the picture." Rylan rubbed his forehead, eyebrows low and head shaking. "They knew I'd been getting my nose into their business. They didn't want to take me out at the estate—"

"Not Mordan's golden soldier boy," Denny scoffed.

"—so they left clues for me to check out Rook's, and knew I'd be on my own. I'm guessing they set the lure and hoped an eidolghast would finish me off for them."

And it almost did. Or at least, left him so weakened that the second ghast he faced that night practically killed him.

The vivid memory of Rylan's torn body bleeding out on the street still made ice crystals grow through Everly's chest. "Okay, so it might have been them who were after Rylan, but why set a lure at my place that night, too? They didn't know me. I'd only just come back to town."

"Maybe they aren't lures. We're just guessing here. I might not be remembering right from when I was a kid, either," Callan offered. "It was a long time ago."

Lian leaned back in her chair and closed her eyes. "I wasn't on the Darkfreys' good side, but there was no reason for the Mesmans to go after us back then. It doesn't make sense."

"That was well before they lost Blaise, too," Rylan added. "They've been messing with this stuff for ages."

"And how? How are they actually doing magic? Shadyrs haven't been able to since interbreeding with humans after the crossover," Tammy said.

Jasper tilted his head. "It was ten years ago that a number of relics went missing, blamed on the Gorhanmere shadyrs."

"Who only actually had the Bane," Everly squeezed in.

Jasper nodded. "And that wasn't long before Rylan and Callan joined the estate."

"Blaise said they had more artifacts than just the one we tried to close a shroudpool with," Tammy said. "So they've had them all this time, and are somehow using them to do old shadyr magic?"

"And they have one more artifact now too—the Bane." Cherry's voice cut across the room after staying quiet for so long.

He kept his head turned away from Jasper, refusing to even look in his direction.

Jasper gulped visibly. "Vonny sought it out especially. I don't know what for."

"Do they know its connection to the dragon?" Rylan's gaze went straight to Everly.

Everly shrugged. "Maybe they're going to use it for a power boost, like the Gorhanmere shadyrs did."

And Harper.

The strength and energy boost the Bane had given Harper for the short time she'd used it was impressive, but had also changed her. She'd been that much more wild, hectic, edging on bloodlust under its influence. And since the Bane had been taken from her, the withdrawals were equally powerful.

Harper excelled in hiding her weaknesses as she excelled

in so many things, but Everly could tell she was tired and drawn lately. Whether that was simply the effects wearing off, or from the effort of fighting the intense desire to have it again, Everly didn't know.

But she did clearly recall the wild gleam in Kole Mesman's eyes, the knots of muscle barely restrained beneath the massive man's shirt. She wouldn't be surprised if power was what he wanted.

He might already look powerful, but there was never enough for men like him.

"It could also simply be to add into their collection. I'm unsure." Jasper's shoulders lifted then slumped. He stilled Rushelle's hands as she applied a butterfly bandage over a tear on his cheek, nodding to her.

"I've told you everything I know. Thank you for your hospitality, but I won't intrude any longer. I understand my presence isn't wanted."

He couldn't be going back to the estate. That sounded to Everly like a death sentence if he got this roughed up before he'd even delivered stolen intel to the other side.

But she didn't really know much about Jasper beyond what Cherry had shared. "Do you have somewhere to stay?"

"Well ... no. But I'll find my way." Jasper's groaned as he stood.

Lian pushed her chair out to stand as well. "We have plenty—"

"No," Cherry cut in.

Rushelle paused midway packing up the med kit. "At least for dinner?"

"No." Cherry finally turned to stare at Jasper, his dark eyes blank. "He said he'll find his way. That's what he needs to do."

Chapter Two

Stepping out of Howell House felt like stepping out into a lonely tundra. The night wasn't especially cold, but the warmth Jasper felt inside the home had seeped through to his bones.

The smell of the meal cooking, the long farmhouse table set for everyone to eat together, the kindness they'd shown in patching up his wounds—that warmth of family was so distant to the cold, industrial cafeteria, and toughen-up-it's-just-a-scratch culture of Darkfrey Estate.

Howell House wasn't only a halfway stop for outcast shadyrs. It was a home, one filled with love and acceptance. Jasper could feel it to his core, and having to step away from that, from Cherry, wrenched the warmth from his body, leaving nothing but a bitter chill.

One he was sure he deserved.

Jasper carefully closed the front screen door so it wouldn't slam, not wanting to disturb the family inside any more than he already had. The news he had brought would have been hard for them to hear.

He stood there on the porch, staring at the star-spotted sky for a long moment as he pushed his emotions away, and tried, tried desperately, to stop thinking about what life would have been like if he'd left the Darkfreys back when Cherry did. Left *with* him. Stayed by his side, instead of putting his career and goals as a shadyr first.

We could be in there now, together, and happy in that warmth.

We could still be in love.

Instead, Jasper straightened his cardigan against the cold, and wondered where on this plane of existence he was going to spend the night.

There were a few Darkfrey safe houses around town. Maybe he could find one that wasn't occupied, at least until morning. Then he could think about where to go longer term. Staying in Shroudhaven could be risky now that he was on the wrong side of the Mesmans and alone, but what was life for a shadyr outside of this town?

There were the odd few shroudpools out in the world, in other cities, even other countries, that had small bands of shadyrs guarding them. Maybe he could make his way to one of those and hope he'd be accepted.

He also hoped that the Howell team could do something with the evidence he'd provided. Maybe they could fix things. Maybe he'd be able to come back, one day.

Laying the burden of action on the Howells left him feeling guilty, but there wasn't anything he could do with it alone.

And he was alone now. Utterly. Not a Darkfrey, not a Howell, not someone who was loved by Cherry. He wasn't sure what he was anymore.

His chest ached like his ribs were cracked. They probably were. Nilson Darkfrey was a beast. The pain made standing upright a struggle, and imagining scouting the streets of Shroudhaven for a refuge on foot made Jasper's eyes water.

It's going to be a long night.

The old wood of the porch steps sighed as though in sympathy as Jasper walked away. The gravel crunching under his feet almost covered the low whine of the screen door opening behind him.

"I've got to say, I really didn't think you had it in you."

At the sound of Cherry's voice, Jasper's throat tightened. He cleared it, and turned around, trying to hide how his heart was racing. Trying to push down any hope that tried to rise within him.

He came out after me? Why?

Cherry's expression remained stony. Dark, nebulous

eyes assessed Jasper from under strands of bright-red hair.

Jasper cleared his throat again, but it had gone dry. "That I had ... what in me?"

"The guts to turn on the Darkfreys, finally. I'd come to accept that would never happen, and then you go and surprise me. And all it took was discovering that your brace buddies were psychopaths trying to bust their own personal hole into a hellish dimension of monsters."

"I should have left them for less."

Cherry raised his eyebrows.

"I mean ... not that you're less. I mean—" Jasper winced and ran a hand through his hair, trying to pull himself together.

One corner of Cherry's lips twisted. "I know it was hard for you. I know how much you wanted their acceptance, and when you thought you had it, you didn't want to lose it. Not for anything, or anyone."

He leaned against one of the porch posts and folded his arms. "But did you ever think you were looking for acceptance in the wrong place all along? You'll never truly belong with people who treat you as ... *less* ... just for being who you are."

"I don't think of you as less. Never. That wasn't my intention." Jasper's voice dropped away under Cherry's cool glare.

It dared him to answer all the unspoken questions. If

he didn't think that, then why? Why didn't he leave with Cherry? Why couldn't he be himself? He didn't think of Cherry as lesser. Cherry was truth and bravery and sincerity bundled in human form.

It's me. I'm the one I've always thought was lesser.

Before the sting of that realization could fully pierce Jasper's heart, Cherry spoke again. "Growing up with the Darkfreys and their hateful culture, it's easy to think that's how the whole world is. That everyone's out to get you, so you better stick with those you've got. But it's not like that."

Cherry turned, staring up at Howell house. "You've told me many times how brave I was for coming out and then leaving the Darkfreys, but it was only hard *because* of the Darkfreys. It was easy to be myself once I left. I'm with good people now, where acceptance is *normal*, not some impossible dream."

Jasper nodded once, but he didn't really understand. He couldn't fathom the concept of acceptance, of not having to hide major parts of himself from those he considered family until he had forgotten how to even accept himself.

His head hung heavy, a dull throb behind the growing bruises around one eye. He nodded again, more to himself this time, relating to the words *impossible dream*.

That was what he saw in front of him. Cherry, silhouetted by the warm glow coming from the home behind him. "I'm sorry. I can't apologize enough for taking so long ... too long. I don't expect forgiveness."

"Good, because I have none for you." Cherry's shoulders lifted then fell. "Still ... there's a place for you here, if you need it. You don't have to be alone."

A pinprick of warmth burst inside Jasper's chest and his dry lips parted but couldn't form words.

Cherry fixed a firm stare his way. "But before I let you back inside, I need to know that this isn't some setup for more betrayal, that you aren't going to hurt us ... the good people here, again."

It was the last thing Jasper wanted. If he could go back in time and rewrite every instance he'd hurt Cherry to wipe it from history, he would.

It was a hard promise to make, because life was unpredictable, and sometimes people got hurt no matter how hard you worked to avoid it, but he wanted to try. He wanted to be as brave as Cherry and do his best to make things right. His body ached as he straightened himself up, and his heart ached as he held Cherry's gaze.

He didn't get a word out before Cherry's eyes widened and he leaned to look over Jasper's shoulder. "Or is this some kind of ambush already?"

"What?" Jasper spun around to see where Cherry was looking.

Out in one of the overgrown fields that surrounded the homestead, only a stone's throw from the front porch, a shadowy figure stood still.

"I came alone, I swear." Jasper squinted at it, urging his shadyr night vision to gather more details.

The silhouetted form didn't move, and Jasper scanned around, spotting another close to the other corner of the property.

Did I bring trouble here? Have the Mesmans sent people after me, or come after me themselves?

He was their enemy now, and he knew how they dealt with their enemies based on what they attempted to do to Rylan. Jasper shuddered at the thought that he might have brought danger to the Howell House doorstep.

Cherry eyed him skeptically.

Jasper set his jaw, refusing to be the cause of more pain for him. "I promise, I will do everything I can to keep you all from harm."

He set off at a disjointed jog toward the closest figure.

"Don't go out there alone, you idiot!" Cherry's footsteps hurried behind his.

"Get back into the house," Jasper called over his shoulder.

He knew it wasn't smart, but the sting of too many regrets had skewered his chest and he wanted to be reckless, and brave, and take any action he could to keep that warm home behind him safe.

He picked up his pace, stomping through knee-high

dry grass and dodging clumps of berry brambles. The figure stood in the shadow of an old, half-dead oak tree. As he grew closer, and his vision pierced the darkness, it became clear his target was not a human.

He hadn't seen one of the bone lures in person before but recognized it now from the sketches he'd stolen.

Obsidian-shaded bones of human appearance had been melded together into a horrific effigy. A tangle of spines swirled up the middle, forming the figure's base. Ribs fanned out with fingerbones studded along the edges.

More than one jawbone created a mockery of a crown at the top. Worst of all, it *moved*. A shimmer and a sense of dripping, like looking through an intense heatwave that affected only those blighted, blackened bones.

"Is that what I think it is?" Cherry gasped.

Jasper spun around, scanning the fields and the view down the lane to the rest of the town, then back up behind the house to the forest in the distance.

"There's at least one more over there. I can't see or sense a ghost nearby yet. They may have only just been set up."

Looking at the bone lure made him feel ill, a nausea that burrowed through his skull. He reached for one of the dry branches overhead and snapped it off, then swung it at the effigy like a baseball bat. A hail of broken wood and bones sprayed out from his blow.

"Go back and let the others know. I'll get rid of these

and check for more."

Cherry hovered for a moment, face tinted green as his gaze locked on the half-smashed statue. Then he gave a single nod and ran back to the house.

Jasper watched him go before letting the wince of pain reach his face. Nilson's beating left him sore in a way that didn't agree with being part of the sharp impact between wood and bone.

He dropped the makeshift club and kicked the effigy, taking it out at the base so that it fell backward into the weeds and scattered acorns.

He stomped the remaining pieces with a satisfying crack, over and over until they stopped moving. Jasper hoped that meant it was no longer working its dark magic.

He only hoped he stopped it soon enough.

Breaking the effigy apart left his battered body aching and sweat beaded on his forehead.

He turned to where he'd seen the other lure, as the deep, churning heat of his shadyr shift warned him an eidolghast was nearby.

He stepped out from under the cover of the oak tree but still couldn't see anything moving within the field around him. Even the tugging magic of the shift felt different, unlike the usual vasmire or weroth changes.

Where was the eidolghast?

What was the eidolghast?

The world grew darker, as something above Jasper blocked the dim moonlight. He turned his face up as a massive shape swooped in a dive directly for him.

Chapter Three

The news Jasper brought about the lures, and their purpose, caused Everly's anxiety to spiral, and set a low rage simmering. All that suffering, all those families torn apart, made a desire for vengeance rise within Everly. She locked it down before her rampant emotions could let loose the creature inside her.

She could feel that the Coruscare liked the concept of revenge, could feel its encouragement, like a warm hand on her back, pushing her toward an edge she might never come back from. She could be a wrathful god of vengeance. She could rip the lives and souls from all those who had done them wrong. She had the power ... she just had to set it free.

No. That's not me. And you are not in control, dragon.

Everly collected Harper and Neri from the loungeroom once Jasper had gone. She caught them up on the new information about the plot to open a shroudpool as they headed back for dinner. Neri didn't understand, and that was probably for the best. Everly wished she didn't either.

Birdie had fallen asleep on her well-worn spot on the old lounge, and Neri threw besotted glances back to the little dog as they left.

Everly had noticed Jasper eye the newest member of their group curiously, and it was safer to keep Neri away from too much attention until they were certain Jasper could be trusted. Cherry clearly wasn't happy about the Darkfrey loyalist being around, although he did slouch past them in the hall, heading outside after his ex.

Rylan and Callan were still pouring over the Mesmans' notes and diagrams, speaking together in low voices. Tammy had excused herself as no longer hungry, despite Rushelle's pleas to stay as she fixed place settings and returned to bringing out the meal.

Everly took a seat beside Lian, who was staring dully into the distance. Learning that her husband may have died in a purposeful attack would need some processing, and there were still so many questions unanswered.

Everly attempted to focus on what she could do to keep her friends and family safe in the here and now.

She leaned a little closer to Lian and asked gently, "Do you know anything about a Portia Darkfrey?"

Lian blinked a couple of times. "Hrm?"

Harper and Neri moved into seats across from them, and Harper placed her rose-gold tote bag onto the table. "We found a lot of belongings of Portia Darkfrey's in Ev's attic. A bunch of shadyr and Darkfrey gear. Including this gorgeous darling."

She reached into the bag and pulled out the segmented weapon that had been coiled inside like a rope. "We were hoping you could tell us that it's safe to use and mine all mine."

"Portia Darkfrey?" Lian reached for the glossy, dark weapon and held it to her face for inspection. "Yeah, I knew of her. As a shadyr you tend to know everyone from the Darkfrey family line, high and mighties as they are."

Everly waited, expectantly.

"Didn't know her personally though. She was an older woman when I was a kid back in my days at the estate. I remember the fuss when she left. I don't know why she did though. Some said she was kicked out, some said she deserted. Either way, it was clear she was someone who didn't fit into the Darkfrey mold. Gossip wasn't tolerated though, so before long, it was like she never existed."

"You ever see her around town?" Everly asked.

"Maybe once? She kept very much to herself, and we were instructed to consider her invisible, too. It's funny, after I left the Darkfreys, I started thinking about her again, feeling like I understood more about the many reasons one might leave. I considered trying to find her, reach out in solidarity and all. Never did though. What was her stuff doing at your place?"

"Dad bought it. We found invoices from her estate sale and a clipping of her obituary. She died sixteen years ago."

Then not long after that I broke the crystal that was part of Portia's estate and let the Coruscare into me. And it killed my father.

Such a powerful object, lost into obscurity until it ended up sold off with a bunch of bric-a-brac, as though it had just been a household decoration for Portia. Even the piece of Coruscare from the lighthouse, and the one in Barry's maze, they were used for the residual powers they exuded, but no one had any idea what they truly were.

Everly wished someone had worked it out, had kept the fragile shard that held a third of a malevolent deity locked away, out of reach of a curious toddler. Her life could have been so different.

"Whatever the reason was that Portia left, there must have still been bad blood there, since she seems to have died very much alone." Harper pouted in disgust. "Which doesn't surprise me from what I know about the Darkfreys. But what does surprise me is that they didn't swoop in to reclaim her gear when she was gone."

"Well, that was back before Mordan was in charge. He's kept a tighter hold on anything deemed valuable than his predecessors did. A lot of those who leave the Darkfreys do so with just the shirts on their backs, which sometimes includes the body armor. The Darkfreys have enough resources that they don't really care about a few basics going missing. Portia must have taken more of her own valuable collection with her though, because this beauty …"

Lian let out a low whistle, brushing her finger carefully along the sharp edge. "This is something else. There's old magic in this one for sure."

"*Safe* old magic?" Everly pressed.

Harper pulled a pinched face that threatened getting a tongue poked out.

Lian tilted her head from side to side. "Hard to say. If Portia was actively using it, and she died when you say she did, she led a decent, long life—for a shadyr at least—so I doubt it was doing her harm. From the looks of it, this is an early shadyr weapon, possibly pre-crossover considering the materials it's made from. Materials not of this realm."

"So, it's safe?" Harper bounced a little in her chair.

"I'm not sure that's exactly what she was saying," Everly sighed.

Lian smirked and handed the whip sword back to Harper. "I'm saying it's made by shadyrs, *for* shadyrs. Like my sword. Which is the big difference between this, and something like the Bane which was made by who knows what for entirely dark purposes."

Harper's smile faded as she took the weapon. "But I'm not a shadyr."

Everly struggled against the negative words trying to force themselves out, against the idea that her best friend running around with even a *mundane* whip sword didn't sound like a safe prospect.

But she knew how much Harper wanted this, and Harper had never been less than completely supportive of her.

Everly took a deep breath to still her anxiety and smiled. "Shadyr or not, it's yours now, and if any human can make it work, it's you."

Lian patted the back of Harper's hand. "And if something goes wrong, you've got a bunch of shadyrs at your back."

"And a shadyr god," Harper added, grinning at Everly.

Everly's smile strained. She still had very complicated feelings about the being of light inside her.

Her dragon. The Coruscare. The others only saw its sheer power, and how that could be used. They didn't feel how malevolent, hungry, and self-obsessed the being was. As though it would consume the whole world if it were allowed.

It had been quiet since rejoining with the second piece of itself. In a way that brought Everly no comfort.

As though it were simply biding its time.

Its power had grown, but so had her own. She understood that being, and herself, so much more now. There hadn't been opportunity to really test the limits of her control since then, and she wondered whether her confidence was justified.

Whether she was still a threat to her friends' very souls.

A light tingling in her hands signaled to Everly that a panic attack was on its way, so she pushed her chair back, looking for a distraction. Rushelle was still bustling around in the kitchen, so Everly headed that way.

"Anything I can help out with?"

Rushelle smiled sunnily, tucking a blond curl back up into her fifty's pinup-style hair. "All done, love, just can't find the bottle opener. I betcha Denny's left it in the living room again."

"I'll go have a look." As she walked away, Everly ran a finger up and down the digits of her other hand, breathing in and out in time with the action, bringing herself back from the edge of unnecessary panic.

She'd never get used to how her attacks could come at any time, for no apparent reason, but she'd gotten used to the warning signs, and as long as she acted fast, she could normally ward them off.

She spotted the bottle opener on a side table, and when she turned back, she ran face-first into Rylan.

Oookay and back comes all that anxiety again.

His warm, green eyes, sprinkled with the faint hint of stars that shadyr eyes took on at night, searched her face. "Hey, can we talk for a bit?"

Everly fidgeted with the bottle opener. "We can. We should."

I have to tell him.

She still wasn't sure how to let him know that the entity inside her had held just enough of his soul captive to make him feel protective of the being, and her, for most of his life. That the things he felt for her, the words he'd said in her dreams, in the flooding sea cave, came from that forced bond.

She could *never* tell him how much she wished his profession of love was real, how she felt about him in return.

How could she after what she and the Coruscare had done? She wasn't sure she could even trust her own feelings. But that was why Rylan needed to know the truth. He needed the information to know which of his feelings he could trust, too.

Rylan wet his lips and opened his mouth, but Everly held up a hand.

"No, let me go first. I—I have to tell you something. And you're not going to like it. And I hardly even know how to ... but—"

The front door to the house slammed open, and Cherry

yelled breathlessly, "There are ghast lures, all around the house!"

"What?" Rylan burst into action, dashing down the hall.

Everly hurried close behind. "Where's Jasper? Was this him? Did he set us up?"

Cherry held the front door open as they went through, with more footsteps coming behind them. "No, I don't think so. He's out there trying to take the lures down."

"Any sign of eidolghasts yet?" Rylan paused on the front porch, scanning the area as Cherry pointed.

A sound somewhere between a foghorn and nails on a chalkboard came as a reply. Out in the field, a pointed, dark shape plummeted from the sky toward Jasper.

"Look out!" Cherry shouted, sprinting down the steps.

Black mist swirled around him as he ran for the field. Jasper ducked and rolled, disappearing in a similar puff of dark smoke as Cherry reached him.

The huge, winged creature crashed down over them both.

Chapter Four

Everly held her breath, staring at the spot where Jasper and Cherry had stood a moment before. The eidolghast screeched again, turning on the spot. From a distance, in the low light, it seemed like an oversized bat, but its body was unnaturally slim between the wings.

Harper, Neri, Lian, Rushelle, Callan, Denny, and Tammy all pushed out onto the porch, trying to gather what was happening. Seeing what they were facing, jackets and shirts were hastily shed.

"There. They're all right!" Rylan pointed to the side of the monster, where Jasper and Cherry popped up behind a patch of brambles. "Come on, we need to get out there and help them."

"*Flying* monsters now?" Harper sounded half annoyed, half excited at the concept.

"Herrelspurn," Lian said, dropping her gray cardigan on the porch. "Uncommon, but I've faced a few. Watch out for its fire."

All the shadyrs apart from Neri nodded in understanding and headed toward the monster.

Neri's shadyr change had already engulfed her, bright sparks shimmering in the misty magic around her.

As it faded away, Neri stared over her own shoulder in horror. "Wings? I'm still having problems with *legs*."

The leathery membranes had sharp hooks at the end and had torn out through the back of Neri's dress. Her skin had changed too, from a warm brown to a rich, deep red. It wasn't quite the same as the dragon form Rylan had taken fighting the drowned zombies, but it clearly had some part in it.

Harper stepped closer to Neri as though she were about to embrace her. Instead, she pursed her lips into a small smile. "Stay here and take cover. There are plenty of us to deal with this flappy beast. Don't worry at all, okay?"

Neri glanced from Harper to the house and back again. She nodded and stepped inside behind the screen door, wings bumping against the walls.

Everly put a hand on Harper's shoulder. "Ready?"

"Am I ever." Harper grinned back and thrust out her whip sword. It clicked back into a rigid blade with a *shnnnkk*.

Out in the field, the shadyrs all took on the red, winged form. Rylan, Callan, and Denny had shed their shirts entirely to save them from being shredded. They looked like classical demons, emerged from the fires of hell. Cherry and Jasper didn't have time to consider their clothing, and their wings poked out through ragged holes at their backs.

The shadyrs swarmed around the herrelspurn, catching at its wings with their hands. The beast moved fast, twisting away and taking flight.

As it lifted from the overgrown field, Everly got a clear look at it in the dim moonlight. Its flesh was like smoky glass, lit red from within along its narrow, spindle-like torso.

The bat-like wings were tipped with overlong wriggling fingers, but the most disturbing part of the creature was its face.

Atop a mess of dozens of thin necks that twined together between the body and head, there was a face that seemed far too human, and yet not. It was smooth, with no eyes, but all the right proportions and shape of a person, like a porcelain mask. Its nose sniffed, and the human-lipped mouth opened to reveal rows of needle-sharp teeth. It released another bone-chilling scream.

"Oh my ghast," Harper gasped as they ran to join the others.

She held up the whip sword. An aura of golden light shone around the edges of the blade. Looking from it to

Everly, her eyes were glossy.

"This is the best present anyone's ever given me."

"Eye's up, kiddos!" Rushelle's voice came from above them.

She, Tammy, and Lian had one of the creature's wings pinned in midair, and it was tumbling out of the sky above them.

Harper dove left and Everly dove right. The shadyrs leaped off the herrelspurn a moment before it hit the ground, letting their wings catch them.

Dry blackberry canes snapped and crunched as the ghast rolled over, swinging its head to where Everly was getting back to her feet. It hissed and flung out a wing toward her, its vast wingspan reaching farther than Everly expected. She dropped herself onto her back again, but the long-fingered tips scraped across her face and neck like razor blades.

She inhaled sharply at the sting, shocked for a moment as the herrelspurn reared back and glowed brighter.

"Evie!" Rylan dropped from the sky on top of her.

The following burst of air stirred up dust and dried grass. He grabbed her, holding her close. One of his deep-red wings fanned out around them like a shield as the roar of fire filled Everly's ears.

Flames tumbled and danced around the edges of Rylan's wing, the translucent skin shining bright as the sun. Everly turned her eyes to Rylan's face, terrified for the pain he must be in. She found him looking back at her, concern writing lines across his forehead.

"It's okay, it can't burn our wings in this form," he said, and his breath blew hot against her cheek. He reached a hand to her neck, and she saw him swallow. "You're already healing."

Everly blinked, confused. The distraction of nearly being burned alive in Rylan's embrace made her forget that the creature had sliced her skin.

The pain had already passed, and the buffed-up Coruscare seemed to have come with the perk of rapid healing, similar to what it had given Neri from living near it her whole life.

"Yeah, yeah I'm okay."

Rylan had one arm wrapped around her waist, and his face bent close to hers. His eyes glittered like a god's view of a galaxy. The scent of burned grass filled Everly's nose and she coughed on the smoke. The crackle of flame ceased, and Rylan unwrapped his hold.

He stared at her for a long second, and she was sure he was going to tell her to run, to hide, to stay safe. Instead, he nodded to her once, and launched himself at the monster.

Okay?

Before she let her mind spiral by over-analyzing Rylan's behavior, Everly did a situation check. Rushelle's bright-yellow tank top was like a beacon in the dim light, stark against her now red skin. She and Lian had backed off, destroying something in the distance—probably one of the other lures.

Rylan, Callan, Denny, and Tammy were trying to keep the ghast grounded, but it kept slipping free of their hold. Harper stood back from the fight, cursing about it being her first fight with the sword, and it had to be against something that could *fly*.

Cherry had Jasper back on his feet, and they seemed to be arguing, with Jasper hobbling toward the fight as Cherry gestured angrily at his side.

None of the shadyrs were dressed for battle that night. But Jasper looked the strangest—an incubus in a beige knit cardigan.

The herrelspurn was in line with the roof and gaining height. Everly tentatively let the Coruscare's powers out. Starlight glowed around her, and her feet lifted from the ground, hovering above the scorched dirt.

The glowing tendrils emerged, but the sense of hunger, of control being taken from her, didn't come with them. The Coruscare remained quiet, compliant, as she directed those lashing strands of light at the flying monster.

We're just going to hold it. Just hold *it. This isn't a meal.*

She caught it around one wing, carefully avoiding the surrounding shadyrs. The herrelspurn shrieked again, a sound that drilled up Everly's spine and into her teeth. She winced.

The creature flailed its other wing, knocking Tammy out of the air. She spiraled, her wings tangled uselessly around her. The herrelspurn breathed fire again, jets of red flame shooting from its throat.

Jasper launched into the air and snatched Tammy before she hit the ground. He wrapped them both in his wings as the flames spread over them.

One shoulder of his cardigan caught alight, and as he reached the ground, Tammy gave him an awkward smile and patted the flames out for him. Rylan, Denny, and Callan landed beside them, not far from Everly.

Rylan's gaze traced the shimmering strands from the herrelspurn all the way to where Everly floated. "Can you bring it down?"

"Maybe. But I don't want to ... I *won't* let the Coruscare eat it. And I don't know if I can control that fine line between kill and consume." Everly's top lip curled with effort as she lassoed the beast with another scintillating string.

She could feel the Coruscare's hunger again now. It would eat everything they touched if it could. But it wasn't pushing back against her control the way it used to. She told it no, and it recoiled, allowing her to guide their actions.

"You don't have to kill. That's our job," Rylan growled.

"Just hold it still for us."

Tammy shook out and stretched a shoulder. "So how do we kill this thing?"

She'd left her black hooded jacket behind, but had sacrificed a cobweb-laced shirt to her shift rather than stripping off more. Everly figured she'd choose the same with someone like Denny around, but it sucked Tammy had to deal with ruined clothing because of him.

Callan swiped his long hair back from his face. "The weak point is one of the necks, but there are so many. Seriously, why so many necks and only one head? We could be hacking away for ages before we find the right one."

"It's not the one that's glowing?" Harper stepped beside them, her narrowed eyes locked onto the herrelspurn, which writhed in Everly's snare of light.

It loosed another stream of flames, skimming not far over their heads. They ducked in unison.

"Duh, there isn't one glowing," Denny scoffed. "For someone who looks damn good, you don't *look* very good, do ya?"

"There is, hidden more in the middle, but you can see it sometimes when it twists around." She held up her sword to point, its aura dull compared to Everly.

Callan shrugged. "If I've learned anything in this town, it's to go with the weird. So if you can see it, you can go for it. Worth a shot?"

"I'll try to keep it still, but the fire is a problem for Harper." Everly strained to reel the monster to the ground.

"I'm on it," Rylan said, and dark magic swirled around him.

He ran toward the herrelspurn as the shift enlarged his body. He emerged from the sparking mist twice his normal size and covered in scales—his combined dragon form. He'd gained so much control over the changes Everly's presence caused him, she'd almost forgotten he could still draw from that to choose any number of shadyr forms.

He tackled the downed creature as another gust of flames blasted free. He caught it in a headlock, trapping its humanoid face between his chest and massive arm, clamping the jaw closed. The large beast reared back, and Rylan lifted from the ground, steadying himself to keep hold.

"Go on, jump in whenever you're ready," Callan urged Harper.

"It's too high up for me," Harper said, her voice strained. "I don't have that strength anymore."

Callan grinned at Tammy. "Let's give her a lift."

The two of them grabbed Harper under her shoulders on each side. Wings pumping, they drew her off her feet.

As they circled over the huge bat-like creature, Callan called, "Dropping the Bellsy bomb in three, two, one."

Harper's hair flew behind her as she fell a few feet onto

the back of the creature, Everly's bonds lighting her from below. She grunted fiercely as she thrust her sword deep into the creature's tangle of necks.

With a click, the sword sectioned out again into a flexible whip. Harper kept hold of the hilt as she jumped off the beast's back. The blade wrapped around a portion of the necks, and Harper's momentum sliced through them like a guillotine.

Gurgles of smoky blood spurted from the wound. Rylan let go of the semi-detached head. He snatched Harper and flapped backward in one giant step as the herrelspurn collapsed in an explosion of blood-like lava.

Everly kept the ghast tangled in her light until it stilled completely before she withdrew those tendrils. The glow around her faded and she landed as easily on the ground as if she'd simply taken a step forward.

As the scorching blood sizzled away into the earth, the shadyrs, Harper, and Everly stood together, catching their breaths.

No one spoke, but in the bright-eyed gazes shared between them, a heavy satisfaction was clear. They'd fought as a team and fought well.

"I'd say that confirms the use of those bloody bone effigies as lures," Lian muttered as she and Rushelle rejoined them.

They had already shaken off their demon-like forms,

and the other shadyrs joined them, returning to their human shapes.

Across the field, the front door of the house clanged, and Neri jogged awkwardly toward them, still red. Her wings flapped lopsidedly, giving her small boosts of speed that left her stumbling.

"I've never done herrelspurn form before," Tammy said, looking over her shoulders as though she already missed her wings.

"You and your all-black outfit pulled off the look the best, I have to say," Harper grinned.

"Eh, clashes with my hair," Cherry muttered with a smirk. "Why can't we take some kind of cool Coruscare shadyr form?"

"Hrm, that's a good point," Lian said. "The Coruscare is a creature from the Everdark after all. But we don't seem to have any reaction to it."

"Because whatever the Coruscare is, it's not an eidolghast." Rylan's voice was low. "Shadyrs only react to eidolghasts. We don't shift in reaction to creatures from earth, either."

Everly let out a huff of air. She hadn't ever thought of it that way before. She still considered the thing inside her to be a monster, but it was at least a little comforting that it wasn't *that* kind of monster.

She glanced over at Harper who was beaming at her.

The sword had stopped glowing once the herrelspurn was defeated. It seemed to react to eidolghasts, too.

Could it be what let Harper see the weak spot?

"I don't suppose you're seeing any glowing weak spots on me?" Even if the sword no longer seemed active, Everly wanted to be sure.

"No weak spots at all." Harper's eyes wrinkled as her smile grew. "Oof!"

Neri stumbled up against her, clinging on to steady herself as her wings kept flapping of their own accord. "Did you get hurt? There was so much fire."

She warily eyed a patch of grass that still smoldered.

Harper's cheeks colored, and she backed away from Neri by a small step but held her arm out to keep the girl from toppling over. "All good here. Thank you."

"I think our newest household member might be feeling a bit rough still." Cherry shrugged toward Jasper, who had slumped over with his hands on his knees.

Jasper straightened up and tried to tidy his hair. "Just ... tired."

As though a strong gust of air had hit only him, he swayed on his feet, then folded onto the ground with a thump.

He shook his head from where he sat. "Okay, very tired. And sore."

"Don't worry, little duck, you're with us now. We'll

look after you," Rushelle said, smiling from him to Cherry. "If that's okay with everyone."

There were nods all around. Neri's eyes widened. "Does that mean I can use my ... *talents* now too?"

"If you want to," Harper said.

Neri gave a firm nod.

Jasper shook his head and his nose wrinkled as Cherry helped him up. His voice was a raspy whisper.

"Thank you, for letting me stay. For everything."

Cherry's lips raised in a half-smile, but his gaze remained cool. "Jasper, this is our new friend Neri. Just wait until you hear what she can do."

As Neri began her song, Everly looked out over the field where the lures had been. The haunting strains of the mermaid-girl's voice renewed Everly physically, but she couldn't shake off the worry that had permeated her.

They could bring Jasper in, they could give him their trust, but how long were any of them going to be able to stay safe when their enemy could send monster after monster their way?

CHAPTER FIVE

A hot ember of concern had settled into the pit of Rylan's stomach since Jasper came to them with his information about the Mesmans.

He'd suspected someone had tried to have him killed. He suspected there were dark magics being played with. But having those suspicions confirmed flipped his world over like a rowboat on a wild sea.

It had to be set right.

After the death of his dad, Rylan trusted Mordan Darkfrey to train him so that he'd never feel useless as a loved one died, ever again. He'd put every ounce of his trust into the Darkfreys. He left his home and family. He pushed Everly away.

And now Callan was talking about the possibility that their father's death wasn't simply a tragic ghast attack.

That it was one of the Darkfreys' own who caused their father to die.

Mordan had to be told what the Mesmans were doing.

He would deal with them, and the division they had caused could be repaired. He, Callan, and the others could rejoin the Darkfreys.

Is that what I want?

There was a part of him that deeply missed belonging to that institution. He had been part of something bigger. He'd been one of the best. Mordan had treated him like one of his own children.

He only left because he knew someone there wanted him dead, but the others at Howell House left for their own reasons. Reasons that wouldn't change with the end of the Mesmans' plotting.

He doubted any of them would go back if that was all that changed. Maybe Denny, if they'd take him.

Could I go back to the Darkfreys without the others?

Rylan huffed as he slid back his jacket hood, his breath coming out in a white cloud. He was getting ahead of himself. First, they needed to tell Mordan and see how he was going to handle the issue.

They arrived at The Crow's Nest, and Shroudhaven lay in an eerie stillness. Low clouds created a glary gloom, but no rain fell. The wind that often rushed up the streets like a howling banshee was absent, and the temperature was cold enough that Everly's nose and cheeks turned pink. The rosiness against her white hair had her looking so beautiful that the breath caught in Rylan's throat.

She noticed him staring and averted her eyes. Ever since the cave under the lighthouse, when he opened up to her, shared how he truly felt, she'd been avoiding him.

Is it some kind of twisted revenge for how I pushed her away for so long?

No, that wasn't like her. There had to be something more going on. His lips still tingled with the ghost of their icy kiss in the caves, and the memory of the more heated kiss in Everly's dream.

Since waking up, he felt differently toward Everly than before. Less of a fierce protectiveness, and more a fierce desire to be with her. To feel her lips on his again, and again. But maybe that wasn't what she wanted. He told her he loved her, but did she feel that way about him? He knew they had been good friends, and that pushing her away had hurt her deeply.

But he didn't know whether she felt *more* for him than that. After all the years putting her safety ahead of his feelings, maybe he'd blown his chance with her for good. Misty air huffed from his mouth again, coming out in a shiver.

Lian locked the car, then turned to where they stood on the cracked footpath. "You think he'll show?"

Rylan nodded once. He had Mordan's private number and had set up the meeting away from Darkfrey Estate so the information could be relayed in a neutral location. He didn't want the Mesmans getting wind of things too soon, before Mordan could make his move against them. Mordan had seemed happy to hear from Rylan which was an undeniable relief that he hadn't lost Mordan's favor entirely.

"I still don't get why I have to be here," Tammy mumbled, tucking her blackened hands deep into the pockets of her coat.

Lian pushed the heavy, dungeon-like front door open, leading them inside. "You're part of our evidence. You heard Blaise talk about his parents having a number of stolen artifacts."

Tammy scoffed. "In case them trying to kill us all multiple times isn't enough for Mordan to want to do something about them."

Warm air met Rylan as he stepped inside. The Crow's Nest was always cozy, comforting, and cluttered, with swathes of beaded, multicolored curtains and rainbow light cast through stained-glass lampshades. The smoky remnants of incense and smudge sticks mixed with the scents of alcohol and deep-fried food.

Mismatched tables held groups of people, some in Darkfrey jackets, others looking like average Shroudhaven citizens. But all would have been shadyrs. A few looked up but quickly returned to their own conversations and drinks with little more than an eyeroll at the presence of the Howell team.

"There he is," Rylan said, tilting his head toward the far end of the bar.

Mordan sat on his own by a small coffee table. His slick, satin lapel jacket contrasted with the frayed corduroy of the old armchair he'd claimed.

On their way there, Crowea swooped over to their side in a jingle of bracelets and swoosh of long skirts.

"Got business with the old man?" She raised her eyebrow over her one good eye. "You know I don't tolerate conflict in my house."

"We won't cause any trouble," Rylan grunted.

Crowea fanned a gloved hand at him almost like shooing a fly. "Trouble follows you like a vengeful ghost, boy."

Lian pursed her lips. "Hopefully this will be the end of some problems."

She nodded to Crowea and turned away.

"One moment." Crowea grabbed Lian's arm. "In case you haven't heard yet, Candace Zathory passed away a couple of nights ago. I know you two were close, many years back."

Rylan recognized the name too. A woman of his

mother's age, still active in the Darkfreys' ranks. While she looked like a formidable shadyr, she wasn't in a brace herself anymore, and instead ran some of the classes at the estate.

Lian's shrewd gaze softened. "How'd she go?"

"In her sleep."

"Lucky. Plenty of worse ways for a shadyr to go." Lian patted Crowea's gloved hand.

"I'll bring you some drinks, on the house." Crowea jangled away to the bar.

"Are you okay?" Everly asked Lian.

Lian sighed, but her smile returned. "I was friends with Candace back when we were kids but hadn't seen her in decades."

"Loss is still loss though," Everly replied.

"That it is." Lian pulled her ankle-length gray cardigan a little tighter around herself as she led them toward the leader of the Darkfreys.

"Mordan, I'm surprised you came alone." Lian dragged her chair a little farther away from him before sitting down.

Mordan smiled, fine lines creasing around his eyes. "Oh, a Darkfrey is never alone in Shroudhaven."

His grin broadened as his gaze took in Rylan. "Good to see you up and around, my boy."

Rylan took a seat directly across from Mordan, finding himself smiling in return, although he did notice Lian bristling at the term of endearment. Everly and Tammy shared a small two-seater lounge beside them.

Mordan clapped his hands together. "Now, I know you're not a fan of niceties, Ms. Howell, so would you like to get straight to it?"

"I would." Lian's eyebrows raised, but she reached into her bag and drew out the papers Jasper had brought them as evidence of the Mesmans' activities. "A couple of your shadyrs are messing around with dark magic. Creating lures to draw in eidolghasts. Trying to open their own shroudpool."

Mordan bent forward to look at the loose pages, rubbing his white-and-gray-streaked goatee. "Ah, the Mesmans."

Rylan shifted to the edge of his chair. "You know?"

"Oh, I'm sorry. Did I ruin your big reveal?" Mordan's eyes twinkled.

Rylan shot a look at Lian, who frowned back at him.

"If this is all you've come to see me about, I'm afraid you're wasting your time. They aren't the villains you think they are." Mordan moved to pick up the papers, but Rylan smacked his hand on top of them, pulling them back.

"So, they didn't try to have me killed?" Rylan spoke through gritted teeth, and the ember in his gut seemed to burst into flame.

"Well, yes. They did go a bit off script there. I'm sorry."

"You *knew*?" Everly glared intensely at Mordan and

light flared around her. Everyone else stilled, watching her warily. With a shake of her head she muttered something to herself, and the glow flickered and faded.

Rylan swallowed, as though he could put out his own fire burning within but didn't have as much control as Everly had just shown. Swirling thoughts and implications clouded his mind like smoke.

Mordan knew. And he's acting like it was nothing.

Mordan cleared his throat and continued. "They thought they were doing the right thing to keep some important secrets. I did discipline them at the time. But generally, they provide great value to our shadyr mission, so I have to overlook some things."

Lian sneered. "Value? How could luring eidolghasts to innocent family homes be valuable?"

The realization hit Rylan like brass knuckles to the sternum. He wasn't the only shadyr child who ended up with the Darkfreys when one or both of their parents died in an eidolghast attack.

Annabeth had a similar story, and many others over the years since Rylan moved to the estate.

And it wasn't always children. Sometimes those with shadyr blood would be drawn back to Shroudhaven without realizing what they were but would very quickly find out when a ghast showed up at their home.

Rylan's tone was low and gravelly. "You've been using

the lures to identify shadyrs. To motivate them to join the Darkfreys."

Mordan's eyes narrowed, but his smile remained. "The Mesmans' magic has proven to be the perfect tool to help bring reluctant shadyrs into the fold. A very successful recruitment method, in fact."

Lian straightened in her chair. Her cardigan opened to the side, revealing her hand resting on the hilt of her sword. "You had my husband killed for *recruitment*?"

Mordan sighed. "I had to do something when it became clear you weren't making any efforts to train your sons. I couldn't very well let two strong shadyr boys of the Pimey line go to waste. I understand it seems cruel, but so is this world and the monsters in it that we are at *war* with. The results have been worth it. We have built the biggest shadyr army in history. I've done what is needed to make us strong enough to fight back the darkness."

Rylan couldn't breathe. He'd left his home, his family ... He had been a child, thinking he was doing the right thing, going somewhere he could learn to be a good fighter, so that he could protect his loved ones from the fate that took his father.

But his father had been killed by the very people he turned to. He spent half his life working for them, being the best soldier he could be, and it had all been built upon a lie.

Rylan couldn't think straight as the ember inside him

boiled the blood behind his eyes. His whole body heated, and in such close proximity to Everly and the powerful eidolghast essences she radiated, he almost lost control of his change.

He only had so much control because of what the Darkfreys had taught him. He hated that the parts of him he thought were the strongest were now tainted by their cause.

Who would I be now if the Darkfreys hadn't recruited me? Everything, everything would be different.

His breath came in deep pants that left him dizzy.

A hand rested upon his, squeezing gently. Everly had reached over, locking eyes onto his face. A shiver railroaded up Rylan's spine. He clenched his teeth and made an effort to not explode.

By his other side, Lian sat deadly still. "You are *dripping* with blood. How many have died for your cause?"

"How many would have died without it?" Mordan asked back, sincerely.

"Less, if you weren't busy killing your own." Rylan couldn't look at Mordan.

The sting of shame joined the white-hot fury burning inside him. It wasn't just the betrayal of how he became a Darkfrey that hurt him. It was the fact that they tried to have him killed, and Mordan knew. He *knew* all along and he didn't care. As twisted as they were, the Darkfreys were his family.

He'd felt special there, important. But he was expendable to them.

"I never wanted to lose you," Mordan said. "You really were one of our best. You and your brother would still be welcomed back, if you can put this all behind us."

"You set lures at my home again just last night! You tried to kill us all, and you want them to put it behind them?" Lian's knuckles turned white in their grip around the hilt, but she remained statue-still.

Mordan steepled his fingers and tilted his head almost bashfully. "After Jasper left how he did, there were concerns you all knew things that you shouldn't know. We had to make efforts to stop the spread of sensitive information. But when you reached out for this meeting, I hoped we could come to an understanding."

Rylan's mouth was too dry to speak, and the others simply stared, aghast. Mordan continued, "I've been upfront with you all. I'm hoping that you can understand the logic and honor in our actions. I know your losses have been personal, but we must think beyond ourselves. This is for the greater cause, as is everything I have ever done."

"How is opening a shroudpool part of the greater cause?" Tammy hugged her thin chest tightly, and Rylan could see her shivering despite the warmth of the room.

Mordan flicked his fingers dismissively. "That's just

the Mesmans' pet project, and honestly, I doubt anything will ever come of it. Now, I'm sure you realize that the information we've shared can't go any further. Many won't have the capacity to grasp the work the Mesmans and I have done. I'm hoping that you can. Do we have an understanding?"

Rylan tightened a fist around the pages on the table, scrunching them in his hand. He glared at the mad scribblings and sketches, unable to loosen his grip as his fingers shook. Everly still squeezed his other hand, and his mother remained still and pale.

His whole life he'd trained to fight monsters. But he was only now feeling the cost. Life couldn't only be death and loss. And he couldn't be part of an organization that lived that way, that accepted those tragedies as normal. They were no better than the monsters he'd learned to kill.

He whispered, "No. I don't understand."

"Hrm. That's a shame." Mordan shrugged and snapped his fingers.

Every other shadyr in the establishment stood up in a clatter of chairs and downed drinks. They closed in, forming a wall between the Howell team and the exit. From behind curtains toward the back, Rylan's old brace, or what remained of them, stepped out—Nilson, Annabeth, and Vonny Mesman.

Rylan shot to his feet, the others behind him.

Lian's sword sang as she unsheathed it halfway in warning. Rylan knew she wouldn't draw it entirely until she needed to strike, because she'd be blinded by its magic the moment it was out of the sheath.

"What is this all about?" Crowea's voice rose from behind the bar. "This is a safe space for all."

"This space, as with every space in Shroudhaven, only exists with my permission," Mordan barked back.

He got to his feet with the slow actions of an old body, but Rylan knew he was as deadly as any shadyr around them. "And traitors to our very race and the safety of our entire dimension won't be tolerated."

"Can you clear a path out for us?" Rylan whispered to Everly.

When she didn't immediately reply, he turned to find her looking green, bent as though punched in the stomach.

Rylan grunted, spinning back to the approaching Darkfreys.

Vonny smirked at him from between her blond bob as she strode forward, unwrapping a bundle of old parchment in her hands to reveal sharp, diamond-shaped metal that oozed dark blood.

"Ghast dammit," Rylan muttered.

Beside her, Nilson held no weapon, and Rylan imagined he'd be pleased to kill them all with his bare hands. Annabeth followed a couple of steps back, eyes red-rimmed but firm.

"Make a break for the front door? Or try for the back?" Lian whispered.

Before Rylan could reply, Tammy stepped in front of him and snatched Lian's hand into hers. *Tammy.*

He guessed what the girl was planning and hoped she could pull it off as she had in the flooding cave. He quickly put a hand on her shoulder, keeping the papers held tight in his other.

Vonny watched the way they came together with her teeth bared, pausing for a moment to sneer at them.

Tammy reached across to Everly, and as her black hand touched Everly's skin, the lights flickered and a *whomp* of magical mist burst from them.

Rylan hadn't noticed that reaction when they were in the cave, but he'd also been up to his eyebrows in icy seawater and watching as Everly came far too close to death.

He didn't have long to take it in this time either, as a moment later a tug jarred him, like someone had put a shark hook through his heart and pulled. Sensations of twisting air, being dragged through mist, of *being* only mist overwhelmed him, until they were gone seconds later, and the four of them stood together at the Dark Corner shroudpool.

Everly took a deep breath beside him, the color quickly returning to her now that the Bane wasn't nearby. "How could they? They're evil, all of them."

Rylan's chest hurt, and he squinted his eyes closed. "No. You don't understand how important defending this world against eidolghasts is for shadyrs. Some would do *anything* for that cause. They aren't evil. They're fanatics."

"Same thing, I'd say," Lian muttered. "And no matter what we call them, they now want us dead."

CHAPTER SIX

Learning that the death of Rylan and Callan's father had been a purposeful attack almost pushed Everly over an edge into a rage she wasn't sure she could come back from.

It had been a strange sensation, similar to a panic attack with the same racing, clenching heart, but with a determined strain deep in her muscles that urged her to take action. Take *revenge*.

She wasn't sure how much of that was her, and how much was her dragon. But for a few moments, the idea of ripping the soul from the man who caused them all so much pain seemed like the most sensible course of action. It would have been good. He deserved it.

Maybe he did, but Everly didn't think she had the right to make that judgment or execute such a punishment. She managed to reel those emotions back in, whether they were her own or the Coruscare's.

Callan picked them up in Lian's SUV, and the return to Howell House was somber and quiet. All in all, attacks on their lives included, they were back home by midafternoon.

Rushelle made everyone hot drinks, and they gathered around the long farmhouse table.

Everly held her chamomile tea under her nose and breathed in the grassy, apple scent, hoping it would help ground her, or bring her some inspiration as to what they could do next. "Do you think Crowea is okay?"

Lian shook her head, but replied, "I doubt they'd hurt her, and as much as she'll be furious about it, I don't know what she can do. Mordan was right in a way. The Darkfreys own this town."

"I'm sure Crow will get back at them in her own way. She must have some witchy hexes up her sleeve," Rushelle said.

"She'll probably close for a week to smudge away all the bad conflict energy." Harper chuckled, but her mirth faded almost instantly. "I can't believe they did that. All of it. I knew the Darkfreys weren't the best people in a lot of ways, but still ..."

Tammy had her head on the table, resting on folded arms, muddling her voice. "What can we do about it?"

There was a resignation in her tone, as though she

already knew the answer. *Nothing.*

Trying to come up with a solution to offer, Everly stared at the top of Tammy's head. The goth girl had previously kept her hair trimmed in a soldierly buzz cut, but over the last week or two she hadn't seemed to have cut it, and the black hair had a thicker, shaggy texture. Did she just want a change? Was she giving up on the strict guidelines of being a militant shadyr? Or was she just ... giving up?

Lian leaned her elbows on the table, cupping her mug between her hands so the steam drifted up in front of her face. "We have to think about our safety first. Whether we can stay here."

"I'm staying," Callan said firmly.

Although there were enough seats at the table, he remained on his feet, leaning on a hutch behind Tammy.

Rylan mirrored him on the other side, standing in front of the kitchen counter with arms crossed over his chest. He nodded in agreement, and the motion spread around the others in the room.

Lian sniffed. "You're brave kids, but if I think we have to leave to stay safe, we're going. This is just a building. You are all family."

"We need to stay so we can put a stop to what the Mesmans and Mordan are doing," Rylan growled.

"And how are we going to do that?" Lian shot back. "Frontal assault the entire Darkfrey Estate? If Mordan considers the Mesmans valuable, he's going to keep them protected. Kole never leaves the estate as it is."

"Do we really think they even can open a shroudpool? Is that really a risk?" Everly asked.

The lures were a crime, but they could keep an eye out for them now, put a stop to them when they showed up. Opening another shroudpool right in the middle of Shroudhaven was something else.

Jasper still wore the same clothes he'd arrived in the night before, but had cleaned himself up, and been healed by Neri's singing.

He spoke a lot more confidently than before. "They are building the structure for it now. I'm sure that's what I saw. Whether they can activate it, and how, is the question."

"Eidolghasts open new shroudpools if they stay in one area for long enough," Cherry said. "Maybe they're keeping some ghast pets somehow as part of it?"

"At Darkfrey Estate? All the shadyrs there would sense them if they were," Denny scoffed. "I reckon they can't do it. Even if they've got a bit of old school shadyr magic happening. If they *could* do it, they would have done it already. It's been years since their kid punched a one-way ticket to the Everdark."

A soft groan came from where Tammy had her head down.

"Could you try for once to not be the biggest dick in

the room?" Callan snapped at Denny.

"Impossible. And I'll prove it if you like." Denny grabbed at his fly.

"For ghast's sake, that's—"

Tammy raised her head, her mouth open as though in terrible realization. "Do you know why? Why Blaise wanted to try to close a shroudpool?"

Denny opened his mouth again, but Callan slapped the back of his head before he could speak.

Tammy continued, her voice almost a whisper, "Because so many kids were losing their family to eidolghasts. He wanted to find a way to close the shroudpools for good, all of them, so that no more kids would have to lose their parents. So *he* wouldn't lose his parents. He was so scared something would kill them, but it was them! It was them all along ..."

Lian reached across the table for Tammy's hand. Her blackened fingers twitched, but she didn't pull away. "All this time they've been blaming it on you, never knowing it was the price they paid for their own actions."

"It was never your fault," Callan added.

Tammy's face scrunched, and she shook her head. But any reply was cut off by a knock at the front door.

Around the table, eyes scanned about as though doing a head count. They were all there, even Neri, sitting wide-eyed beside Harper, trying to take in as much as she could of all the new information.

Everly frowned. "You think they've come for us again?"

"But why knock?" Harper asked.

Lian got to her feet, striding toward the door with a no-nonsense *humph*. Every other chair scraped against the floor as the rest of them followed.

Through the screen, backed by the fading light outside, a single person stood silhouetted.

"Careful," Rylan hissed as Lian opened the door.

A young red-headed woman gawked back at them all crowded in the entrance.

"Annabeth?" Rylan nearly coughed the word.

"Um ... Hi?" she said, tucking a strand of curling hair behind a freckled ear. Beside her on the grayed timber of the porch was a black rolling suitcase.

Lian stepped out past the woman, her hand on the hilt of her sword and eyes narrowed on the surrounding fields.

She turned back to Annabeth. "You were there today, with Vonny."

Annabeth stood straighter as though at attention and gave a sharp nod. "They told us you were traitors, working to destroy us. I went along with orders even though they didn't make sense."

"Typical Darkfrey," Cherry muttered from the back.

Annabeth's shoulders lifted toward her ears. "I'm sorry. As soon as I got Jasper's message ... Things make sense now. I packed and left right away. I couldn't stay there." She chewed at her bottom lip. "I couldn't stay with the people who killed my parents."

"Jasper's message?" Lian asked.

Jasper winced and directed his explanation to Cherry, despite how everyone looked at him. "When Mordan's recruitment methods were revealed, I believed sharing that intel with Annabeth was the correct thing to do. I'm sorry. I promise I'm not making a habit of divulging secrets to the enemy anymore."

Rylan had kept his eyes on Annabeth. "Annabeth isn't the enemy. She's one of our brace."

Her bottom lip pouted, then she pulled it in, her back straightening even more.

Everly wondered how long the young woman had been trained as a soldier, at what age she'd been 'recruited.' Everly didn't understand brace dynamics, or how long she'd been in Rylan's, but it was clear they had formed a bond. From having both lost parents, and no doubt more.

Everly also knew how Annabeth felt about Rylan. And a dark, mourning place within her heart told her that maybe Rylan would be better off with Annabeth. Someone who truly understood his experience as a shadyr. Someone who hadn't messed with his soul and emotions his entire life. Someone who wasn't capable of doing it again.

We could. We could take him again, make him be ours.

Why not have what you want?

Everly shivered at the voice that shared space in her mind. It sounded so much like her own, but the urge behind it was cold and alien.

Or was it? She yearned to be close to Rylan, to have him for herself, to be the soulmates she once dreamed they were. How could she separate those feelings from the urges of the entity that possessed her?

Jasper nodded in agreement with Rylan but continued to look to Cherry with seeking eyes.

Cherry bit his bottom lip. "You were right. She deserves to know. They all do."

"I'm sorry for showing up here unannounced, but Jasper said you were very welcoming, and I hoped …" Annabeth's hand shot to her neckline and fidgeted with her necklace. "I mean, I understand if you don't want me here. I didn't do enough when Rylan was missing. I haven't been on the right side."

She twitched as though mentally slapping herself, then released the necklace and returned to a rigid stance of attention. Only her round, red-rimmed eyes revealed a deeper vulnerability.

Everly's heart softened for the girl.

"We all make mistakes. Especially when we put our trust in the wrong people. There are still a couple of spare rooms here, right?" she asked Lian.

Lian nodded slowly, and checked with Rylan, "You vouch for her?"

Rylan gave Annabeth a scrutinizing look but nodded.

"Okay, come on in then," Lian muttered.

Annabeth lifted one foot and seemed to hover for a moment before bringing it over the threshold. She deflated as her tense shoulders released.

"Hey, I like your necklace," Everly offered as she moved to make room.

The pendant had fallen on the outside of Annabeth's button up shirt after she'd played with it. It seemed made of an opalescent crystal, carved in a single, thin point as small as a fingertip. It was a dark, smoky color, with bright highlights like sparks from a fire.

Her hand went to it reflexively again. "Thank you. It's a family heirloom. A piece of true pre-crossover shadyr bone. It's all I have left from my parents."

Everly smirked. "Sweet *and* creepy. I like it."

Rushelle pushed her way in beside them. "Oh, I do like new people! Let me get that for you."

She reached for Annabeth's luggage, grunting as she dragged it toward the stairway. "Wow, did you escape the Darkfreys with a bag full of gold bullion or something?"

Annabeth helped lift the other end as they made their way up the stairs. "I might have, um, stolen a bunch of books."

"Ha!" Rushelle barked. "A reader, huh? I don't suppose you like erotic satire?"

"Rylan, you should show Annabeth around," Everly said.

The words came fast, as though she had to chase them out before they stuck. "You and Jasper, you know her best. Help her feel at home."

"Good idea," Lian said. "And keep an eye on her for a little while too. Just in case."

With the threat of danger passed, most of them had already drifted away, either back to the dining room, or off to their own rooms, in the case of Tammy. Everly took the chance to slip into the living room, feeling the need for space to take some long, deep breaths.

She stood in front of the vintage TV cabinet, staring at photos of the Howell brothers as young boys, when someone cleared their throat behind her.

She turned to find Rylan there, standing close enough to see the warm golden flecks in his olive-green eyes. "Aren't you going to show Annabeth around?"

He shrugged but didn't break eye contact. "Jasper and Rush are on it. Denny also volunteered so I let him take my spot."

"Denny? Nooo, why? Do you hate Annabeth?"

Rylan huffed a laugh.

"Anna can hold her own. Besides," his lips pulled tight,

and he licked them, "we need to talk."

Everly took a long, shaking breath. Her body reflexively took a step backward, but she came up against the cabinet, making the frames rattle.

Rylan gently reached for her chin and turned her to face him again. "No excuses. No running away. No interruptions. I just ... want to know why you're avoiding me. I know I probably deserve it, but—"

"You don't. You don't deserve any of it. That isn't why I've been avoiding this. It's just hard. What happened, it's so awful I haven't known how to tell you."

"What's happened?" Rylan's hands moved to her shoulders, his grasp firm through her red bomber jacket. "Are you okay?"

Everly's chest stung like it was wrapped in barbed wire. *He's still so protective. It hasn't faded.*

She swallowed away the pain and pressed her feet firmly downward to ground herself.

She had to tell him. Now.

"When the second piece of the Coruscare joined with me, I learned so much, about how it behaves, what it can do. It doesn't just eat souls. Sometimes, it can steal a small fragment of a person's essence, to bind that person to it. It enslaves them, making them want to protect the Coruscare at all costs."

She stared into Rylan's eyes, hoping he would

understand. There was a wrinkle between his eyebrows as he stared back, but he didn't speak.

"That night, when the vasmire almost killed you, that wasn't when I first stole your essence into me. It was when we first met, lost in the woods. The Coruscare has bound you too me ever since then."

Rylan's hands dropped and his eyebrows pressed low over his eyes. "What does that mean?"

Everly exhaled slowly, fighting the sting in her nose and her eyes that threatened to burst into sobs. "It means none of your feelings for me are real. It's how the Coruscare has made you feel so that you'd help keep me, its host, safe."

Rylan took a step back. He didn't seem angry, just confused. His eyes roamed the ceiling as though seeking answers, then returned to her.

"Are you sure?"

"It's why I always dreamt of you, every night since we met. Part of you was always with me." Everly winced at how that sounded, almost romantic, so she added, "Stolen, without your consent."

He shook his head fiercely. "But you haven't dreamed of me since you woke me up, since you freed me with the Bane. You must have freed all of me then, right?"

"Yeah, I think so."

"How I feel about you, what I told you in the cave ... That was when I was free. And I've felt that way for a long time. It hasn't changed." He pressed a thumb to his bottom lip thoughtfully. "Not a lot. Feeling protective of you was one thing, but ... I feel so much more than that now."

Everly clenched her teeth in an effort to force back tears. Everything she ever wanted was right in front of her, so close she could see his pulse beating in his neck, and it was all wrong.

"It's not real. The soul bond has been messing with your emotions, our emotions, for fourteen years. It's going to take a while to really know what's real."

"No. I don't need a while. I pushed you away for so long, thinking distance is what would keep you safe. Maybe that was the bond, making me think protecting you should come above how I felt about you. I don't know. Honestly, I don't care. I'm free now and I *know* I want to be with you." Rylan's throat moved as he swallowed, and his eyes locked onto hers. "I just need to know if you want to be with me too."

It felt as though time collapsed around Everly. As though she could stand in that moment for eternity, lost in Rylan's longing eyes, avoiding having to form an answer that would ruin her.

As a child she'd loved him so deeply that she imagined their love would last lifetime after lifetime, soulmates seeking each other out in every new reincarnation, for all of eternity.

He had been everything to her. Her best friend, her savior, her first love.

But she was only a child. Even if she'd carried those foolish romantic dreams into adulthood.

She swallowed her heart, pressing it deep down into a vault of stone. "We don't even know each other. Not really. Not anymore. Not after so many years apart, and everything that has changed."

Rylan's lip twitched and he took a small step closer. "But what do you *want*? How do you really feel?"

I love you. I love you with every heartbeat.

She couldn't say it. She couldn't bind him to her like that again. Not while the *thing* inside her remained. But denying those feelings was a lie she couldn't produce on her stuttering lips.

A stream of light curved in through the living room window and gravel crunched outside.

Lian's voice came from the hallway. "Looks like more visitors."

Rylan groaned and pushed the curtains aside to look out.

Everly peered around his shoulder to see not just one car, but a slow stream of vehicles coming up the drive.

Rylan cursed under his breath. "An attack?"

"Maybe. Maybe not." Lian joined them in the living room, looking out the second window beside them.

"Annabeth said she may have told a few others about what's been going on. And word can travel fast."

The first Darkfrey-marked van came to a jolting stop, and a kid that looked too young to be driving hopped out, followed by two even younger children. They hovered near the car in a huddle, looking around as though unsure what to do next. The occupants of the second car were also climbing out, older teens, acting no more threateningly.

Lian sighed. "I guess being worried that Mordan will come after us to keep his secrets is a moot point now."

"Looks like the damage has been done," Everly agreed, as the teens nervously approached the porch, and the younger kids skittered after them.

"Why in the Everdark are they all coming here?" Rylan muttered.

Everly turned to Lian, who stood tall and slim in the beam of a headlight breaking into the living room. Her wrinkled expression was set like a solid wall, but one built from strength and compassion.

Everly smiled. "Because they know this is a place shadyrs can come when they have nowhere else to go. They know they will be accepted here. No matter what."

She just hoped it would remain a place they could all be safe.

Chapter Seven

Everly missed her dreams with Rylan. Even when they were nightmares, they were better than the dreams she'd had since.

Now, she shared her sleeping mind with the Coruscare.

I'm dreaming, she told herself, although it was easy to tell this wasn't real life. The landscape she saw before her wasn't even this *dimension*.

Most of her dreams now took place in the Everdark, before it had become the Everdark, when the Coruscare still ruled over the shadyrs. She seemed to share the entity's memories. And since it had many thousands of years of memories more than her, those were the visions that now dominated her mind.

A swirling, seasick feeling of movement accompanied the dreams, and Everly winced as her body lurched through the yellow-tinted world, the sense of motion disturbingly mismatched to the direction she moved.

She'd seen visions of this dimension from when the Coruscare was at the height of its power, but this was different. The crystalline forests and pillar-shaped mountains burned, blackened and cracking, as eidolghasts swarmed in large mobs.

There were so many of them. Vasmires, weroths, auerdaxes, herrelspurn, and many more that Everly couldn't name. They squabbled and tore at each other, dark gore carpeting the ground.

They did not originate from my realm.

Everly looked for the source of the words, but the Coruscare didn't bring itself before her in visible form. Still, its voice came through as clear as a spike of ice to her eye.

"There are so many of them." Everly shivered. Were there still so many of these creatures in the Everdark? Were there *more*?

My dark mirror, shadow twin, assisted their encroachment. Made them tools to betray and destroy this self. Take this self's power.

Everly's nose twitched. The Coruscare liked to paint itself as the great victim, but she didn't buy it. She'd seen how it used and abused the entire race of shadyrs for its own power. Whatever this shadow twin was, they were probably as bad as each other.

"I thought it was the Bane of Teeth and Stars that broke you?"

A rattling hiss thundered so loud Everly covered her ears.

Forged by the shadow twin. Wielded by. Endless eons we contested but never found triumph, never for either. No comprehension how dark twin destroyed this self, but have seen, since awaking in this vessel.

Vessel was said with a heavy disdain for how it viewed her and her body, but Everly was used to this. She also knew what it meant by having "seen."

Not only did she share the Coruscare's memories, but they also seemed to be able to access the memories of some of the beings it had consumed the life essences of. It made for scattered, confusing dreams, like looking out through the eyes of multiple insects, a kaleidoscope of perspectives patched together.

A tug shifted her untethered consciousness, like a wave pushing her about in the ocean, as the Coruscare took her through the space-time of the dreamscape. The sensation of movement felt so real it left Everly's stomach churning.

The sky darkened, something vast and black shadowing the realm. Beneath the coal-smoke sky, masses of eidolghasts congregated. They moved in wild, hectic motions, as a force dragged them all toward a central point.

"They're terrified," Everly gasped.

This self has seen, from essence consumed since waking. One that saw and survived.

The ghasts clawed and ripped at each other, stampeding desperately to escape the pull, but they were drawn ever inward. There had to be thousands of them. Everly narrowed her eyes, trying to see what was in the middle that they were destined for.

A sickly green orb hovered there, above an immense altar where the Bane lay. The sphere wasn't much larger than a basketball, and it drew eidolghasts to it as though it was a black hole.

And then it would *pulse.*

It enlarged, expanding so much that multiple eidolghasts could fit inside. The crystalline green material that formed it fractured into a web, and eidolghasts were drawn *through* it, shredding them in the process. Then it collapsed in on itself again.

The mass of the victims it had drawn in seemed to vanish, and from the bottom of the sphere, a single drop of thick, dark blood dripped onto the Bane.

The process continued. The sphere expanded and contracted, like a Hoberman sphere toy in the hands of a hyperactive child.

Everly stared, open-mouthed in horror. It was harvesting thousands of eidolghasts, and crushing them into ... what? Some sort of essential oil of monster?

"That's why it hurts you," Everly wondered out aloud. "It's just too much energy. That's why it bleeds constantly. It contains more power than it possibly should."

And the blood was a mix of so many eidolghasts, as Lian had observed in Gorhanmere.

Bane must be destroyed. Have let foes take control of what can end self.

Everly nodded. She could at least agree with that. She didn't like the idea of Vonny being in possession of a weapon that totally incapacitated her. She didn't seem shy about using it either.

Everly couldn't watch the massacre any longer. Even if they were monsters. She turned her eyes away, staring up into the darkened sky.

And the sky stared back at her.

Everly pitched forward on the lounge, gasping into consciousness. Her heart raced and her sleeping bag rustled as she pushed it off, trying to cool her overheated body.

"You all right, duck?" Rushelle leaned in from the hallway.

She had a sparkly toiletries bag in one hand, and a toothbrush sticking out one side of her mouth.

"Yeah, fine. Just a bad dream." Everly gave Rushelle a reassuring smile, thankful for her presence.

After the lures and open conflict with the Darkfreys, Lian had wanted Everly, Harper, and Neri to move into

Howell House, at least for a while. But Everly couldn't handle the idea of even more time spent around Rylan.

It was hard enough seeing him at all but living under the same roof would be too much.

She reassured Lian that the three of them would be fine. They were right around the corner, and Everly could deal with almost anything except the Bane.

Still, Rushelle had volunteered to stay over for a while. Just in case. For Lian's peace of mine. Everly was happy with that, even if it meant Rushelle got her old bedroom and she continued sleeping on the couch in the living room. To be honest, she wasn't sure she was ready to move back into her old bedroom anyway. It had never been a happy place.

"Thanks for staying with us," Everly told Rushelle, as she had every day for the last couple of weeks.

Rushelle waved it off, her sunshine-yellow, boa-hemmed nightgown puffing around her fingers.

"It's been no trouble. I mean, I'm not getting to see as much of my boyfriends, but you loves are worth it." She passed Harper in the hall as she stepped back into the bathroom.

"Did she just use the plural?" Harper blinked groggily.

Everly shrugged, still half asleep herself.

Harper yawned and leaned on the ladder-stairs going to Neri's attic room. She'd still been so tired since using the Bane to empower herself. Everly frowned at her friend, wondering whether beneath the already done makeup, she'd find dark circles under her contact-colored green eyes.

"You okay?" she asked.

"Yeah," Harper said through a second yawn. "Neri had a bit of a rough night again. I'm surprised she didn't wake you too."

"I didn't hear a thing. I must have been out hard." Everly pulled her jacket on over the old T-shirt and leggings she wore as makeshift pajamas.

With the four of them sharing one bathroom, she could wait until later in the morning to get in a shower and get dressed properly. "You want me to cover the pack and ship this morning? If you want to get a bit more sleep in, that's okay."

"You're sweet. But I'm okay. Just poke me with a stick if I nod off."

The two of them headed downstairs and Harper made coffee. Everly checked the plate of meat she'd set out for Zozo the night before, but it hadn't been eaten. She still set out food each night, and some nights it would go.

She couldn't be certain it was the undead cougar that ate it. But she felt good on those mornings, and worried on those when the food was left untouched. Then she and Harper went into the antiques store to get a bit of work done.

It felt strange to Everly, acting as though life was

normal, going about such mundane motions as printing invoices and packaging antiques for the mail. She could still feel how her dream of the Everdark left her skin crawling, how the eidolghast filled the dimension to overflowing.

And dread burbled in the pit of her stomach at the thought of a doorway to that hellscape being opened in the middle of Darkfrey Estate.

But time passed, and nothing happened.

Life fell into a holding pattern of daily activities, so normal it was disturbing. Although there had been some huge changes as well.

After getting the most urgent customer service work completed for the day, and Everly got her time in the bathroom, the four of them headed over to Howell House where the differences to daily life were more obvious.

The residence was now packed with Darkfrey defectors. Every spare room was full, and the front yard and nearby field looked like a tent city, with shadyrs living out of cars and makeshift shelters. Harper even donated her campervan to the housing efforts.

Although many of the shadyrs had their own homes around Shroudhaven, it quickly became clear that the Darkfreys weren't going to let the defectors live peacefully after leaving. There had been violent attacks, and more use of the bone lures.

There was safety in numbers, and the number of

shadyrs making Howell House their home had grown significantly.

How long can this last?

This couldn't be the long-term solution to the divide between shadyrs. There just wasn't enough space or services for everyone there. Everly was suddenly grateful that it was only the four of them sharing one bathroom at her place. Lian had her come over to fix the plumbing in the old homestead once already.

Darkfrey Estate still held the balance of power—in the shadyr conflict, and the town as a whole. As long as they were retaliating against those they considered traitors, the temporary living arrangements would remain.

Rushelle waved as she headed to the kitchen to help out with the constant work of making meals for everyone, and Harper and Neri split off to join in with a daily training session. Rylan was running a lot of those himself, so Everly went in the other direction.

He hadn't pushed her again for an answer to how she felt about him after they were interrupted last time. She hoped that meant what she'd told him had sunk in, that he'd examined his own feelings and realized they weren't as real as he thought. Even if that left a churning black hole of despair in Everly's chest, it would be the right thing.

Everly adjusted the tool belt slung around her wide waist, and made her way to where Callan was unloading some timber and metal sheeting from a truck. She'd already helped build one temporary shelter, and they'd just brought in supplies for another. It was something she had the skills for, and she liked being useful, even if the shadyrs often watched her with wide eyes and barely concealed whispers.

The information about her possession by the Coruscare had gotten out.

Jasper was a suspect at first, but the trail of gossip led back to Denny bragging about having a god on their side.

It was clear a lot of the Darkfrey defectors weren't entirely sure about this new alliance, and reliance, on the Howells.

Many questioned the existence of the Coruscare, as though Everly were making it up to seek attention, and others still considered Tammy to be a murderer. They acted as though it were beneath them to be cowering together there with these misfits.

And yet, there they were.

Rylan, Callan, and Jasper helped bridge the gap. They had all been well-respected in the Darkfrey ranks, and it was clear some of that respect still held.

"I can take those." Everly looked up to where Callan unstrapped some two-by-fours on the truck bed.

The invoice stapled to the top of the timber with a logo for Pimey's Hardware had been discounted to zero.

It seemed as though Lian was pulling favors from

family. Everly knew there had been a divide there too, when Lian left the Darkfreys, married a human, and became a Howell. But with the new revelations of the Darkfreys' actions, some of her relatives in the Pimey line were opening back up to Lian and helping out where they could.

That was the last of the building materials, and Callan jumped down beside Everly. His gaze kept shifting over to the porch, where Tammy stood rigidly in front of an older couple and two children.

Cherry and Jasper brought over a miter saw and rolled out an extension cable. A few shadyrs close to Tammy's age walked by, chatting in low and gossipy voices.

Everly caught the end of a sentence. "... I wouldn't forgive her, she's cursed."

"Hey!" Callan barked. "We don't act like that here. Tammy's done nothing wrong, and if I hear you giving her a hard time again, you'll be answering to me."

Everly's eyes widened. She'd never heard him speak like that before, sounding like a drill sergeant rather than his usual, cheerful self. He was only a couple years older than the teenagers, but they looked like they were ready to drop and give him a hundred. There were some mumbled apologies, and they bumped into each other in a rush to back away.

"Who is Tammy talking to?" Everly asked.

His expression softened immediately into his usual

lopsided grin, tickled at the edges by long, feathery hair. "That's her family."

"Oh. Is that ... is she okay?" Everly examined the people surrounding Tammy, looking for resemblances.

With her dark-rimmed eyes and short hair, it was hard to pick, but one of the kids could have been her brother. He was the first one to step forward and wrap Tammy in a hug. Her eyes went wide, and she almost impossibly became more rigid, straighter and stiffer than the two-by-fours Everly had just unloaded.

When her mother and father joined the embrace, Tammy's face scrunched in on itself. She flickered—there, then not there—but she didn't vanish entirely. Her blackened hands rose ever so slowly up around her parents, and then pulled them in tight.

Callan tilted his head, his eyes glossy. "Yeah, I think she's going to be okay."

Cherry plugged in the saw and stood up to join them. His gaze turned down the long, tree-lined driveway, as Everly had seen him do many times since Darkfrey shadyrs started showing up. There were no new arrivals.

It was obvious what he was looking for, but Everly didn't know how to comfort him without drawing attention to the fact that his parents hadn't joined them, hadn't offered him any apologies, or asked his forgiveness for casting him out.

Jasper watched Cherry for a long moment, as though

taking the opportunity to do so while Cherry was distracted. Everly doubted the two were back together, but Jasper often hovered close by Cherry's side.

"Tammy's parents only showed up this morning," Callan addressed Everly, but she figured it wasn't really meant for her. "Some shadyrs are needing a bit longer to change their thinking."

"I thought I saw the brace we met at Gorhanmere on the way in. I didn't know they were here," Everly said.

Callan brightened. "Yeah, Lucas's team. Him, Molly, Benson, and Parker. They arrived a few days back. Lian's old friend, Bob, came with them too. And Jasper's ... parents ..."

The four of them stood in an awkward silence until Jasper cleared his throat. "They're over there."

He pointed along a lane formed between tents to a very clean-cut couple with medium brown skin and silky black hair. The man had a strong Roman nose matching Jasper's.

Cherry sighed and stuffed his hands into his pockets.

Jasper's gaze flickered to him, then he lifted his chin. "You know, it took them that long, and they don't even ... well, I haven't come out to them yet."

His bronze skin warmed across his cheek bones, and he cleared his throat again. "Right then. I think I'd best go and do so."

Cherry's jaw hung open as Jasper marched away. Everly looked from one of them to the other with wide eyes.

Cherry closed his mouth and he flipped his hair nonchalantly. "He can be *such* a weirdo."

As they'd been chatting, Annabeth had moved closer to them, hovering at the edges of their group. When Jasper left, she shuffled into his space, offering a bashful smile as greeting.

"Can I help out?"

Callan turned from checking on Tammy again to greet her. "You're not joining in the training?"

Rylan had taken the group of younger shadyrs, including Neri and Harper, over into the field beside the lane.

"Mm, I'm probably getting a bit rusty, but to be honest I was always more into the academic side of things than active brace duties." Annabeth turned deerlike eyes onto Everly.

"What are they doing down there?" Everly asked, trying to see through the patchy birch trunks.

Callan smirked. "We found a dead vasmire out in the field this morning. Not sure who took it out. We haven't really got any formal patrol rosters and reporting set up yet. Still, we figured we could use the corpse for some of the younger shadyrs to practice their shifting before we clean it up."

Everly made a face. She could still so vividly recall the exact pungent scent of rotting vasmire that filled the

Boderleth residence not long ago. "Ew, but I get it."

In the field, Rylan had Neri separated from the others and was crouched in front of her. He seemed to be giving her some kind of pep talk, but his body language came across as gentle and non-threatening.

Not at all the task master Everly might have expected. Neri was a special case. She was having a hard enough time adjusting to being human. Finding out her body could become all sorts of different shapes and sizes was overwhelming. Everly's chest tightened, and her cheeks warmed as she watched Rylan in his crouched pose, the soft smile on his lips, and head moving in slow, understanding nods.

It had been easy to tell herself he'd changed, that she didn't know him anymore, that he grew up as a soldier under the Darkfrey's influence, and that any of her old feelings made no sense.

But he had taken that same posture, made those same gestures, back when they were kids, to comfort her. It had been one of those times that she first truly realized her feelings for him were more than just friendship.

It didn't matter though. Even if he was still the person she used to love, and still did, that only meant she was less willing to risk the Coruscare hurting him again.

Rylan stood back up, and Harper and Neri split off from the group, wandering along the lane. Everly waved to catch their attention, and they headed her way.

"Do you need to do any special training?" Annabeth asked, wide eyes glued to Everly.

"Oh, not really? There isn't exactly a guidebook for me to follow. I only have dark, whispering urges and disturbing dreams to go by."

Annabeth's eyes managed to widen even rounder. "I saw you at Rook's Hotel that night. It was so amazing. I should have guessed then what it was. Not that it had even seemed a possibility at the time ... I mean, the *Coruscare!* I can't believe I'm standing in front of it, right now."

Her words stumbled rapidly, and she put a hand over her mouth. "I'm sorry, I'm so fangirling."

A chill of anxiety ran down to Everly's fingertips, leaving them numb. There it was again, the Coruscare. For the last couple weeks, that had been the only interest anyone had shown in her.

Fair enough, it was something straight out of shadyr mythology. They would be interested. But for those who believed, the reverence that came with the interest made Everly deeply uncomfortable.

"It's okay, just don't think of it as some kind of benevolent deity, all right? The things I've seen from its memories of the Everdark are not—"

"You share its *MEMORIES*?" Annabeth practically yelled. "Oh my ghast. That's huge. HUGE! We have so little in the way of historical records from before the crossover."

Harper and Neri reached them. Neri's skin was silvery, and she pouted over sharp vampire teeth.

"Historical records?" Harper asked.

"Pre-crossover shadyrs didn't even have a written language. A few symbols used for their magic, but records only really start once they integrated with human culture. By that point, the oral history was fragmented, and often contradictory. Studying shadyr history can be like reading different versions of the Bible from every culture and trying to pick out the facts." Annabeth's eyes glowed.

Everly's stomach lurched. She hadn't really considered how hosting the Coruscare could be important in that way. How the visions and memories she shared with her dragon would be things that shadyrs would want to study.

Which would make her the one to have to break to them exactly how awful the Coruscare had been to their kind. Enslaving their whole race, using them to hunt for its food, or even sacrificing themselves to its never ending hunger.

Everly's chest ached, and she pressed a thumb between her collarbones and took a deep breath. And behind the strain in her lungs, she felt the stirring thoughts of her dragon. It queried why she let this bother her, why she let anything bother her? She could consume, enslave, destroy as she pleased, but she chooses pain.

Take what we want. Take everything. We can.

Annabeth didn't seem to notice how the blood had rushed away from Everly's face. "Do you think we could go over what you know about the Coruscare sometime? Would you mind being recorded? I'd want to keep thorough records of the interview. I wouldn't want to miss *anything*."

"Anna?" Rylan had stepped up behind their group.

His brow was furrowed as his gaze slipped away from Everly toward the redhead. "Can you come and help me out with the training?"

Annabeth paused with her mouth open. "Oh, um, sure."

She cast one more eager glance at Everly before jogging over to join Rylan.

As the two of them walked away together, Everly settled herself with a few more deep breaths. There wasn't much distance between their shoulders, and Everly's rising anxiety distilled into a cool lump in her gut. Maybe Rylan's feelings for Annabeth had changed recently.

It'd be for the best.

Callan watched them leave as well, his small frown softened by a half-smile. "Rylan told me she was into shadyr history, but she is *really* into shadyr history."

Harper chuckled and nudged Everly with her hip. "Aw, and here I thought I was your biggest fan."

"I don't think it's exactly me that she's a fan of." A tremble came out with the words before Everly could hold it in.

Harper tilted her head, assessing Everly. She reached out and tucked a bit of white hair behind her ear. "They're the fools if they can't see the truth though. You may have a god inside you, but you're the woman that *controls* that god."

Everly snorted a laugh. "Well, when you put it that way."

She had felt in control lately. Able to use the Coruscare's powers how she wanted them to be used. No souls consumed. No lives taken. But the urges, the sheer, overwhelming energy inside her burned in a way that made her worry it wasn't sustainable. And somehow the soul-eater felt like it was growing stronger each day, and she didn't know why.

She might be in charge now, but for how long?

She may as well have a leash on lightning.

Chapter Eight

There hadn't been many dinners shared together at the Boderleth house. Certainly not any happy ones.

Even on normal days that weren't interrupted by some hellish new catastrophe, Everly and Harper either snacked on the go while working in the antiques store or had dinner over at the Howells'. Although the kitchen was technically functional, the appliances might as well be in the antiques store themselves.

Sitting with Harper, Neri, and Rushelle around the retro laminate and chrome table brought up a feeling Everly couldn't quite pinpoint. A warmth, but also a deep sadness.

Had her family ever eaten dinner at this table together, before her father died? She couldn't remember. It certainly never happened afterward.

But now, at this time, with these people, it was right. It

felt—Everly's eyes washed over with tears—it felt like *home*.

Rushelle had brought some pasta casserole over from the Howells' and Everly managed to get the old oven going well enough to reheat it. Harper insisted on eating together and set the table with mismatched plates and cutlery. Neri picked some miniature roses and dandelions from the front yard to go in an old milk bottle in the center of the table.

Everly scraped up her last forkful and smiled. "We should do this more often. Maybe I could cook something tomorrow?"

Harper raised her eyebrows. "You're a woman of many talents, but cooking isn't one of them. I'm sorry. Unless we all want to eat instant noodles."

"*Instant noodles*?" Neri said with an awe that suggested they were discussing some kind of pasta-manifesting magic.

"I can cook some things," Everly said defensively, knowing entirely well that even when they'd had the time and a full kitchen back at their apartment, Harper had prepared most of the meals.

Healthy, veggie-filled dishes from family recipes she learned cooking with her mom. Everly only ever learned 'fend for yourself' from her mother.

"Okay, fine, I can follow directions on a packet. But that counts."

"I love instant noodles. With a deep, romantic, love," Rushelle said with a grin.

Harper sighed dramatically, scraping up her last mouthful. "I mean ... me too. Who doesn't?"

A knock came from the back door, in a familiar pattern that Everly hadn't heard since she was a kid and Rylan would show up and rescue her from this house.

Everly put her cutlery down on her empty plate. "I'll get it."

She couldn't be sure it was him, but a million scenarios and worries flashed through her head as she went to answer. She opened the door to Rylan wearing a gray hoodie and holding a Pimey's Diner takeaway cake box. His shadyr eyes glittered under the dim light of the candle-shaped fixtures in the hallway.

"Hey," he said.

"Um, hi. You need something?"

"I grabbed this on the way back from town. Thought you might like to share with me." He held up the box, opening the lid a crack.

The scent hit Everly before she saw inside. A toasty caramel and cocoa aroma, rich and buttery, that shot her straight back into her childhood.

"Is that ... Dutch funny cake?"

One of Pimey's Diner's signature desserts, it wasn't really a cake. It was more like a sponge cake and a pie had a baby, with a thick, fudgy layer of chocolate thrown in. It used to be Everly's favorite.

Did he remember?

His satisfied smirk said he did.

Behind Everly, Harper, Neri, and Rushelle came out into the hall to check on her, since they still worried about unwanted visitors.

"We were just finishing dinner. Is there enough for everyone?" Everly asked.

"Oh, I am stuffed," Harper cut in. "Couldn't fit in another thing. We're going to head upstairs and work on Neri's reading."

"She's teaching me fairy tales and how terrible they are," Neri said through a wide grin.

Harper pushed Neri from behind, driving her up the stairs. Neri turned puppy dog eyes back at Rylan as the delicious fragrances hit her, but Harper kept maneuvering her away.

"Me too." Rushelle yawned dramatically and finger waved as she followed them. "Oh boy, just *really* sleepy tonight."

Everly gave them all a deadpan glare before turning back to Rylan.

She sighed. "Come in."

On the way down the hall, Everly's ears tweaked to a scraping sound below her.

Ugh, rats in the basement again.

"I didn't get any ice cream, so it won't be the complete

experience, sorry."

Everly's heart raced.

Exactly what experience is he expecting from this? It could be a peace offering, a way for him to say he wanted to be just friends again and he'd fallen head over heels for Annabeth, because why wouldn't he?

Maybe the funny cake was a way to soften the blow when he told Everly he'd thought about it, and yeah, he could see now that it was the soul enslavement all along. She should tell him to leave, make some excuse now so she didn't have to hear those things. Even if they were good. They would be *good*.

Enough. Everly pressed a palm against her temple to calm her overthinking. Whatever he had to say, he deserved to say it.

Rylan took a seat at the table as she made her way to the freezer.

"Harper was introducing Neri to ice cream yesterday so—" Everly opened the lid to find the tub scraped clean. "Yep, all gone."

"Who puts an empty container back in the freezer?"

"Neri's still learning," Everly said defensively, keeping secret that it was one of Harper's few flaws.

Turning back to see Rylan sitting at her table forced the flutter of butterflies up her throat. The others had already cleared away after dinner, so she couldn't use that as a way to keep busy and delay sitting down with him.

Everly set out some plates, spoons, and cake knife—which she was a little surprised to find considering she had precisely zero memories of cake existing in that house—and lowered herself into her chair with a withheld sigh.

"Sorry about Annabeth the other day." Rylan extracted an entire pie from the box and gestured to the size of slice he should cut, waiting for Everly's approval.

Everly indicated bigger, bigger, enough. "About what?"

"She looked like she was being a bit full on with you. I know she can be a bit ... zealous when it comes to her passion for shadyr history." He served her piece then cut one for himself the same size.

"Is that why you called her away?"

Rylan smirked and shrugged.

He did it for her? Everly held her breath in case she exhaled butterflies. Then she couldn't wait any longer and ate a spoonful of the cake-pie hybrid. A small groan of pure nostalgic pleasure escaped her throat.

Rylan chuckled and took a bite of his.

Her cheeks flushed with heat.

Too busy worrying about imaginary butterflies then I go and make sexy food sounds.

Rylan said, "You remember we used to get slices after school, then go and sit by the river? You would fight off the ducks so they didn't steal any."

"It would have been bad for them," Everly pointed out. "Also, I did want it all for myself. It's sooo good. I haven't had funny cake since ... around then."

Rylan's smile dimmed and he stabbed at his slice with the tip of the spoon. "I'm really sorry. For pushing you away after Dad died. I don't think I ever properly apologized for that. I thought I was doing the right thing, but I was wrong, and it was cruel."

For a long moment, Everly could only stare at him. It was long enough that Rylan stopped looking at his plate and turned his gaze up, seeking a response from her.

"If you can't forgive me for that, I'd understand," he said.

Everly blinked, snapping herself out of her head. "Oh, no, of course I can. I mean, if you can forgive the whole soul bondage thing in return, I think we're good."

Rylan chuckled. "Pfft, no problem. What's a little bondage between friends?"

Everly choked on a bite of funny cake.

"You all right there, Boderleth?"

He used to call her that when they hung around his other friends, as though going by her last name made her seem more like one of the guys. He'd always been popular, but he had been her only real friend.

She used to wonder why he made time for her, the scrappy kid from the wrecked home. What did he see in her? She knew why now. It had never been about *her*, but the thing inside her. She couldn't quite reconcile whether that was better than her other theory—that he'd just felt sorry for her.

"Yeah, I'm okay." Her voice sounded sad, even to her own ears. "Thank you, for this."

She finished her last bite and stood up, taking the plates to the sink. She hoped this would indicate that it was time for Rylan to leave. She didn't really want him to go, but it was for the best.

Rylan followed her, wandering slowly across the kitchen, hands in his pockets. "Look, I honestly can't say what feelings are my own, or how to make sense of the knowledge that there was something else affecting my behavior for so long. But ..."

He stepped ever closer, moving in a straight line toward her in a way that suggested he wouldn't stop. "I do know that I missed you. When I left for the Darkfreys, then when you left town, I missed you every moment."

He stopped just inches away. "Even now, when you're standing right in front of me, I *miss* you, like you're still too far away."

Everly wished he'd take another step and close that gap. All other worries and doubts were smothered by that same feeling—missing him. He was close enough that a deep breath could bring their chests together, but he might as well be another dimension away for how much she craved him. It would be so easy to close that gap, to have what she always wanted.

Everly's lips opened, her body drawn forward.

And the lights went out.

"Every. Damn. Time," Rylan growled.

Everly could no longer see him, but he was still so close his words gusted over her cheek. "Can't talk to you for five minutes without something coming up."

"We live a hectic and catastrophe-filled life," Everly sighed. "Can you see? There's a flashlight in the drawer near the fridge."

Her night-blindness hadn't improved any with her increase in Coruscare powers. She could feel her way over there but figured Rylan could find his way more easily.

She heard a few steps and some rummaging, then a beam of light flashed on.

Everly glanced out the kitchen window.

That I saw Rylan almost die through.

She shuddered. "There are still lights on down the street. I think it's just us. I'll go and check the fuse box."

"Where is it?" Rylan handed her the flashlight.

"The basement. I thought I heard some rats chewing down there before, maybe they tripped something." She bit her lip, trying not to remember the last time a fuse box put the lights out, at the hotel at Gorhanmere. She hated rats, but hoped it wasn't anything more.

"Rats?" Rylan frowned. "You want me to go?"

Everly shivered, but stepped out into the hall, keeping the flashlight beam steady in front of her. "I'll be okay. I think after everything that's happened recently, I should be able to face some rats. Also, how much do you know about old fuse boxes?"

Rylan followed on her heels. "If something is flicked down, flick it up?"

"Hopefully that will do it, but with how old and dodgy the wiring in this house is, I better check it out too."

As they headed to the basement door, Rushelle, Neri, and Harper appeared on the stairs from above. Everly cast her flashlight over to check on them.

Harper held her sword in one hand and used her phone as a light in her other. "What's going on? Blackout?"

"Yeah, something's tripped. Going downstairs now to try and get the power back on," Everly said, opening the door to the basement.

Harper squealed. "Oh no, this feels like that moment in a horror movie when the killer is hiding under the stairs."

"I'm going with her," Rylan said.

"Ugh, like she needs your protection. She can kick one thousand more asses than you."

"I didn't mean ..." Rylan exhaled roughly, then swore under his breath. "Rush, you feel that?"

Everly turned her light back toward them.

Rushelle's blond curls had been let down for the night and they jiggled as she shook her head. "Oh dear. Yup, I feel the tingle. Something incoming."

"Something?" Everly asked, but she knew they meant eidolghast. "Something that likes to have the lights out?"

Harper's mouth opened, then slammed into a pout. "Another auerdax? I really don't like them. Last time was so much cardio."

Rushelle pulled her phone from her pocket and was speaking to Lian within seconds.

Everly turned to Rylan. He had even more reason to hate that kind of eidolghast. His jaw was set tight, and he pushed passed Everly and down the basement steps. He quickly moved out of the range of her flashlight.

She hurried after him. He might not need the light to see, but if an auerdax was nearby, she didn't want to leave him in complete darkness, where the creature was strongest.

"Ghast dammit. There's a lure down here. The window looks like it's been forced," he said.

He struck out at the bone effigy, snapping it apart and crushing it beneath his boots.

The sound sent a ripple of moving shadows racing across the floor toward the stairs where Everly stood.

Rats. She held her breath, frozen in place, as the critters vanished silently into the clutter under the steps.

Once they were gone, she closed her eyes.

It's okay. It's fine. They're normal, harmless, clever little mammals. They can't hurt you anymore.

When she opened her eyes again, Rylan was right in front of her. "You're okay."

There was no question in his tone. She exhaled through an O-shaped mouth. "I'm okay."

The side of Rylan's lips pulled upward.

Then the house shook like it was hit with a wrecking ball. A thunderous smash echoed down to them, followed by screams.

CHAPTER NINE

Rylan became a ghost.

His skin and even the clothes he wore turned translucent with a soft, eerie glow. The urge to reach out and touch him, to see if her hand would go right through him, almost overwhelmed Everly, but the crashing upstairs continued.

Rylan's shift confirmed what they were facing. An auerdax, that would be at full strength and solidity in the darkness upstairs. One of the toughest eidolghasts to kill, as it phased in and out of reality depending on the brightness of light around it.

But the last time Everly faced one, she was different. She was too scared then to use the Coruscare's light because she couldn't control it enough to keep it from also consuming her friends. She didn't have that problem anymore.

She sprinted up the stairs, bringing the Coruscare's glow out around her along the way. It lifted her so that by the time she reached the top, her feet didn't land on the steps.

Instead, she floated out into the hall.

"It's coming through. It's smashed in the window, and half the wall!" Harper yelled from near the kitchen doorway.

"Come over here with me," Everly called to her. "I'll keep the lights bright until Lian gets here with her sword."

Rushelle and Neri also appeared to be ghosts now. Neri sat at the back door, with two phones on the floor in front of her creating a small pool of light, staring through her hands in horror. Everly rolled the flashlight to her to add to her shield of illumination.

The Coruscare's glow brightened the hallway more than the dull electric lights would have, but it didn't hurt to have a backup.

Harper dashed away from the kitchen doorway as a chair flew out and smashed against the side of the stairs. The auerdax's twisted, whiplike arm lashed out into the space she'd been standing.

She ran to join the others, and they crowded together in the orb of Everly's brightness. With everyone so close, she kept the scintillating tendrils tucked safely away entirely, just in case.

Beside her, Rylan sneered at the creature with pure hatred.

The auerdax reached through the doorway again, and then pushed the rest of its bulk out, cracking the doorframe as it went. Everly only got a glimpse of the bone-and-slime asymmetrical torso before her light made it fade away.

She hated knowing that it was still *there*, just incorporeal.

"I think I saw something. Like with that flying eidolghast," Harper said in a rush. "A glowing spot."

"A weak spot?" Rylan asked.

Harper nodded confidently. She pointed her blade, currently set rigid, to where the creature was last visible. "I think it's this sword. I think it makes them visible to me. Ev, would you dim the lights, just a bit?"

"Are you sure? We can wait. Lian won't be long."

Harper's bright-green eyes gleamed, reflecting Everly's white glow. "The bone lure is busted. What if that thing decides we're not interesting anymore and wanders over to a neighbor's place? Do we want that on us? We can't even see where it is right now. I think we can take it out. I think we should."

Everly held her gaze then nodded. Concentrating, she closed away the Coruscare's power, the aura around her dimming. Her sock-clad toes brushed the old carpet as she lowered to the floor.

In the half-light, the auerdax materialized before them,

much closer than before. No face, no head, just a misshapen torso on clumpy legs, formed from inhuman bones and black ichor.

"Rush? Help me hold it back," Rylan called.

Rushelle rolled up her sleeves and vaulted over the banister. "On it."

The auerdax flung out one of its long, elastic arms, aiming straight for Everly. Rylan snatched it from the air, pinning it between him and the hallway wall.

It was clearly solid enough not to pass through objects with this much light, and the shadyrs seemed to be affected similarly by the illumination level.

From the skulls floating within its chest, it loosed a scream like the keening of eagles.

Soul eater. Star-toothed abomination! It squealed in a language only Everly could understand. Deep within her, she could feel the mocking disdain of the Coruscare in return. And a twinge of hunger.

Harper stood beside her, a narrow glare fixed on the ghast. "It's the shoulder joints! Both of them."

"Righteo!" Rushelle hollered and was down the hallway in three leaping steps.

She grappled the second whip-arm and lifted off her feet as she held tight.

"Keep it still for a few seconds!" Harper raised her sword and moved in.

The massive eidolghast swayed its body, and swung the arm Rylan clung to, smashing him from the wall to the banister and back to the wall again. In his ghostly form, he passed slightly through, but the way he grunted suggested it didn't cushion the blows entirely. He growled and readjusted his hold.

Harper dodged around him and swung. The sword lodged into the shoulder of the limb Rushelle held, sliding deep between two skulls into the eerie slime. A sickening pop and crackle sounded as the arm detached, and a stream of shadows poured from the wound.

The amputated arm writhed like a headless snake, knocking Harper onto her back and Rushelle into the corner. The detached limb didn't reform and grow back the way injuries to the previous auerdax they had faced did.

As clotted darkness tumbled from the ghast's shoulder, it keened again and launched itself at Everly, dragging Rylan with it.

On instinct, Everly loosed a glittering tendril at the beast, slashing it toward the second shoulder joint. But as it neared, the auerdax faded away, and the Coruscare's powers cut uselessly through the air.

"Harper said both arms!" she yelled.

With a feral snarl, Rylan's shadyr change swirled around him as he pulled from the eidolghast essences within Everly and added the strength of werewolf form into his ghostly visage.

He let go of the end of the creature's limb and pounced onto the monster's back. He thrust sharp claws deep into its shoulder, furred muscles straining as he wrenched.

Slime oozed and coalesced around his hands, trying to reform as the tear grew larger, until the last few strands snapped.

Like ghosts fleeing hell, shadows burst free, rushing from the injury. Rylan leaped back as the auerdax fell. Skulls and bones from all sorts of creatures tumbled loose in a pile.

The back door burst open, and Lian stepped through, hand on the hilt of her sword. She took in the situation before her. "I thought you needed my help?"

Callan peered past her shoulder. "It's already over? What the Everdark?"

Rylan straightened up over the crumbling ghast. "Just 'cause you took days to deal with the last one."

"We had the help of Harper's weak spot vision this time around," Everly explained.

"Unfair advantage!" Callan pointed an accusatory finger at Rylan.

"This isn't a competition," Lian muttered.

"Yes it is," Rylan and Callan said simultaneously.

The sound of crunching debris came from the kitchen, and Lucas's brace stepped through. Lucas sighed at the ghast's body. "Damn. Thought we'd get a second shot at adding an auerdax to our kill score too."

"Thanks for bringing the cavalry." Rushelle climbed to her feet and shifted back to normal. "It's still appreciated."

"Probably worth it too," Lucas said, thumb-pointing over his shoulder. "We scared off a bunch of Darkfreys that were hanging around, no doubt waiting to pick off any survivors."

"Yeah, this wasn't a random attack. There was a lure. Down in the basement." Rylan forced his change back to human as well.

Harper picked up her sword and winced as she stretched out her arm. She bent to look past the brace of shadyrs.

"The kitchen is trashed. Aw, come on! I just repainted!"

Everly took her flashlight from Neri. Shining it around the hallway, she saw a significant amount of damage in there, too. Several balusters on the stairs were cracked.

The wall where Rylan had hit was also pushed in, and the light fitting dangled freely. Plaster crumbled around the ruined doorframe. There wasn't much kitchen remaining. Despite Harper's Bane energy-fueled paint job, it probably was due to be ripped out and renovated, but it hurt Everly to see it like this just after the happy moments from earlier that night.

The house had been a trash heap when she first came back to town, but at least the bones of it were still good.

As Everly surveyed the damage now, her heart sank. Half the front of the house had been smashed in as the auerdax barreled through, drawn in by the lure. It would need a complete rebuild. With that much damage, she wasn't even sure if the second story over the kitchen—Harper's bedroom—was safe.

"I don't think you can stay here anymore," Rylan said near her ear. "I'm sorry."

"I can fix this," Everly said. "I've got some tarps we can put up temporarily and—"

"It's not safe," Lian cut in. "You were targeted, and I know you're strong, all of you, but that's not always enough. That's why you need others at your back."

Everly looked away and into the kitchen again, finding her eyes suddenly stinging and trying to hide them. "Is there even any room still?"

"We'll make room for you one way or another." Lian chucked her under the chin. "It's no problem at all. Go and grab a few things and we'll take you back with us now."

Lian turned and spoke quietly to Lucas for a moment, who then left with his brace.

Neri, still ghostly, skittered over to Harper. "We have to go?"

Harper tilted her head. "Yeah, but we'll still be together."

Everly closed her eyes to the devastation in the kitchen.

We have to go, but we'll still be together. Leaving felt like saying goodbye to that sense of home that had so recently awoken within her. But the people who made it home were going with her.

And you'll be closer to Rylan.

The thought came unbidden, and she gave it an internal groan. It was what she'd been avoiding for weeks now. She couldn't go down that path. Could she? He did so much for her, considering what she needed, what she wanted, and it was just *him* now. Not the Coruscare's influence. Maybe she could have what she wanted.

Everly opened her eyes and stared at the remains of the funny cake, smashed on the linoleum. She tried not to see it as an omen.

She forced a smile. "Okay. Let's grab what we need for the night. We can come back for more later."

Rylan, Lian, and Callan remained on guard downstairs in case of any fresh attacks, while Everly, Harper, Neri, and Rushelle went to pack bags.

Rushelle had been living out of hers while staying with them, and Everly realized that she'd never really moved beyond living out of her duffel bag either, never thought about setting up more than a sleeping bag on the couch.

She sighed as she collected the few belongings that weren't in her bag already and stuffed them away. The lights were still out, so she spotlighted the flashlight around the room, trying to see anything she'd missed.

"You need a hand?" Rylan moved through the doorway, taking slow steps in, edging closer.

"Almost done." Everly noticed her toiletries case on the coffee table and packed it away. Once she zipped up the bag, Rylan was beside her. She stared up at him, her mouth suddenly dry. "My ... my tool bag is already at your place. So this is it."

There was a scrape across one of his cheekbones from the fight, and Everly reached up, her fingertips hovering above it. "Are you okay?"

He shrugged. "Ribcage got a bit hammered, but I'll survive."

She hated seeing him hurt, acting as though bruised ribs were normal. She wanted him to shift into vampire form so he could heal, but it felt weird to suggest something Rylan would no doubt have done, if he wanted to.

The gray hoodie he wore was a bit too small for him and hugged tightly around his shoulders and biceps. Everly wondered if he'd borrowed it off someone, whether he'd even had time since waking up to sort out the basics of life like his own wardrobe. She wondered what he had left behind at Darkfrey Estate.

She wondered what his lips felt like, when they weren't deathly cold or drenched in seawater.

As close as he was, he took another step closer, and

stared down at her with an intensity that left her breathless. "I know you dreamed of me, when we were apart, but did you ever think of me?"

All the time. Everly nodded in a way that was more a tremble.

"I used to think about you, too. When you left town, I used to lie in bed every night and wonder what you were doing with your life, how far you'd gone, whether you were thinking about me, or if you'd fallen in love with someone."

She'd tried. She had a few relationships in her time away from Shroudhaven. Tried to move on from her feelings for Rylan and find someone else to love. But they never worked out. Her heart was locked in a cage to which only Rylan had the key.

"I thought of you the same way. But we don't know if that was really us."

"I'm completely free now." He put his hands on her rounded shoulders, and she lifted her chin. "And completely in love with *you*."

Their lips were a breath away from each other, and it was Everly who closed the gap. She pushed up on her tiptoes and grabbed the front of his hoodie to pull him down and her whole body shivered in a suppressed sob of emotion as her flesh met Rylan's.

He gasped as he opened his mouth to hers. Her soft body pressed against his firm chest, and he held her with an insatiable strength.

He was warm, and real, and himself, and he *wanted her*. She could feel it through the heated trails his fingertips left on her cheeks, neck, back.

There was nothing else but him. Her world finally felt right, whole, in a way she'd dreamed of her entire life.

Why couldn't she have this? Why shouldn't she? She could no longer think of any excuses. There was no Coruscare, or Everdark, no monsters, or dark plots. No overthinking. No panic. Just the fiery flush of love and desire so long yearned for.

"You need any more light in there, love? I've found another flash—whoops!" Rushelle stepped into the room then pirouetted around on the spot. "Sorry!"

"Every. Ghast. Damned. Time." Rylan breathed, taking a step backward.

His gaze remained locked on Everly's lips, hungry.

Harper and Neri appeared as well. "We're all done. For tonight anyway. I'll do a second round on makeup and camera gear tomorrow. What's going on?"

"Nothing. We're all done too." Everly gave them a thin-lipped smile.

Her heart still hammered in her chest, as though it wanted to burst free and join Rylan's. She hefted her bag onto one shoulder.

"Okay, let's go."

They loaded into Lian's SUV for the short drive back to Howell House. To avoid staring at Rylan and doing nothing but relive that kiss in her head and question the implications, Everly focused on the luggage on her lap along the way.

So weird that I've lived from this bag for weeks now.

She still had some belongings in storage back at their previous apartment. Some clothes, furniture, a few pairs of fancy shoes she'd only ever worn once or twice. Harper had left a lot more behind. This move had been meant to be temporary.

When they hadn't gone back in time, Everly lost her superintendent job.

Harper had her income from views and sponsors and had offered to cover rent while they worked things out. Luckily, the online sales of antiques had been going so well that Everly had managed her living expenses in Shroudhaven and kept up on the rent of their previous apartment too.

And part of her had always believed they would be going back there, some day. Until Shroudhaven started to feel like home.

Until Rylan had kissed her. Not in her dream. Not when she was dying. He'd kissed her in her mundane living room with a mouth that tasted like dreams coming true.

Maybe it was time to make a decision and settle

somewhere permanently. With the Boderleth residence in ruins and still so much going on, it was a hard call to make. She wanted to be here, with all her new friends, and with Rylan, but she didn't know if it was the right choice.

Could she dare make this place her home?

Chapter Ten

When Tammy's family showed up at Howell House, she had so many designs on how she would ignore them, disown them, rage against them in revenge for how they had treated her.

They abandoned me, didn't defend me when the Darkfrey's kicked me out.

She'd considered all the cruel things she could do in return, like tell Lian to turn them away.

Instead, she gave them her room.

Sucks for them, two adults and two kids sharing that closet space. It wasn't really the vengeance she'd once dreamed of, but she found that maybe she didn't really have those dreams anymore.

Tammy folded her futon-style bedding in the living room and stacked it beside Rylan's, Rushelle's, Callan's, and Cherry's.

Cherry let Jasper and his family take his room, and last night, Rylan had given his to Everly, Harper, and Neri. Rushelle had her own place but was happy to join the living room squad for now.

It wasn't too bad sleeping there. The close proximity of the beds reminded Tammy of the dorms at Darkfrey Estate. And it still seemed better than camping out in the front yard. Sure, she'd be surrounded by a lot of shadyrs, but sleeping outside at night in Shroudhaven just didn't sit right with Tammy. There were some brave souls out there.

They had filled the house to bursting before they started telling the defectors they'd have to work something out in the surrounding yard. There had been a few spare rooms in the beginning, which they gave priority to for the underaged orphans, of which there were too many.

That was when Callan moved to the living room. Annabeth got a room as the first comer, but now shared it with two others. Even Lian shared her bedroom to help fit more in.

Only Denny hadn't given up any space in his RV to anyone else. He claimed he was saving it for when Alexis showed up.

As if that's ever going to happen. The creep was delusional.

Tammy had to admit, she'd been feeling delusional herself lately. Sharing sleeping quarters with Callan had been hard at first. She would be so focused on the sound of his breath or every small movement he made that she couldn't sleep.

She found herself staring across the room at him in the dark, trying to force down and crush the romantic notions his high cheekbones and kind, goofy smile raised in her, but was unable to even turn her eyes away. Which was how she caught him looking back at her, more than a few times.

But it's not the same. He wouldn't be thinking anything romantic. Not about me. He's just checking to see if the kid of the team is okay.

But the delusional part of her would remind her that she was only a couple years younger than him. Would remind her how he carried her when she couldn't stave off her mermaid shift at the lighthouse. Would remind her of how his body felt, pressed against hers.

"Last call for breakfast!" Rushelle poked her head around the doorway, her blond curls stacked in a perfect beehive. "Boy, were folk ravenous today. We're almost cleaned out."

"I'm good." Tammy had snagged some coffee and toast earlier.

She was still cringing internally at the guy who joked that her soul was as dark as her espresso. And the other Darkfrey who criticized her lack of discipline for eating before she cleared away her bedding. They all found some way to be on her case.

"Can you go and check on the ladies upstairs? I know they had a rough night, so I don't want them to miss out."

With a nod, Tammy jogged up the staircase, dodging two kids who sat chatting halfway up. They grew silent and stared at her as she passed, whispering in her wake. She was used to it by now. Everyone had their version of gossip about the cursed girl with Everdark-stained hands. None of them really knew the truth. Tammy felt like she was only learning it now herself.

A frustrated squeal greeted her at the door to Rylan's room.

"I know I put them over here last night." Harper searched the bedside table with her brown eyes.

"What's missing?" Tammy asked.

"My contacts. And bronzer. And straightener. And—EUUGH!" Harper screeched and dumped herself onto a messy pile of blankets on the floor.

A rose-gold suitcase was open beside her. Underwear, eyeshadow pans, belts, and shoes tumbled out around it.

Everly checked the surface of the tallboy and on the floor around them. "I can't find them, sorry."

Neri sat on the bed, tugging at her curly brown hair. "It will be okay if your eyes aren't green today, won't it?"

Harper huffed and resumed her search.

Tammy hovered awkwardly at the door. "Well, they're almost out of breakfast downstairs, so if you want to eat, you've got to get moving."

"You guys go without me. I haven't finished my makeup or even started on my hair. I'm sorry, I'd normally be all done by now, but I don't have a lot of energy lately." Harper slapped her hands on the lid of her suitcase. "And I can't find anything!"

Everly sighed. "Come on, come with us. You look fine."

"Fine?" Harper shot her a withering stare.

Neri dragged fingers down her own cheek and seemed horrified. "Should I be wearing makeup too?"

"No, you're perfect." Harper bit her lip. "I mean, you don't have to wear any if you don't want to. It's okay to not wear makeup. I just ... people expect me to be a certain way."

"Fuck people." Tammy's words burst out vehemently.

Fuck them, and their stares, and their whispers, and their gossip.

She couldn't relate exactly to what Miss Princess was going through, but she got the gist. "Seriously, what's going to happen if you went downstairs as is? Would it really be the end of the world?"

"I can't ... I don't know *how* to be anything less than flawless. I don't know how to let people see me ... like that. Even now, with you three." She tilted her head, hiding behind sleep-crooked hair.

"I think you're already perfect, too," Neri offered, seeming more confused than ever.

Harper's ears went red. Tammy figured her cheeks probably were too but were already covered in layers of foundation.

I bet she contours.

Tammy never thought she could be friends with someone like Harper. She'd stereotyped her as a diva influencer the moment they met, but over time, she saw through the layers.

"I think you should let people see you, however you are. Let them stare. Let them talk. Let them cringe. That's a them problem, not a you problem."

Harper shook her head. "I wish."

"Tammy's right." Everly had a wicked grin growing on her face. "You know what you need? An anti-makeover."

"A what?"

"You're going to let us help get you ready. Don't worry. We're just going to ... enhance the real you," Everly said.

She knelt beside the overflowing suitcase and grabbed a bag of makeup removal wipes. Pulling one free, she approached Harper gently, as though she were a wild animal.

"It's going to be okay. It's not going to hurt at all."

Harper cowered. "Can't I just—"

"Come on. This is going to be great. Trust me." Everly

reached out and wiped at Harper's cheeks, clearing away the contoured foundation.

Harper whimpered melodramatically, but remained still, letting Everly remove the makeup.

"Great idea." Tammy picked one of a selection of hairbrushes to join in. "You can do this. You're tough as coffin nails."

She grabbed a nearby water bottle and dripped water across the bristles. Stepping forward, she hesitated. Brushing Harper's hair was a step too intimate, so she handed the job over to Neri.

Neri beamed as she pulled the brush through Harper's long black hair, wetting it down. Then she ruffled the damp locks in her fingers like throwing confetti.

Harper sat statue still, eyes round. "You're seriously not going to leave it like that, are you? To dry *naturally*?"

Horror dripped from the word.

"Yup," Everly said.

She leaned close to Harper's face, examining her eyes. She made a pincer motion with her fingers toward the long lashes.

Harper dodged backward. "Oh no, those are firmly attached."

"What else then? Clothes?" Tammy suggested.

Harper had already dressed into leggings and a strawberry-print shirtdress of flouncy soft fabric that puffed around a glittery belt and hung elegantly off one shoulder, but Everly found one of her old T-shirts for her to change into.

They all turned around for a moment, and when they turned back, Harper was trying to tie the excess fabric to one side.

Everly slapped her hand. "No styling!"

"Just a belt maybe? Or …? Fine." Harper stifled a breathy grunt, her expression indignant. "Do I at least get to see what I look like? The grand reveal in front of the mirror?"

Everly swished her head left to right. "You look like *you*. And you're amazing. That's all you need to know."

Harper stilled, and her face softened.

With a soft pout, she murmured, "Thank you."

Neri played with a strand of Harper's wavy, damp hair. "You look just like when we first met! Messy and wet and beautiful!"

Harper's bare cheeks turned visibly red that time. She covered them with her hands.

"It is kind of nice, taking it all off. It feels … lighter. I mean, I do still love my makeup though. I'm not going to give it up. But it's good to be reminded sometimes that I'm worthy without it."

Tammy nodded, and her voice caught as she said, "You are worthy, no matter what anyone else thinks."

Harper's eyes turned shiny, and she wrapped Tammy in a hug before she had a chance to dodge.

She whispered almost silently, "You are too."

Harper thankfully let go before it got weird. "Come on then, let's go see if there's any food left."

"I'm so hungry," Neri said, and hummed the jingle from a local bakery's radio ad. "I hope there's still bread."

Tammy followed them down the stairs as Everly told them all about the funny cake, and that she wished Neri and Harper could have tried some.

"It looked like you and Rylan were getting along pretty well," Harper said with a leer.

Everly shrugged in a way that was clearly meant to seem casual but came across as awkward and mechanical. "Um, yeah, I guess. Just getting to know each other again really."

Harper pretend-coughed out the words, "Getting to know each other's tonsils."

Tammy's eyes widened. That was a development. She remembered how Everly had consoled her at Gorhanmere, about the two of them being in love with the Howell brothers who they could never have.

But if Everly and Rylan were getting together, then maybe ...

No. That didn't mean anything about anything. There was no correlation there.

Ghast dammit, why does my brain have to be so dumb

about this? About Callan?

"Okay, maybe things are going *pretty well*," Everly conceded. "But I'm still not sure it's the right thing. I'm still worried about the Coruscare—what it's done, what it could do. It seems to be under control now, but I have such strange dreams ... I don't know."

Harper hesitated on the last step. Tammy could see her take a deep breath before nodding to herself and following Everly and Neri to the kitchen.

Tammy smirked without any humor. The woman had charged a weroth with nothing but garden shears, but being out in public without makeup terrified her? The world was so screwed up.

There were some stares and whispers that followed Harper. Tammy hoped she'd be okay.

She split off from them there, since she was meant to be helping Callan with training some of the younger shadyrs that morning. She wasn't sure exactly what value she could add. Maybe it was his way of making her join in for training he thought she still needed too. Or helping her 'make friends' or build her confidence or some other plot to help her out.

Why does he always have to be so ghost-blightedly KIND?

He really had changed lately in how he treated her. Still kind, still caring, but there was a level of respect now that was so sincere it left her questioning everything. Maybe he really did think she could add value to the training. No ulterior motives. Maybe he just believed in her.

At the front door, Lian and Lucas blocked the way out, having a conversation across the threshold. Molly, the youngest of Lucas's brace, stood at attention behind him, her forehead furrowed and a timidness to the set of her shoulders.

Tammy had been jealous of her up at Gorhanmere when Callan had saved her life, but now she just felt sorry for her. Molly was young to be invested into an active brace.

The Darkfreys push too much onto people. Too many expectations. Too much trauma. Tammy found herself for once feeling happy, rather than ashamed, to have gotten kicked out.

"We didn't catch up to those Darkfreys from the Boderleth place last night," Lucas said.

His tone was direct yet polite, the way shadyrs were expected to address superiors at the estate. Tammy raised her eyebrows. Lucas's team hadn't been with them long but was already happily taking orders from Lian.

"Any more bodies?" Lian said.

"Bodies?" Tammy asked.

Lian turned to greet her, nodding solemnly. "The bloody Darkfreys are leaving ghast bodies around town. They aren't even caring about clean up anymore. Almost like a dare, that they are coming out into the public eye in open warfare. Mordan is getting reckless."

"Not just ghasts," Lucas said. "A few shadyrs have been found dead in their homes too. Not defectors, but others living alone. Maybe the Darkfreys thought they were traitors in one way or another or were going to be."

Lian folded her arms. "I can't believe they've gotten so aggressive. They're only going to lose more shadyrs over actions like that."

"Or out us all entirely to the world," Tammy added.

She knew the small local police force was mostly under Mordan's thumb already, and they had influence over the town press too, to clear what was reported and how. Things were different now with social media though. Tammy wondered if Mordan had any idea how that worked. The odd video here and there would be written off as fake, but if they were getting careless with cleanups, that would change things.

Lian muttered, "He could take us back to the good old days of being hunted as monsters."

"Let's hope it doesn't come to that," Lucas said. "Maybe we need to organize some peace talks or something."

Tammy grunted. "Last time we tried that they ambushed us and tried to kill us."

"There are a lot more of us now though," Lian said. "And there are some other older families with a fair bit of influence. If we could get through to them, find some way to get the dangerous individuals under control, maybe you lot could all go back home again."

Tammy shrugged and pushed through to the porch, leaving the two of them talking.

She didn't have a whole lot of interest or hope in peace talks. Sure, her parents had come around, saying a few pretty words and acting apologetic, but things hadn't really changed.

Her heart burned painfully every moment of every day, because at that shroudpool in Dark Corner she'd had the most traumatic experience of her life, thought she'd killed her best friend, and everybody had abandoned her.

Everybody.

Every one of the Darkfreys, with their talk of honor and family and the good of their kind. Her own parents. Blaise's parents. Everybody turned on her.

And it wasn't my fault!

Tammy gasped air in then let it out slowly in a shudder. It wasn't her fault.

Did she actually believe that now? The words had yelled out into her mind before her self-doubt could stop them, coming from some deep, primal place. Already the guilt and shame were making excuses and arguing the blame, but she held tight to those words.

It wasn't my fault.

"Did you see that bliv girl this morning, the influencer

chick? She's really let herself go."

Tammy was halfway across the yard and spun around to give the owner of that voice a mouthful. Two guys stood beside a tent, drinking from Lian's coffee mugs.

Tammy was almost upon them when they continued.

"Still hotter than that black-handed freak though," one of them scoffed.

"What did I tell—" Callan's voice behind her got drowned out by her own.

"You want to see what these hands can do?" Her shroudpool-black finger pointed right into the man's face.

"My hands are stained because I almost got dragged into the Everdark trying to save the life of my best friend. They are a mark of *honor*. What have your hands done lately other than jerk off to your Daddy Darkfrey?"

Tammy could feel Callan behind her, right at her shoulder. His presence gave her strength, but mostly in knowing that he believed she had plenty of her own. And in how he'd helped her start to believe that too.

The grins on the guys' mouths twitched and faded. One looked like he was about to talk back, but instead mumbled an apology and walked away.

"That was amazing! You're amazing. That, wow, you." Callan had his hands out in front of him, gesturing as though trying to get words out. "Seeing you so confident lately, just, just, *wow*."

On impulse, Tammy placed her fingers on his, as though it would shush him before he embarrassed her further.

With a halfhearted eyeroll, she muttered, "You helped. You've helped a lot."

He stared at where her midnight skin touched his peachy flesh, then snatched her hand tight in his, dragging her in close.

And he kissed her.

He's kissing me?

Tammy's eyes were wide, staring into the face so close to hers. She was too stunned, too overwhelmed to even consider kissing back.

He's kissing me, he's kissing me, repeated over and over in her head, growing in volume and speed in time with her heartbeat, as though her brain was trying to make her believe that this impossible moment was real.

That she could feel his soft lips on hers, feel his warmth and smell the pepper and hot chocolate scent of him.

Her cheeks flushed and her eyes filled with tears and her nose stung and her lips only wanted more, but her body had frozen and couldn't move, despite how her heart punched against her ribcage.

Callan's lips peeled slowly off hers, and he seemed almost as surprised as she was.

"I'm sorry, I should have asked first if that was okay."

Tammy couldn't reply to tell him it was okay, it was more than okay, because she flickered and vanished.

CHAPTER ELEVEN

Rylan stood at attention on the porch while Lian grilled him over the incident the night before.

"And you definitely found a lure?"

He nodded.

"Why were you around at Everly's so late?"

"Just ..." Rylan swallowed and sweat beaded on the back of his neck. "Visiting."

"I want more details about how you took that auerdax down so fast."

Rylan nodded briskly again. He was about to speak when Lian turned shrewd eyes upon him.

"Visiting?"

Does she know? How could she know? Oh no, I bet Rush said something.

Rylan cleared his throat, but when he opened his

mouth, he wasn't sure what to say. He had no idea what his mother would think about him and Everly being together. If that's what was happening. Everly hadn't told anybody else about the Coruscare soul bond.

What Lian would think of *that* detail was another mystery. Everything was so complicated, so tenuous.

It didn't really matter what Lian thought of any of it. Rylan was an adult now and would do what he wanted. And she hadn't been in the position to be a mother to him for so many years anyway, since he left her for the Darkfreys. It felt weird to expect her to take that role now.

But somehow, since returning to Howell House and learning about the person Lian was, he found himself wanting her approval. Not only because she was his mother, but because she was a good person who he looked up to.

Rylan titled his head. "Mom—"

"We need a pickup for Tammy!" Callan came sprinting over.

"What happened?" Lian snapped.

Callan rubbed a hand on the back of his head. "She just, umm, got emotional, I guess?"

Lian fixed him with a piercing stare. "Rush has my car out on a grocery run. Hers is only a two-seater, and I'm not keen on anyone going anywhere alone right now."

Everly pushed the screen door open and stepped out onto the porch, chewing a corner of toast.

Her gaze caught Rylan's briefly and she smiled bashfully before looking away. "Want me to go? I can drive Harper's van. I'm sure the couple staying in it won't mind as long as we're back with it soon."

Rylan regarded the large front yard and field. There were a few other cars and vans that had been liberated from the Darkfreys, but they were being lived in too, and had lean-to-style tarps attached that wouldn't be easy to move. Harper's camper at least wasn't pegged down.

"I'll come, too," Rylan and Callan said at the same time.

Lian shook her head and pointed at Rylan. "Annabeth wants you for something, sounded important." Her fingertip swung over to Callan. "And don't you have some training to be running right now?"

"But, I, um ..." Callan winced.

Everly reached back inside and grabbed the keys off a hook in the hall, then sat on the steps to pull her boots on. "It's okay, we'll be fine. I think it's my turn to do a Dark Corner pickup anyway, like a rite of passage."

Lian strode over to where Harper's campervan was parked and flagged down its residents to let them know.

Callan pulled his hair back tight then let it go, mumbling something under his breath before wincing again and heading to where they held the training classes.

Rylan crouched beside Everly. She hadn't braided her hair today and the pale gray waves sparkled around her face. "Annabeth can wait."

She smiled back at him. "I won't be long. We'll talk when I get back, okay? No interruptions."

Rylan stared at the worn and weathered timber of the steps. He still felt the desire to be beside her, keep her safe, but he also knew now how strong she was.

And how if he expressed his yearning to protect her, she'd worry it was coming from the influence of the Coruscare. He chewed his bottom lip.

"Hey." Everly's eyes turned to Lian's back, then checked the house behind them before coming back to Rylan.

She placed the whisper of a kiss on his cheek. "I miss you, too."

Rylan almost pulled her into his arms then and there, but Lian called to Everly, and she jogged away, waving back to him.

Does that mean she feels the same about me? Rylan's heart felt full to overflowing, as though it expanded, pressing against the inside of his ribcage. He already longed for her return. He wanted to talk with her, no interruptions, just time spent alone, the two of them together. He wanted to feel her lips again, he wanted more. He wanted all of her.

The campervan vanished down the driveway between the long morning shadows of the trees. He'd have to wait. Every moment until Everly got back to him was going to feel like forever. But he'd already waited this long.

The skin on his cheek still tingled as he headed into the house to find Annabeth.

"Oh good, hi, come in." Annabeth barely turned her head from where she sat on one of the mattresses on the floor of her shared room.

She had some very ancient-looking tomes spread out around her, lying open. In her hands she held the notes that Jasper had taken from the Mesmans.

"Are these the books you stole? I thought you meant textbooks or something, not priceless relics." Rylan stepped carefully between them and took a seat on the bed nearby.

Annabeth looked at him properly then, smiling sweetly. "Well, when Jasper told me what was going on, with the recruiting and the Mesmans trying to open a shroudpool, I figured I needed books that actually had info about shadyr magic in them. None of our modern textbooks have that."

"Fair enough. What did you want me for?"

"I've been going over and over these, but I can't work out how Kole is doing it. Getting old shadyr magic to work, that is." She pointed to some of the man's handwriting on the notes.

"This here? This is written in the old shadyr language, or at least a phonetic representation of that spoken-only language, and I think it's literally a spell. Seems to be about activating the lures from what I can translate. And this here too, one for improving vision. I can read it, and

I can say it, but nothing happens."

"Because we don't have magic like the pureblood shadyrs anymore." Rylan frowned, still unsure why she needed him.

Annabeth got to her feet and hopscotched through the laid-out tomes to come and sit beside him. "Right. I mean, we have some artifacts that behave magically, but actually casting spells doesn't work. So how are *they* doing it? I was hoping you'd tell me about what you saw that got them trying to kill you in the first place. Maybe it will answer the question."

"I didn't see much, really. Some bones, which they must have been using to make lures. I tied that to the missing bodies that I was looking into, but honestly never had any idea of the scale of what they were doing, or how. Sorry."

"Oh. That's okay. Would have been nice to get a lead though. I'm going nuts trying to work it out." Annabeth sighed in a way that slumped her whole body.

She had only been part of his brace at the Darkfreys since Callan left, but she'd always been diligent and took failure very personally.

"Hey, it's okay. Maybe even with what magic they have, they still can't open a shroudpool anyway. I mean, with their secret out in the open, you'd think they'd get it done as soon as possible. But it's been weeks, and nothing has changed. Maybe there's something they're still missing.

You don't have to stress so much."

Her blue eyes glossy, she half-smiled, then looked back at the books.

"Everly's really nice," she said out of nowhere.

"Uh, yeah?"

Annabeth sighed and tucked her red hair behind one ear. "As soon as I saw you two together, it was obvious that she was the one, that it was her who had your heart this whole time."

Oh. Rylan had wondered at times whether Annabeth's feelings for him were more than normal brace companionship, although never thought much of it. He'd been cluelessly lost in his own emotions, but it seemed she had him clocked.

Even now, he was only crossing the threshold of understanding, of being honest with himself, and others.

He laughed wryly and shook his head as he tried to form that understanding into words. "No. I never really gave her my heart. I was always too busy trying to protect it, by pushing her away. I was so scared of losing someone I loved again that I denied how I felt and focused only on protecting her, to protect myself."

How much of that was the Coruscare's influence, he didn't know. Without it, would the desire to love and be loved have won over the desire to protect? Without its influence, would he and Everly even have become friends in the first place? He only knew that he was free now, and everything he thought and felt was his own.

"I think that's changing now though. I think I can finally give her my heart, freely."

Annabeth nodded once. "You should. You deserve to be happy."

Rylan bumped his shoulder against hers. "Hey, you too."

Her freckled nose scrunched and she looked away.

Rylan stood up slowly, the mattress rising with him. "Let me know if you need any more help going through these. My ancient shadyr is rusty, but you don't have to do this alone."

"Your ancient shadyr is *non-existent*." Annabeth laughed. "Although I don't know how good mine is either, honestly."

She reached down and pulled one of the books onto her lap. "Like this passage here about when the shadyrs first created the portals to this dimension. It uses the term 'the Beast of Teeth and Stars.' Like those are words that make any sense together."

A chill ran along Rylan's body, so cold it seemed to stick his feet to the floor with ice. "It says what?"

"I mean, there was an artifact with a similar name that went missing from Darkfrey Estate some years back, but it was a Bane, not a Beast. So, I'm thinking I'm just translating it wrong. I'm probably getting the whole thing wrong, but every way I look at it, it says beast, monster, abomination—"

Rylan's voice was rough. "You don't know about the Bane?"

"Not really? Just its name?"

Rubbing his hands across his close-cropped hair, Rylan paced in the small patch of bare floor. "It's the artifact that freed me from Everly. It affects her in that way because of the Coruscare. That's another name for it—the Beast of Teeth and Stars. An eidolghast called Everly that—she could understand it—that's how we made the connection."

His words tumbled out, his thoughts churned around by fear of the other connection that was being made.

"The Coruscare *is* the Beast of Teeth and Stars?" Annabeth sought confirmation as her face grew pale.

Rylan stopped pacing. "What does the passage say?"

Annabeth's jaw worked but it took a moment for words to come out. She turned back to the book, reading along with a finger. "That—that the shadyrs used ... used pieces of the Beast of Teeth and Stars, used its magic to break through the shield between dimensions to flee from the eidolghasts to a new world."

Rylan's fingers shook as he whipped his phone from his pocket. Every second felt too slow as he brought up Everly's number.

The call rang, rang, and rang out.

"No answer? It could just be bad reception." Annabeth had gone white, and she hovered beside Rylan, checking on his phone screen as the second call timed out.

Rylan shook his head and tried Lian's number. It rang, and rang, and—

"Hey, what's up?"

Rylan exhaled in relief. "Where are you now?"

"On our way b—" static crackled. "Got Tammy, but there's a tree d—SSHHHKKKK—on the road. We won't be lo— Mmff MMFF!"

"Lian? Mom?"

A loud pop and crunching sound came through the line, and the call disconnected.

Lian's heart only felt at ease once she got Tammy in the car with them.

After the attack on Everly's home the night before, and every attack on her loved ones leading to that night, her emotions were tightly strung.

She knew the world could be cruel and loss happened, even to those who were most protected, but this wasn't chaos and chance.

This was the cruelty of a few power-mad individuals targeting her and her family.

A humming fury had grown in her, like she'd swallowed a live wasp every time someone she cared for was put at risk.

Tammy had vanished from their home of her own accord, even if she hadn't meant to, but Lian didn't want her out on her own a moment longer than she had to be.

The drive on the way to Dark Corner with Everly was quiet. And given the red, sullen expression on Tammy's face when she climbed into the van, Lian expected the drive back to be equally so. Tammy folded her arms and glared at the wall of the campervan in front of her, occasionally shaking her head as though disagreeing with some internal argument.

I wonder what set her off.

The dirt laneway leading back from Dark Corner was rough, and Everly took it carefully in the rattly vintage vehicle.

"When did you learn how to drive?" Lian asked, curious.

Years back, she had imagined teaching Everly when she taught her boys, but since she lost them all when they were barely teenagers, the time never came. And Lian highly doubted that Everly's own mother would have taught her.

"I had a job at a pizza place when I first moved out. They needed more delivery drivers, so I learned as quick as I could."

Lian did the math in her head. "You wouldn't have been old enough to drive alone."

Everly cleared her throat. "I may have been working off a fake ID."

Lian stared out the windscreen into the dark woods around them. Even at mid-morning the forest was black as the depths of the sea.

She'd been so worried when Everly left home, but also proud. Striking out on her own at such a young age had a lot of risks but staying in that awful home probably had just as many. Lian had meant many times to go to Everly, and offer her support, to let her know that she hadn't been abandoned by the whole family, but she'd been so lost in her own grief during that time.

Before she knew it, Everly had moved away.

"I think your time away from Shroudhaven was good for you, but I'm glad you're back," Lian said, keeping her eyes forward.

"I think I'm glad I'm back too, now," Everly replied. "Although, part of me wonders whether continuing to live my life without knowing monsters are real might have been better."

"I'm glad you brought my son back too. In more ways than one."

"How do you mean?" Everly glanced over quickly

before refocusing on the road.

"It's as though your presence softens him. That first night after he woke up, all I saw was a Darkfrey soldier. But the more time he spends time with you, it's like he's becoming the person he used to be. He's becoming my son again."

A buzzing sound came from the pocket of Everly's red jacket. She pulled out the phone and glanced at the screen. "Speak of the devil."

The phone went back into her pocket, still ringing, and she returned her hand to the steering wheel.

"You don't want to get that?"

"Not while I'm driving. We'll be back soon anyway, and I'll talk to him—WOAH." Everly hit the brakes as they came out of a turn.

The van lurched on the unsealed gravel and shuddered to a stop, inches from a large tree lying across the road.

"Lucky you weren't on the phone," Lian muttered, her hands braced on the dashboard.

"Sorry." Everly winced.

"Not your fault."

"What is it?" Tammy leaned over from the back, shaken from her sulk.

Everly unbuckled her seatbelt and clicked her door open. "There's a tree on the road."

"I can see that *now*," Tammy mumbled.

Everly called back to them from in front of the van. "It's not too big, I think the three of us will be able to drag it out of the way."

The sliding door grumbled as Tammy rolled it open, almost as much as Tammy did. Lian climbed from the passenger seat, adjusting the sword sheathed on her belt. It was an instinct, a security blanket. Up ahead, Everly had paled and placed a hand on her stomach.

Down by her thigh, Lian's phone vibrated in her long cardigan's pocket. She frowned when she saw who was calling. "Hey, what's up?"

It was hard to tell whether the sigh she heard over the line was him or the normal static. "Where are you—SSHHHKKKK?"

Lian walked over to the trunk, eyeing it as though she could gauge its weight. "On our way back. We've got Tammy, but there's a tree down on the road. We won't be lo— Mmff MMFF!"

Heavy fabric went over her head, blocking her vision. Her phone was knocked from her hand. It clattered onto the road, followed by a stomping, crunching sound. Beside her, Tammy shrieked.

Footsteps moved around behind Lian. Two people—no, three.

The roar of an engine approached rapidly, and gravel crunched. Car doors slammed.

"The info was good. We've got the two of them, and the old lady."

"Load them up, quick."

Lian didn't know the first voice, but that one was Vonny.

Lian tensed, still as a statue as she took in all she could of her blacked-out surroundings. Tammy grunted and there was a *thwump* of a punch or kick. Only a soft groan came from Everly's direction.

Hands grabbed the back of Lian's cardigan, forcing her forward. "Vonny? What are you doing?"

"Just picking up some things we need. Took long enough for that cursed kid to show up here, but we figured she would at some point."

Everly groaned louder, her words forced and clipped. "They've got ... Bane."

The two of them ... They're after Tammy and Everly then.

Not a chance in the Everdark was Lian letting them be taken. She hinged at the waist, bending at a ninety-degree angle and ducking away from the hands that guided her to Vonny's vehicle.

Rolling to the side, she drew her sword in the same moment. The few pinpricks of light that sparkled through the bag over her head vanished.

A shoe scuffed in the dirt behind her. She struck out, feeling the air around her blade, the catch of it on fabric.

Heard her target stumble as they dodged. To the right. She struck again lightning fast and met flesh, slicing along in a liquid motion.

A woman cried out, the voice unfamiliar.

"Shit, how's she seeing us?" a man called.

"I don't need to see you to kill you," Lian hissed, charging at the voice.

The ground was uneven, and she wished for good footing. The man crashed across the gravel in his attempts to escape her blade, making him an easy mark. Only a car door slamming saved his life, as Lian whirled toward it, refocusing.

"Leave her, we've got what we came for," Vonny yelled as the engine revved.

The man hurried past her and Lian struck. The blade sliced lightly along his skin. He grunted and ran faster. She tried to follow, dashing to where she heard the car door open and slam.

Her shin smacked hard into the rough bark of the downed tree. She went face-first over it, chin smashing into the hard-packed ground. Her teeth rattled and her sword slid out of reach. Car wheels skidded and flying gravel pelted Lian as she scrambled to her feet and wrestled the bag off her head.

The black jeep sped away from her, vanishing down the winding road, taking Tammy and Everly with it.

Chapter Twelve

Rylan gripped the wheel with choking strength as he raced along the dirt road to Dark Corner.

"It could just have been bad reception," Callan said from the passenger seat, trying again to call Tammy, Everly, or Lian.

They'd had to wait until Rushelle got back with Lian's SUV. Rylan had been ready to go on his own, either take Rushelle's tiny yellow sports car or simply *run* his way there if he had to, but by the time he'd explained the urgency and argued it out with the others, Rushelle returned.

They didn't even unload the produce. Rylan swung himself into the driver's seat, and Callan, Harper, Cherry, Jasper, Denny, and Annabeth filed in. There was a moment of drama with separating Harper and Neri, but Rushelle stayed back to calm the young woman down.

Shadowed by the mammoth, twisted trees on either side, a slim, gray figure jogged along the road toward them.

Rylan brought the car skidding to a stop beside Lian.

He flung himself out of his seat, looking between his mother and the empty road that continued on to Dark Corner. "What happened? Where are the others?"

Lian bent over, hands on her knees, dragging in deep breaths. "Darkfreys. Vonny. Took them."

She straightened, and her face was as grim and gray as her cardigan. A vivid streak of red under her chin contrasted with her pallid skin.

Callan and the others were halfway out of the car.

"Get back in, we're going!" Rylan barked.

"Going where?" Callan stood on the edge of the car on his side, looking over the roof. "They could be taking them anywhere."

"My bet's on the estate," Rylan said.

"Bets aren't going to be worth anything if we end up in the wrong place." Lian pushed Denny back into the car and climbed in after him.

Harper's face was pale, and her lips pursed as she tapped away on her phone, still standing by the car door. Rylan's face turned hot. What was she doing? Posting a damn selfie?

"Ugh!" she grunted. "Not enough reception!"

"Get in!" Rylan roared at her.

Harper's head snapped up and she climbed in fast. "Ev

and I set up tracking for each other, ages back. You know, two girls living in the city."

Rylan nodded, tightening his grip on the wheel. "Keep checking. But we have to move."

The wheels were spinning as Harper shut the door.

Jasper's voice was quiet. "If the purpose of kidnapping Tammy and Everly is to use them to open the shroudpool, it is likely they would take them to the place where they were building that structure I saw."

"Maybe that's not what they are doing? They could just want, I don't know, leverage or revenge or something?" Denny put in.

"I wouldn't be surprised it if was all of the above," Lian muttered.

Tense silence filled the car, the only sound the tapping of Harper's fingernails on the phone screen. They were off the dirt road and back on the highway when Harper gasped.

"They are at the estate," she exhaled the words in a rush, and held up her phone screen where a blue dot pinged on a map.

Rylan pressed the accelerator harder.

"At least we know where they are, but what do we do with that?" Cherry asked, desperation cracking his voice. "What are we going to do, frontal assault the whole damn Darkfrey army?"

"If I have to," Rylan growled.

"I know another way in," Denny sang out.

Annabeth shook her head. "All the gates are guarded and watched lately, even if we didn't take the main drive."

"Nah ah. Not this one. It's a secret way in."

Rylan stared at him in the rearview mirror, and Denny leered back smugly.

"It's down around the bottom of the falls, back where the estate looks over the river. A special little entry only those of Darkfrey blood know about. And how do I know about it then, you ask?" Denny paused dramatically, but nobody asked. "Alexis showed it to me. Made a nice little place for our rendezvous."

Harper groaned, and Cherry muttered under his breath.

Denny raised his voice. "And by rendezvous, I mean hot monkey sex."

"We're going in the front gate," Rylan grunted.

They were near the main street of Shroudhaven, and he swung the car around a corner to avoid an oncoming bus. Speeding down an alleyway, he scraped one side of Lian's SUV against a dumpster.

"Aw, come on man, don't be like that. This is legit!" Denny whined.

"It could be worth a shot," Callan added. "If we can get in without having to fight our way in, we'll get in faster, and also not dead."

The turn to go either up the hill to the estate or around

to the falls bore down on them.

"I know you guys don't believe that Alexis and I are in a deep, meaningful, and hot-as flaming-monster-trucks relationship, but trust me for once. I am what I am, but I'm not a liar."

Rylan gritted his teeth and slammed his hands on the dash. "Fuck!"

He spun the steering wheel, veering off toward the falls.

He spoke through clenched teeth. "This had better be real."

Denny leaned back in his seat. "If anything, I'm too honest, which is why people can't handle me."

He called out directions as they drove along the side of the river. He sent them off to the left, then as the road went from sealed, to dirt, he climbed over the middle seat, and pushed through to lean over into the front.

He waved his finger in front of Rylan's face. "It's coming up here, here! HERE!"

"Where?"

"Turn right!"

Rylan swerved fast. The road they ended up on was more like a goat track, rough and overgrown. Branches smashed against the windscreen as they hurtled along.

"You'll have to stop now before—"

Rylan ground the car to a halt, inches from the edge of a rocky cliff that plummeted down beside a waterfall.

Gasping deep breaths, Rylan peeled his hands from the steering wheel. He glared back at Denny.

Denny slapped him on the back. "Come on, entry's just up ahead."

Drawing a machete from his bag, he slung the pack over his shoulder and was first out of the vehicle.

Rylan climbed out of the driver's seat, his body aflame with raw nerves. The rocks under his feet were slick with spray from the falls and verdant with moss. He backed up, taking in the steep, cascading tiers of cliff and running water. Right at the top, he could see the high walls of the back end of Darkfrey Estate.

Denny had already set off, following what could barely be considered a trail. He hacked at ferns and twigs that crossed the path, even though they would barely have tickled to pass by. Lian and Harper were close behind and the others fell into line.

Callan moved by Rylan's side as they marched after them. His brows were low over his eyes, and his lips fallen from their usual smile.

"Did the stuff you and Annabeth were reading say anything about why they want Tammy?"

"No."

"They definitely wanted both of them," Lian called back, pushing a dripping branch out of the way.

"Doesn't mean they wanted them both for the

shroudpool ritual though." Callan's voice cracked and he marched a bit faster.

"You think being part of the ritual is going to be a better outcome than straight-up revenge?" Rylan snapped a tree limb out of his way. "We have no idea what the Mesmans are going to do with Everly, whether or not she'll survive the process. You've seen what their favorite ingredient in their dark magic is."

Nobody said it out loud, but the word screamed through Rylan's mind.

Bones.

He couldn't lose her. Not now. Not like this.

"Tada!" Denny sang from up front. He stood before a sheer cliff face that Darkfrey Estate sat above.

"What? We can't climb that! Even if we had gear." Rylan stalked toward Denny, ready to smack the dumb grin off his face.

Denny was the only one to have any supplies with him, having grabbed his Shit Hit The Fan bag on his way out, but there couldn't be enough in there to help them scale a cliff.

"Ta. Da." Denny enunciated again slowly and pressed a chipped-out section of stone.

With a dull, echoing scrape, a narrow door-shaped section of rock opened before them.

"Well how about that." Lian gazed into the dark tunnel

ahead. "Even I had no idea this was here."

Denny folded his arms and his face split in a wide grin. "You can all thank me now."

Rylan pushed past him, striding along the rough incline of the tunnel.

"Or later, later is good too."

"Do you guys mind if I put a light on? I realize I'm the only human here right now, I don't want to mess with your dark vision," Harper said from somewhere down the line.

"Do whatever you want, just keep up," Rylan shot back.

"Hey! You're not the only one worried about Everly. *And* Tammy," she snapped, shouldering him out of the way as she took the lead.

Light shone from her phone, illuminating neatly cut-stone walls marked with worn carvings.

Rylan rolled his neck and twitched his nose. He spoke softly but wouldn't have been surprised if it echoed to everybody around him.

"I'm sorry. I know you love her every bit as much as I do."

Harper caught his eye for a moment, but never slowed her pace. "You'd better."

The pitch turned steeper, with steps cut into the dark rock. Veins of quartz sparkled around them, and Annabeth gasped, running her hands over some of the carvings before Cherry and Jasper pushed her on.

Rylan's heart hammered and sweat beaded on the back of his neck.

When what appeared to be a dead end loomed before him, Denny yelled out, "There it is! Just find the switch. No, over on the side, no, the other side! Little knobbly bit."

The tunnel was narrow, and everyone shuffled around as Denny pushed to the front beside Rylan. It took him a moment of feeling around before he found the right spot and the mechanism clicked, setting off a sequence of clockwork sounds.

Harper smiled thinly at Denny. "Thank you. I still don't like you, but thank you."

"You'll learn to love me, babe." Denny grinned, preening his beard.

"And I'm already regretting opening my mouth."

Cherry scoffed, "I bet Denny hears that a lot."

"Can we focus?" Rylan grunted.

This wasn't the time. Every second counted. He tried to imagine that Everly was okay, just held captive but unhurt, that they still had time. But dread pooled molten metal in his throat.

The tall section of wall slid to the side with the sound of a small earthquake, revealing an interior secret passage within Darkfrey Estate.

And at least twenty Darkfrey shadyrs standing guard.

Chapter Thirteen

Vomit dripped down Everly's chin and her head churned like it was filled with an ocean storm.

She'd been dragged, shoved, lifted, kicked, and through the roaring nausea of having the Bane so close to her, she barely noticed. She could feel it, strapped to her chest now, unwrapped and bleeding. Her shirt was soaked through with the thick, slippery soup of eidolghast blood.

The memory of how that blood came to fill the Bane, of the expanding and contracting orb, sacrificing thousands of creatures in its ravenous motion, filled her mind and her throat burned as she gagged again.

Her body flushed with heat then shivered into an icy sweat.

Something sharp jarred into her back and her hands were pulled behind her and roughly bound together.

The bag was ripped off her head, and she blinked, trying to see through her sickness, which blinded her nearly as thoroughly.

Everything was in black and white, formless blobs of light and shadow.

"*Tammy?*" she tried to say, but only a scratchy cough emerged.

"Everly!" The call came back from the blurry, dark blob straight across from her.

It hurt to open her eyes wider, but Everly pushed, lifting them to take in her surroundings. Slowly, her vision wavered back into color. Edges cleared.

Tammy was right in front of her, out of arm's reach, even if her arms were free to reach out.

They were both tied to a large, twisted contraption. Their placement mirrored each other, bound on lower rings of multiple concentric circles formed from bones and sinew, and things Everly couldn't name even if she could see with perfect clarity.

She knew what she was looking at. She'd seen sketches of it. She heard Jasper's description of seeing it half built.

Her mouth felt numb and tasted of bile and blood. She forced it to form the words, hoping Tammy understood.

"Go. *Go.*" She had to go.

If the Mesmans wanted both of them, needed both of them for their ritual ... they couldn't. They couldn't have them both.

Tammy sobbed and shook her head.

"She's not going anywhere."

Everly flinched. She hadn't noticed Vonny was right beside her. She'd put all her effort into focusing on Tammy.

Vonny raised her voice. "You're not going anywhere, are you? Because if you do, you'll never see your friend here alive again."

"Please, I can't control it! Especially when I'm—You can't, don't do it, please!" Tammy flickered, then with a sob of effort, solidified herself.

Kole Mesman moved into Everly's narrow field of view. His bulky, bestial muscles blocked sight of Tammy entirely as he stood in front of the girl. "It's fascinating, these powers you've been cursed with."

"But are they going to work? Are they going to take us to Blaise?" Vonny checked Everly's bonds, tightening them until Everly couldn't feel her fingers.

"Of course!" Kole roared, his voice wildly uneven. "I've worked it all out. The spell has been adjusted. Her link to the Dark Corner shroudpool will take us where we need to go."

Kole moved around in front of Tammy.

She loosed a series of panting shrieks. When he stepped away, she slumped in her bonds.

A river of red streamed down her face.

Tammy. The word caught in Everly's throat. *What did he do to her?*

Her continuing whimpers were both heartbreaking and comforting. At least she was still alive. Kole turned on Everly, stalking forward, a bloody knife clutched in his ham-hock fist.

"And our other ingredient. The Coruscare itself." His eyes were round and bloodshot.

He clutched Everly's chin roughly. With his other hand he brought the sharp blade to her forehead, tracing it lightly over her skin. Everly shuddered but couldn't pull away. She cast her gaze around, seeking aid, anyone who could help her or Tammy. There had been other shadyrs there when they were ambushed near the dormant Dark Corner shroudpool, but it seemed to be just the Mesmans now.

I must be at the estate. Jasper had said the structure was in an old ballroom, but there wasn't much of a ballroom that remained.

The space they were in was huge, and only thin beams of light pierced through arched windows that had been papered over. The remains of hardwood boards were stacked to one end of the hall, and the structure Everly was attached to stood on a level beneath the demolished flooring, built on what seemed to be an ancient ruin.

Dusty, chipped flagstone paved the ground beneath her feet, and low, crumbled walls surrounded them, tumbled down to knee-height lifetimes ago.

The excavated room echoed strangely, but if Tammy's screams hadn't brought attention to them, Everly doubted any help would come.

There has to be something, some way out of this.

Everly tried to draw on her own strength, to bring the light of her dragon out and fight back, but the Coruscare had fled to the deepest place within her, cowering from the Bane that was bound to her skin.

It was hard to even summon enough energy and clarity to keep her eyes open, to speak. She opened her mouth to argue with Kole, to plead for him not to do something so dangerous. He pressed his hand and the knife slid into the skin of her forehead.

Everly screamed but only a harsh whisper emerged.

Kole cut and carved, squeezing her jaw so hard to keep her still that her cheeks split against her teeth. Tears streamed down Everly's face—not enough to clear the blood that ran into her eyes.

She couldn't stop the Mesmans. Whatever they were going to do to her, to Tammy, to the world, she couldn't stop them.

It felt like the end, and all she could think was she never got the chance to tell Rylan that she loved him too. That she loved him from the moment they had met and every dream of romance and passion she'd had her entire life had been about him and only him.

And that dream was just breaking through into reality like a rainbow cutting across a stormy sky and it was already *over*, and it wasn't *fair*.

Kole finished cutting into her skin and let her go. Her chin flopped weakly against her collarbones.

Agony pounded through her head, and the new healing powers she had didn't kick in.

Turning from her, Kole stripped off the white shirt that was stretched over his misshapen skin, flexing his oversized muscles as he did.

The world was stained scarlet through Everly's vision but still his body looked *wrong*.

Dark blotches embedded in his flesh formed complex patterns across his back and chest, revealed as he turned on the spot and raised his hands. Crooked objects jutted from his forearms.

Everly worked to blink her eyes clear, fighting off a wave of panic. They were bones. He had opalescent bones embedded all over his torso and arms. They weren't quite human, not the usual shapes of rib or femur or fingerbone. They spiraled and branched strangely and seemed to ripple with their own motion.

"What have you done to yourself? You're crazy," Tammy blurted from across the room, her voice high and strained.

Kole kept his arms raised above his head. "This isn't madness, this is power. You're seeing the source of my magic. I've made myself one with the ancient shadyrs, so I could bring all shadyrs into a new era of victory."

Tammy thrashed against her bonds. "With your lures? You have no idea what you've done. It was your fault. All along it was your fault!"

Kole turned away from her as though she hadn't even spoken. His deep voice boomed as he spoke in a language Everly had never heard. One that made her vision waver and her stomach heave with the dark power that oozed from each syllable.

The ritual structure moved.

The outermost ring of bone lifted from the ground and spun in slow circles. White light and black shadows swirled along with it, crackling and wailing.

Then the inner section, where Everly and Tammy were bound, shifted. Everly's boots left the ground as the bones she was tied to screeched and screamed like a chorus of human souls in purgatory.

Tammy yelled, panic jittering through her words. "Blaise wanted to close the shroudpool to save you!"

The structure took Tammy off the ground too, leaning her in toward Everly, bringing the two of them closer and closer in the center of the spinning rings. Energy sparked between the two of them.

Kole kept chanting, but Vonny stepped in front of the ritual, her blond bob flying around her face. "It was your fault. You took him out there. What would he think we needed saving from?"

"He was scared you would be killed, like the parents of so many other kids were getting killed by eidolghasts. But it was you doing the killing!"

Vonny took a step backward, her eyes wide. "No. He ..."

Was Tammy getting through to her?

Keep talking Tammy. Make her see.

"Let him go. He's gone. He's gone and we can't get him back," Tammy scream-sobbed.

Vonny's face went rigid, her eyes glittering. "He's not dead! We're going to get him back. You'll see! If you survive. And if you don't, then that's two birds with one stone."

Tammy turned to Everly, open-mouthed and shaking. Everly gazed back, her own body shuddering in waves of sickness and the pull of shadowy magic.

I'm sorry, Everly wanted to say, and she could see those words on Tammy's lips too. The infernal ritual shifted them ever closer to each other.

"What's going on in here?" a voice rang out into the acoustics of the hall.

Mordan Darkfrey stepped out from the shadows, flanked by three braces of shadyrs.

Grasping for strength, Everly cried out, "Stop them,

please!"

Mordan ignored her, stalking over to address Vonny. "I heard you had the Kyrstelle and Boderleth women brought in. What are you doing with them?"

"It's time. They are what we need to open the shroudpool, to get our boy back." Vonny stood at attention, her chin raised and voice strong.

Mordan glanced toward the swirling ritual. "I didn't think you'd pull it off. Still can't be sure you will."

"Don't let them! You can't let them open a shroudpool here at the estate! Look how big it is!" Tammy cringed back, trying to separate herself from Everly as they drew close to touching.

The shadyrs at Mordan's back exchanged concerned glances, but not one of them broke rank or spoke up.

Mordan stared for a long moment at the spinning rings and streaks of white and black magic curling around them.

Then he smiled. "Hrm. Maybe this could be a good thing. A shroudpool under our control? We could foray into the Everdark ourselves, strike at the source of evil directly. Our army, although depleted, is still strong enough."

"No," Everly breathed the word harshly, lost under the thunderous magic growing ever louder. "No! I've seen it, I've seen the Everdark. You can't."

"You have no idea what we're capable of," he shot back. "We are the strongest, the best of what shadyrs can be."

Everly and Tammy shared wide-eyed, terrified looks.

Blood still oozed from Tammy's forehead. They were nearly nose to nose, and Everly could see it was some ancient glyph carved there. The blood now dripped upward, flying and spinning into the tornado of the spell. Everly could feel the tickle of the same effect on her own throbbing forehead, clearing her vision from the tint of red.

"Go ahead," Mordan told Kole, although Kole had not once hesitated or paused in his chanting. "There will be great victories ahead for our kind, and the good of all our world."

Everly's mind flashed with visions from her dreams with the Coruscare. Endless plains of shadow, swarmed so thickly with eidolghasts that it was as though the ground itself was one impossibly large creature.

Mordan thought himself unstoppable, but Everly knew in her bones, if the portal opened, they wouldn't stand a chance.

Chapter Fourteen

Rylan swung the first punch. "I thought you said this wouldn't be guarded!"

Denny swerved his body under a roundhouse kick by a Darkfrey, then brought up his machete to block something hard. A sharp clang echoed through the passage. "Alexis said it would be all clear!"

Callan pushed in beside Rylan. "What the ghast do you mean, 'Alexis said'?"

The hallway was narrow, and the Darkfreys had them closed in on two sides. In the low light, knives flashed, and the spark of electricity glowed at the end of military-style stun batons.

"I texted her on the way in." Denny took down the Darkfrey in front of him with an uppercut. "Thought we could hook up."

"You did what?"

"You absolute idiot!"

"Were you trying to get us all killed?"

"Could you be any more selfish?"

Rylan, Cherry, Lian, and Harper yelled into the fray.

Whatever was going on with Denny and Alexis, whether it was all in his mind or not, the ghast-blighted asshole had ruined their chances of getting to Everly unnoticed.

Rylan had to hold back from aiming his next right-hook at Denny.

Callan groaned, then raised his voice in a commanding yell. "We can rip the asshole a new one later. Let's beat the Everdark out of this lot first."

They had left Howell House in a rush, almost entirely unprepared. Harper and Lian both wielded their swords, and Denny had his machete. Whatever else Denny had in his pack, he wasn't sharing. None of them had their body armor on. They were outnumbered, and outmatched.

But also ready for some payback.

Rylan's knuckles cracked against the cheekbone of one Darkfrey. He yanked the baton-shaped taser from the man's hands as he reeled backward.

That was for the Darkfreys abandoning the search for my missing body.

Electricity popped and zapped as he jabbed it under the man's chin.

That's for lying to me and killing my father.

An elbow caught his cheek and flung his head sideways. He spat blood. Growled. He shouldered the woman into the wall, cracking the long taser across her knees.

That's for trying to kill us at The Crow's Nest.

He pressed forward, breaking away from the line held by Callan, Annabeth, and Denny beside him, and Lian, Harper, Cherry, and Jasper at their backs. He smashed his forehead into the bridge of another man's nose.

That's for sending an eidolghast to Everly's home.

He barreled into the crowd of Darkfreys, arms burning as he struck out with all his strength. He grabbed a head and smashed it into the wall beside them. He thrust the taser deep into a belly. He kicked out the feet of another, bringing the end of the weapon down over their neck as they crumpled.

That's for taking Everly. And that. And that.

Trembling with rage, breath scorching in his throat, Rylan sought another target. Only a litter of bodies lay before him. Back down the hall, the others had stilled, panting and resting against the wall.

Callan swore. "More coming! We've got to move!"

"This way! I know where we are now." Lian slipped past Rylan and took the lead, speeding ahead like a gray ghost in the shadows.

Rylan wasn't sure where they were. He'd never screwed

around in the secret passages and ancient tunnels that riddled the estate like some shadyrs did.

But he knew the old ballroom that Jasper had said was their target. It was in the east wing of an older building. He just hoped Lian could lead them there, and fast.

Footsteps thundered after them as they bolted along the narrow passageway. Rylan's shoulders scraped against the rough-cut stone, ripping his long-sleeved T-shirt.

Lian led them without hesitation through three intersections. Their pursuers faded out of earshot, but Lian didn't slow her pace.

A buzz of energy built within Rylan. A bare tingle at first, but quickly becoming a swell of recognizable power.

"I can feel her, she's close!"

They burst out from behind a faded tapestry and Rylan quickly got his bearings in the long hallway of the abandoned wing. They were right across from the arched double doors of the ballroom, which stood ajar.

Rylan was the first one through, slamming the doors open wide.

He only had half a heartbeat to take in what he saw.

"Everly!" he bellowed.

She was bound and suspended in the center of a massive, dark structure that stood from an excavated basement through to high ballroom ceiling. Her face was as red as her jacket.

Magic streamed and spun like black and white lightning between her and Tammy, who was tied opposite to her. They cringed away from each other but were pushed ever closer.

Kole and Vonny stood at their feet, chanting as bones and darkness wove circles before them. At the door near Rylan stood Mordan Darkfrey and a crowd of other shadyrs.

And then Everly and Tammy's cheeks touched.

Time slowed and *thwumped*. A shockwave of light and dark energy smashed across the room, knocking down everything in its path. Rylan flew off his feet and skidded along the floor on his back, tangling with other bodies. A column of energy shot upward, blasting through the roof of the ballroom. Sunlight streamed in from the midday sky above.

Then everything sucked backward in a rush, timber and plaster flying through the air like bullets.

The world turned dark.

Everly dragged in a sharp breath that scraped into her lungs. Darkness engulfed her, smothering and thick.

She didn't know where she was, whether she was asleep or awake, alive or dead. But she could breathe. That was a good sign. The air she took in was gritty and bitter, leaving a rancid tang in her mouth. The ground beneath her was sharp, and viscous liquid washed against her in a choppy tide, oozing into her clothing.

Her forehead throbbed, but clarity returned to her thoughts. She moved a hand and found it freed. She clasped it to her chest. The Bane was gone.

What happened? Where am I?

"Everly?" Tammy cried out from nearby.

"I'm here." Groaning into a sitting position, Everly fought away the panic and swell of acid in her stomach.

Nothing but utter, inescapable blackness filled her sight.

Need light. Come on.

She concentrated all her effort on controlling the Coruscare's powers, forcing them out from the depths they had cowered into. She flickered like a faulty fluorescent tube.

"Come on!" she grunted, trying again as though turning over the engine of an old car.

A low illumination spread across her fingertips, up her arms. It hardly dinted the darkness, still a solid wall of black encircling her.

"Everly!" Tammy stepped into the light, then crumpled onto her knees.

She reached her stained hands to Everly, but pulled back

before they touched, shivering. Dried blood caked around her eyebrows and down the sides of her nose.

A flurry of tentacles rushed past them, and Everly pushed herself back along the puddled ground, out of its way.

Oh no. No no.

"We're in the Everdark?" she whispered, but she already knew the answer.

"Watch out!" Tammy leaped to her feet and tugged Everly up behind her.

She could clearly see farther into the midnight world than Everly.

A moment later, a weroth three times larger than the one from the theater strode through the edges of her vision.

Everly scrunched her eyes closed with effort, trying to bring more of the Coruscare out. They needed more light. She needed a way to defend them.

But the dragon was weak.

The prolonged contact with the Bane kept it subdued, and she only managed to create a larger dome of light. The usual levitation effect didn't emerge with it, her feet still firmly set on the slick ground, ankle deep in slime. But the light was large enough to see the shroudpool before them, the stream of eidolghasts flowing toward it, and Vonny and Kole standing at the fringes of day and night.

"They're going through to our world. Oh my ghast,

there are so many of them," Tammy whispered, her eyes glittering with stars brighter than Everly had ever seen.

The eidolghasts hissed and howled at Everly's glow as they passed, but the massive shroudpool was too alluring to them, their chance to move from this blighted, used up, and overcrowded world to a new one where they could spread their darkness again.

Some tried to advance on Everly and Tammy in their small bubble of light. Everly struck out a hand, and light crackled across her fingertips. No tendrils emerged, but it was enough to ward the creatures back.

"I can't stop them going through. The Bane really knocked the Coruscare around."

Tammy threw her jacket on the ground, and power surged around her, a swirl of shadows and bright-red sparks transforming her into a red winged demon. "We need to get through, too. Maybe we can help hold them back on the other side."

"Blaise? Blaise?" Vonny and Kole yelled out into the world of monsters and darkness.

Everly's head swung to the Mesmans with a sneer. Couldn't they see what was around them? There was no way their son was here, or anywhere. There was no way he survived this realm for years on his own. She wasn't sure *they* were going to survive it for much longer.

Clearly they couldn't see, because they broke into a

run away from her.

"Come back here! Stay in the light!" she yelled after them.

Part of her didn't care. Part of her still stung, red raw and bleeding from their cruelty. Part of her wanted them to die as *revenge*.

But as she felt the Coruscare growing stronger, its voice curling around her conscience, she refused to listen. She would hold onto what made her human, to what she thought being a good human looked like.

"They're going to die," Tammy said, her voice flat and aching.

"Come on." Everly jogged cautiously after them and Tammy kept by her side.

She swore a string of curses but didn't argue their course.

The Mesmans moved out of Everly's field of light, ignoring her pleas to come back. She strained, her head pounding, making the size of her illumination grow.

The Coruscare had recovered more now, and it pulled her to a stop for a long few seconds as it shot out a glittering tendril. She gasped at the unexpected action as the soul eater made its namesake known, drawing in a feed from a nearby ghast to help it grow stronger. The open wound on her forehead tingled as it knit together.

Then the light expanded to encompass the area ahead,

in time to see the Mesmans being crunched in the five different mouths of an eidolghast that dwarfed the weroth they saw before. The hydra-like beast fought over their torn bodies, tearing free hipbones in an explosion of viscera, chewing thighs with teeth like chainsaws.

Everly's blood filled with ice, and a nausea unrelated to the Bane washed over her. Tammy sobbed a wordless wail.

"We've got to go, we've got to get out of here," Everly said, choking the words out around acid.

The multiheaded behemoth slithered away toward the shroudpool. Everly watched it, terrified for a moment it would turn on them. She dulled her light as much as she dared, hoping not to draw its attention.

Tammy's gaze remained fixed on where the Mesmans had fallen. She moved again, but in the wrong direction. Toward them, instead of their escape.

"Tammy!" Everly dashed after her, growing the light again.

Her feet skimmed the ground, lifting from the sludgy layer of what she imagined was a millennia's worth of blood. Fissures cracked the ground around them, burbling the clotted fluid, and burning with black flames.

"There's something there, something ..." Tammy ran past the Mesmans' corpses without giving them a second glance, to a bundle beside a tumble of broken smoky crystals.

Her bat-like wings fluttered behind her, speeding her steps. Everly worked hard to keep up, fending off eidolghast that approached on each side, her light tendrils under control again.

Tammy landed on her knees with a crack.

"It's him. It's Blaise." Tammy clutched at the ragged bundle, lifting a scrap of fabric with a Darkfrey logo embroidered onto the side.

"How do you know? It could be ... I don't know, has anyone else ever been lost through a shroudpool before?" Everly offered.

She shot short glances at Tammy while keeping her eyes on their surroundings. An auerdax stared at them from the edges of her light for a long moment before turning away.

Tammy shook her head, plunging her hands into the slime and bones before her, her shoulders slumped in a curved arch. "Their spell worked. It brought us to him."

The Mesmans found their son after all, but died seconds before discovering him dead. Everly wasn't sure what the better outcome would have been.

Whether their death was a mercy compared to what would have happened if they had lived for a few moments longer. If they had seen that it was all for nothing. Their son was gone, all along.

"Tammy, we've got to go." Everly lashed out her light whip to fend off a herrelspurn that dove at them from above.

A gust of fire singed the heavy air.

Tammy didn't respond, her hands working in the blood-soaked ground.

The air tremored, shivering across Everly's sphere of light. A sharp blade of fear stabbed her ribcage, making her heart pump double time. Her dragon squirmed inside her as though trying to free itself from the cage of her body.

Something was coming. Something *big*.

Everly floated down beside Tammy. "I'm sorry, I'm sorry you lost him, Tammy, but we have to get out of here, right now!"

"I'm sorry too. But I've already grieved for him all I can." Tammy turned around.

Her face was marked where tears washed lines down her red-tinted skin, but her expression was still, solid. She lifted her hands to show a basketball-sized orb, covered in slick, dark fluid. Her shadyr galaxy eyes glittered.

"This is what Blaise wanted to close the Dark Corner shroudpool with. Even if we didn't close it entirely, this thing at least made it dormant. We could use it to do something about the shroudpool the Mesmans made."

Tammy wiped away some of the blood covering the orb with her sleeve, and Everly gasped.

It's the thing that created the Bane.

That sacrificial machine of mass destruction. She couldn't even think straight. She just wanted to be home, with family, with Rylan. Eidolghasts still threatened their circle. A force that made her skin want to turn inside out on itself approached at a rapid speed.

The thing Tammy held could be their salvation or their destruction. She didn't know what to do, but Tammy looked at her with such hope in her eyes that she nodded and rose back up.

Tammy stood as well, then the needle point of a weroth arm speared right through her shoulder.

Chapter Fifteen

Rylan jumped to his feet. Where Everly had been, now stood a two-story-high rippling pool of pure darkness.

No. No, we were too late.

Debris covered the ground all around the shroudpool, roof tiles, bones, and timber beams lying thick. There was no sign of Everly.

Or Tammy. Or the Mesmans. But Rylan could only seek Everly, could only scream her name. He could only hope she was in there, somewhere under the shattered ceiling, hope that she was okay.

"They actually did it." Mordan dusted himself off beside Rylan, staring wide-eyed at the portal to another dimension.

His mouth gaped, opening fish-like a few times as he

took in the devastation. Then his eyebrows dropped and eyes gleamed.

In a commanding voice, he addressed the Darkfrey shadyrs scattered around him, "To me. You—go and rally reinforcements. We have the Everdark to defeat today."

"What have they done?" Lian hissed.

She helped Harper to her feet, the rest of their team nearby equally horrified at what lay before them.

"Everly," Rylan gasped out her name, and broke into a run toward where he last saw her.

Footsteps clamored through the rubble behind him, but he didn't know or care who they belonged to.

Then the shroudpool bulged.

Like an octopus pushing its way free from a tar pit, a vasmire emerged, almost gingerly, testing its surroundings with twisting tentacles.

That was fast. Rylan's blood chilled. There were a few active shroudpools in the region, kept as well-patrolled and monitored as they could be. Maybe one or two eidolghasts a day came through them and were dealt with as quickly as possible by the Darkfrey shadyrs.

But they were nowhere near the scale of this portal. Most weren't even as big as a regular doorway. This ... this shroudpool was large enough to drive a mining truck through. Rylan shuddered.

Does the size of the shroudpool affect the size of the

eidolghast that can come through?

A cry like booming horn and nails on a chalkboard pierced the air. Rylan ducked as a herrelspurn flew out from the shroudpool above the vasmire. Then a weroth bigger than he'd ever seen stepped through, spearing the vasmire under a needle-like leg.

Ghast dammit. He had to find Everly before they were overrun.

The massive shroudpool must be like a beacon to the beasts.

Rylan allowed his body to change. He could no longer sense Everly's presence, the essences the Coruscare held inside her.

He tried not to think about what that could mean. But with three eidolghasts and counting in the vicinity, he had plenty to draw from, and experience enough to shift with it however he wanted. The strength of a werewolf. The regeneration of a vampire. The wings of a demon.

The shadowy mist of his change cleared as the shroudpool bulged again, and a horde of ghasts burst through. Dozens of them. They squabbled and clawed at each other as they stampeded around him. Some took to the air, flying off into an unnaturally darkened sky.

There was a scream beside him, quickly muffled as a Darkfrey shadyr was bitten clean in half by the mammoth-sized weroth. Her legs fell to the ground, still twitching.

More screams echoed in the distance across the estate.

Rylan growled, rolling under the gelatinous limbs of some creature he'd never seen before in person or in theory.

One massive eye swiveled in the sickly-pink gel that formed a rough, constantly morphing body. His shadyr nerves twitched, trying to pull his change into ghast-knew-what that bizarre beast would shift him into.

It was all he could do to dodge the mass of eidolghasts clamoring through the space, rushing to break free and wreak havoc on his world and tear apart anything that stood in their way.

He caught a glimpse of Lian, Harper, and Denny, backed against the entryway, which had been smashed through and crumbled beside them. Jasper, Cherry, and Annabeth had gotten mixed up in the braces of shadyrs with Mordan, fighting side by side.

No one noticed or cared that the Howell team had joined the mix. It was shadyr versus the darkness and that was all any of them could focus on. Not Rylan, though. It was him versus anyone or anything that got between him and Everly.

Callan appeared at his side, clawed werewolf hands dripping in green ichor.

"Can you see them?" He howled over the sound of smashing walls and cries of war.

A sharp weroth limb lanced down from above and

Rylan pulled Callan to the side. "Not since the pool opened."

He could barely see three feet in front of him, constantly moving to dodge the lashing of tentacles, teeth, and talons. They were overwhelmed, flooded with monsters.

A great cry came from the end of the hall. At the elevated edges of the ballroom, hundreds of Darkfrey shadyrs poured into the space. A surge of hope flamed through Rylan.

One squad took off flying, bat wings pushing them into the gloomy sky to hunt down the herrelspurn and other airborne eidolghasts. Others swarmed in groups of four over the monsters that matched the change they'd taken. The numbers were on their side, but still more beasts clambered through the massive shroudpool.

"Push forward!" Mordan commanded, shifting into pallid skin and pointy teeth.

The Darkfrey braces caught up to Rylan and Callan, bringing down eidolghasts as they went. Mordan fought beside them, eyes sparkling.

Rylan turned back toward where Everly had vanished. Callan pressed in at one shoulder, and more shadyrs came in at his other side. And they pushed.

A wall of shadyrs met the throng of eidolghasts. Fur and acid flew, flashes of flesh, blood, and darkness streaked through Rylan's sight as he charged into the thick of the battle. A teeth-lined tentacle ripped across his back, tearing from shoulder blade to bicep.

He pitched backward to pin the slithering limb between himself and the stone floor. Latching a clawed hand around the tentacle, he tore it free from the body that owned it.

His left arm hung limp but would heal quickly enough. He couldn't let it slow him down. A Darkfrey offered him a hand to help him to his feet. He nodded his thanks, and they pressed forward again.

They were almost there, had almost pushed the horde back to the shroudpool. It felt good, fighting side by side with those he'd lived with, trained with for so long, instead of fighting against them. They'd betrayed him, in so many ways, but they were still a kind of family to him.

They were all dedicated soldiers and fought together like a seamless engine of eidolghast destruction.

Callan caught his eye, a grim smile pressing his lips together. They were close, the shroudpool almost within reach. It loomed over them, a wavering black hole that seemed to absorb all light around it. Wriggling, wormy strands squirmed across the surface.

"Push on!" Mordan yelled from their backs. "Into the Everdark! We will hold them on the other side, then purge their evil for good!"

A war cry of approval sounded from a few of the shadyrs around them, but many others only gawked from Mordan to the portal of nightmares before them.

"Don't listen to him! He'll get you all killed." Lian's voice rose strong over the cacophony of battle. "Do what you can to hold off the ghasts, but don't step through that shroudpool. It's suicide."

The path to the shroudpool was cleared. Mordan stepped in front of it with a brace by his side. But none stepped through.

Rylan clawed into the tiles and timber around the edges, calling Everly's name and searching for any glimpse of her red jacket or pale, ashy hair. Callan mirrored him, yelling for Tammy.

"Go through, I said! That's an order!" Mordan bellowed.

One shadyr took a small step forward, then quickly retracted. Mordan growled, stalking toward her.

"Cowards!" His hands thrust against her chest, throwing her across the room.

She landed beside a vasmire, which rolled its tooth-covered tentacles over the top of her before she could get back to her feet. Her screams were muffled, disappearing beneath sickening chewing sounds.

Mordan's sharp teeth bared as he snapped at the remains of her brace. "I've ordered you to go through and fight the Everdark, and I will not suffer disloyalty."

"He's mad, can't you see? He doesn't care about any

of you!" Lian yelled from across the battlefield, working with the other Howell and Darkfrey shadyrs to hold back the scattered eidolghasts.

Rylan took in what he could of his periphery as he clawed through the rubble.

"I can't find her," he cried to Callan.

Callan's werewolf snout wrinkled, and he shook his head. "You think ... you think they ended up on the other side?"

Mordan swung his attention to them, grin widening. "Didn't you see? Them and the Mesmans, they were all sucked through when the pool formed."

Rylan's heart compressed with a pressure that could form a diamond. "No ..."

"Go after them," Mordan goaded with a sharp-toothed smile. "Go. Be my first soldiers to set foot in enemy territory. Show these other cowards what bravery looks like."

Rylan stood from his crouched position. He crunched across the debris, the shroudpool in his sights. If Everly was in there, he was going. Mordan could be lying ... but Rylan couldn't sense Everly's presence.

Either way, she's not here anymore.

If there was even the slightest chance she was still alive on the other side, Rylan had to go to her.

Then he noticed Callan matching his trajectory. Rylan stopped and grabbed his brother's arm.

"What are you thinking? You aren't going through."

"I have to. If Tammy is in there ... I have to."

Rylan froze, hand clenched around Callan's skin. He had every intention of going through himself. He was going after Everly, had only thought of Everly. But he didn't want his brother stepping through to a place no one had ever returned from.

He shook his head at Callan. "If I find Tammy, I'll bring her back too. But you're staying here."

The massive weroth came crashing to the ground across the room, taking out half a wall as it was felled. Skirmishes still raged all around them and flowed out into the grounds. Mordan screamed at the shadyrs, but none approached the shroudpool.

"Are you kidding me? If you're not letting me through, I'm not letting you. You think I want to lose you, too? That's what will happen if you go alone. At least if we're together ... we're together."

Rylan's jaw twitched. When Callan had left the Darkfreys before him, it felt like a betrayal, but the loss of his brother then would be nothing to losing him to the hellscape of the Everdark.

"I don't want you to get hurt. There's basically no chance we come back from this. Not without a miracle."

Callan nodded slowly, never breaking eye contact with Rylan. It was clear in his firm gaze that he understood the risks entirely.

"Then let's keep our fingers crossed for one."

Shoulder to shoulder they marched toward the shroudpool.

"Rylan!" Harper's voice screamed from behind. "Lian! What are they doing! Where's Everly? RYLAN WHERE'S EVERLY?"

Rylan looked back but kept walking. He saw Lian physically restraining Harper, who screamed and strained toward him. He saw Annabeth and Cherry, fighting back-to-back, turn to catch his eye, mouths dropping open in shock.

And then a churning slick of shadows washed over him.

Everly swooped forward, catching Tammy with one arm as she hung skewered by the weroths leg. She thrust her other arm out, lashing the weroth with a strand of light.

It squealed, rearing back. Its long, spidery limb slurped out of Tammy's chest as it pulled free. The orb Tammy had collected smacked onto the ground. Her full weight fell onto Everly, pressing her down onto the slippery stones. Energy crackled where Everly and Tammy's flesh met, and Everly shifted her weight so her jacket created a barrier between them.

The weroth roared and snapped at them, and Everly directed her light toward it again. The tendril shot out in a flash, trying to capture the creature, to consume it. The weroth moved faster, skittering away into the surrounding dark.

"Tammy?" Everly cried, high-pitched.

Tammy's head lolled. "Mmf."

"Hey, hang on, okay?" Everly readjusted Tammy's weight so she could hold her more comfortably.

Eidolghasts surged around them, pressing into the edges of Everly's light, as though driven to a frenzy by the scent of Tammy's blood. Everly loosed a second tendril, then a third, swatting and striking at the creatures. She was hyperaware of Tammy's closeness, her body, her soul, pressed against Everly's chest.

Right there, like a snack for the Coruscare.

Beads of sweat flushed her face and neck as she directed its wrath and hunger outward. She found it easier to do with the motions of her arms, but needed one to keep Tammy held up. It would have been even better if she could get two arms around Tammy, lift her properly so she could make her way back to the shroudpool and escape this nightmare.

But the ghasts kept up their threat, and Tammy remained slumped against her, and Everly could barely take a step forward while splitting her focus on both.

"Tammy? Hey, can you teleport yourself out? Can you get back to Dark Corner?" Everly urged.

If Tammy could go, Everly could put all her energy into fighting through to the portal, get back to their world, and hopefully get someone to Dark Corner in time to give Tammy the medical care she needed.

"Try for me. Don't you dare even argue, just try!"

"Mmf," she said again, her mouth muffled against Everly's shoulder.

She moaned a low, long note that juddered out into a sob.

Her words were a rough breath. "Can't. Not working."

Her head flopped backward. The red skin and wings of her demon form seemed to grow dull and retract, as though her body was failing to hold the form. Everly had seen similar in Rylan, the night he almost died on the street in front of her house.

He had looked like a vampire, but when his body had taken more damage than it could handle, he faded back to something more human. He was lucky that there was enough regeneration power left even in that form to help him hang on.

"Change!" Everly cried out. "Change into vampire form, so you can heal. Come on, Tammy, please!"

There had to be a vasmire out there in the storm of monsters.

Tammy's head wobbled limply; her face turned up to the endless black sky.

Everly's mind raced. Could she try to take Tammy's soul into her, like she did with Rylan? Keep it safe until they could return her to her body? But what if her body didn't survive? She could feel the urging of the Coruscare to let it do it, let it consume her, but with that urging came no reassurance that it would be saving her.

She tried to rouse Tammy, to feel for her pulse, but had to return her attention to a new weroth stabbing its saber legs at them. It opened its huge maw, the internal glow eerie in the dark world, like a deep-sea predator, luring its prey.

Behind it, outside of the reach of her light, came the sounds of another scuffle. Everly lassoed the weroth with two tendrils together, and flung it away, just as a dismembered head of a herrelspurn bounced onto the ground before her. A few other eidolghasts that had been testing Everly's defenses scattered.

"Everly!" came a voice that made her heart backflip.

"Rylan?" she replied in a squeal.

Two massive, humanoid forms strode into the light. If it hadn't been for his voice, Everly wasn't sure she'd have been able to recognize Rylan as he stood before her.

Monstrous, three times his normal mass, armor plated and ridged with spines. His skin glittered a metallic blue where it showed through his torn clothing.

Rylan lunged toward her, stopped short by the view of the lifeless girl in her arms.

"What happened to Tammy?" The second voice was Callan's, in a form matching his brother.

"A weroth got her, her shoulder. I don't know ..." Everly stuttered, eyes stuck on Rylan.

"I'll take her," Callan said, reaching out arms almost as thick as Tammy's torso.

He lifted her and cradled her against his chest. She'd faded back almost entirely to human form. Her head rolled to the side, and she let out a low moan. Alive. For now.

With her arms free, Everly stepped into Rylan's. His skin was hard as steel, like embracing a knight in full armor. "What are you doing here? How?"

"We came after you," he whispered into her hair, bringing a hand up to brush the back of her head.

"You're crazy," she whispered back, flushing from a gratitude and relief she had no idea how to express.

"Watch your six!" Callan growled, and Everly pushed away, shooting her strands of light at a vasmire's tentacles that slithered and whipped around them.

"We need to move. What happened to the Mesmans?" Rylan's voice growled over their name.

"Gone. Dead. We found Blaise though. His remains. And this." Everly bent to collect the intricately carved orb.

She felt sick handling it so she passed it to Rylan.

"Tammy thinks it might be able to close the shroudpool the Mesmans made. Or at least make it dormant. Just ... be careful with it. I'll explain if we get out of here."

Rylan looped an arm around her, bringing her close to his steel-plate chest, and placed a firm kiss to her cheek.

The heat of his lips left a tingling mark behind. "Let's get out of here then."

Without Tammy's weight, and with the Coruscare near fully recovered, Everly blazed bright, launching off the ground until her feet floated near the brothers' heads.

"I don't even know what you two are at the moment, but I hope it's fast."

Rylan nodded. "You set the pace and we'll keep up."

"Faster than I've ever been. Yay for my first time in super-multiform." Callan grinned wryly, but it didn't meet his eyes.

He checked Tammy, then set his sights forward to the shroudpool.

Everly took off, her light spreading around the brothers below her. Shooting-star tendrils stepped around them, stilt-like, forming a protective cage as they ran.

"On your right," Rylan yelled, and Everly struck out.

A thick chain of light sliced deep into a surreal creature of crystalline daddy-longlegs limbs and clockwork eyes.

"What in the Everdark was that?" Everly asked.

"I'll explain if we get out of here." Rylan smirked back,

keeping his eyes on guard. "Up front!"

Everly attacked and Rylan spotted, again and again, pushing their way into the flow of monsters all trying to get to the same destination.

The Coruscare's powers renewed with a vengeance, followed by the odd sensation of fullness, satiation, glee, as Everly smashed their way through the monsters.

She hadn't intended the powers to consume any ghasts, hadn't allowed it, hadn't even noticed it happen. But somewhere in the mad melee of whipping light and nightmarish beasts, the Coruscare had fed again.

The thought unsettled her, but not as much as the understanding deep in her core that destruction was coming for them, like a tsunami on the horizon.

She cleared their path to the shroudpool with a burst of light and Rylan stared at her in awe. "Maybe with you on our side, we could take on the whole Everdark."

Sweat drenched Everly's chest and she shook her head firmly. "We need to get out, and we need to close the door. Eidolghasts aren't the only thing here that's a threat."

"Something worse?" Rylan's eyebrows furrowed, wrinkling his shining blue skin.

"You remember the dream we shared that time? With the being of darkness that obliterated everything it touched?"

"Oh," Rylan said flatly.

"WHAT?" Callan said.

They reached the shroudpool, and Everly formed a fence of light to hold off the eidolghasts trying to press through around them. "Big. Bad. The Coruscare's dark twin. And I think we've attracted its attention."

Callan turned wide eyes from her and carried Tammy through the dark portal.

Rylan hesitated.

"I'll be right behind you." Everly drew herself down to his level.

"No, together," he said.

Everly bit her lip and nodded. They stepped into the wriggling slick of magic.

And came out together on the other side.

Everly gasped fresh earth air into her lungs, and it tasted of blood. There were bodies scattered around what was left of the room. Fights still raged between Darkfreys and ghasts, spilling out into the now visible grounds. Mordan Darkfrey stood before her, teeth bared and eyebrows high as he took in their sudden appearance.

Harper called out, and Everly turned to find her friend.

Then every hair on the back of her neck rose so high her skin twinged painfully. The Coruscare shuddered within her.

And from the shroudpool behind her, a mass of infinitely black nothingness burst through.

Chapter Sixteen

Like a nightmare made real, a maddening brume of darkness swirled above the shroudpool. Everly gazed up at it, her and the Coruscare's shared panic short-circuiting her brain.

It's here. It followed us.

"What is that?" Mordan spat at her.

Dark twin. Infuscur. Void. Destruction. The end. The Coruscare answered from within, its light flickering. Everly couldn't speak.

The *Infuscur* spun like an empty galaxy, filling the sky. And then it rushed down at them.

Rylan caught Everly with one arm. He pulled her to the side in a tumbling leap. Callan took Tammy, dodging in the other direction.

Darkness fell over Mordan like black ink poured into

water, obscuring him entirely. As the midnight cloud contracted, Everly was sure she'd find Mordan gone, erased from the world.

Instead, the dark being rushed into him, pouring into his eyes, ears, nostrils, mouth. His body twitched and jerked, joints turning at wrong angles as he hovered over an ebony-stained crater.

He stilled. An aura of juddering darkness ran like ribbons around his body. His fully black eyes turned to Everly, and he smiled.

"Oh shit." Everly brought up a shield of light with less than a second to spare.

Darkness lashed at her, clashing against the glittering strands with sizzling energy. Her defense held, but the force of the attack threw her backward. The soles of her boots clattered across debris as she steadied herself.

The Infuscur's tendrils were similar to the Coruscare's but inverse. Long ribbons of blackness that seemed to suck in the light rather than sparkle. It whipped out again, striking three Darkfrey shadyrs who stood closest to what had been Mordan.

It passed right through them, and in its wake, the shadyrs crumbled, falling into powdery pieces, then faded into nothing.

It made them nothing at all.

Everly's mouth hung open but she couldn't breathe.

She'd had this nightmare, too many times. It had scared the life out of her even in her dreams, and now it was here, real, in front of her.

Rylan attempted to drag her away. Callan ran to Lian, Harper, and the other Howell House shadyrs at the end of the hall. Tammy remained cradled in Callan's arms, her life ebbing away with every jostle, every second her wound was untended. Cherry, Jasper, Annabeth, even fucking Denny—she couldn't see any of them turned to *nothing*.

And I'm the only one with a chance of facing the Infuscur.

"Get to the others and get out of here. Now." Everly didn't give Rylan a chance to argue.

She sped forward, burning like a comet toward the Infuscur.

Mordan raised himself off the ground, shooting back at her with glee in his dark eyes. But Everly was sure there was nothing left of Mordan in that expression.

Their energy smashed into each other's, and the buildings around them shook.

Everly struck with everything she had. Her glowing tendrils were caught easily in dark ribbons, wrenched, and swung. It flipped Everly around it and flung her to the rubble-strewn ground.

Everly hit hard, even with trying to cushion the fall with her light. Her skin burst on her temple, shoulder, hip. Bones crunched. She was still shaking off a view full of stars and spots when the Infuscur struck at her again. She dragged herself backward, onto her feet, and the black ribbons struck where she'd been. Fallen walls and roof tiles crumbled and vanished under their touch.

One ribbon looped around her boot. She screamed as she shot every bit of power out around her. She forced the darkness off her in the miniscule gap of time between her shoe disintegrating and that same destructive force touching her flesh.

It's too strong. We're no match for it.

The Coruscare and Infuscur may have been some twisted kind of twins, paired entities of light and dark, but Everly only held two-thirds of the Coruscare.

Mordan held the Infuscur at full power. And it was throwing her around like a ragdoll. She couldn't beat it. Not like this.

Everly burst upward, pushing as high as her powers could lift her, breaching the broken roof of the ballroom.

She had only a moment before the Infuscur chased after her. Long enough to see her friends checking back with worried glances as they made a dash away from the battle of opposing energies.

Good. She just needed to buy enough time for them to escape, then try to get herself clear. She hardly finished the thought before darkness lashed in front of her nose and she reeled backward, hitting the edge of the broken roof and sliding out across the tiles.

The Infuscur kept close pursuit, harpooning the roof around her. Beams and shingles evaporated, and a car-sized section fell out from underneath Everly. She took the opportunity to go down with it. Dust exploded around her, filling the room.

Shutting off every bit of her light, Everly scrambled over the fallen roofing. She could barely see, her eyes and lungs stinging with grit.

She aimed on instinct for the gap in the wall she'd seen from above. The sound of lashing ribbons came from behind her. The Infuscur sought her with the reach of its void-touch tendrils, stabbing them through the obscuring cloud.

Everly's hand landed on the edges of broken bricks, and the dust cleared. She stared out into the training yards of the estate.

It couldn't be much past midday, but the world had become dark as an eclipse. The screams and blows of skirmishes echoed from every direction, and shadyrs, herrelspurn, and other flying eidolghasts clashed in the sky.

And still more eidolghasts emerged through the shroudpool. The Darkfrey line there was scattered, and she couldn't do anything more while the Infuscur sought her destruction.

Everly took off, sprinting toward the shadows of a

nearby covered walkway, hoping it would conceal her.

Her heartbeat pounded in her throat and her face burned as she ducked between a thick pillar and hedge. She took a chance to glance back.

The Infuscur raised itself high over the shattered ballroom, lashing at the building as though it could find her by obliterating everything around it. With its attention remaining there, Everly fled.

She headed in the direction she'd last seen Rylan and her friends running.

She went left up a side path and almost smacked face-first into a weroth that chewed on the body of a Darkfrey shadyr. It took a significant effort to keep her light inside. She couldn't risk attracting the Infuscur again.

She skidded the other way, across a garden bed, her one bare foot punctured by woodchips. Bounding up entry steps to the main building, she spotted the Howell team down the hall, filing into a secret passage she and Lian had used once before. They fretted and argued, Rylan's growling voice echoing down the corridor.

Harper spotted Everly first and ran to meet her halfway. She threw her arms around her, squeezing tight. Everly squeezed back, panting hard.

"Did you beat it? Is it gone?" Harper questioned with fierce eyes.

Everly could only shake her head. She had no breath

left for words.

Harper chewed a lip for a moment, then took Everly's hand and dragged her to join the others. There was a pat on the arm from Lian, and a nod from Callan, still holding Tammy close to his now more werewolf-shaped form.

Rylan reached for the fresh blood near Everly's temple. The torn skin there had already closed, but his fingertips came away glossy and red.

A rumble from the other end of the building heralded a rout of Darkfreys coming their way, something large on their tail.

"Out, quick!" Lian hissed through fanged teeth, waving them into the passageway. They bolted in, running together in a tight group.

It was bizarre seeing the team in all different shadyr shifts. Normally they all changed together, all vampires, or all werewolves. But with so many eidolghasts around, each shadyr had their own type, or mix of types.

Cherry had ghosted out, while Annabeth and Jasper seemed to be varying mixes of vampire and demon. Denny and Lian stuck to straight-up vampire.

Rylan had held his mammoth, armored form, but their escape tunnel required something smaller, and shadows obscured him momentarily as he shifted to a combination of vampire and nyevmer.

Pale skin and fangs, with the hint of sparkling blue

scales forming a smooth protection across his shoulders and down to clawed hands. Everly doubted a nyevmer had swum free of the shroudpool. He must have been drawing its essence from within her, within the pool of eidolghast energies that the Coruscare had absorbed over eons.

Everly wished the shadyrs could take on some kind of Coruscare form, or that all of them had the power to use the essences within her to change into whatever they wanted, like Rylan had been imbued with since his soul was freed.

Anything to give them an advantage over what felt like frightening odds. For now, Everly would be happy if they could just get out of there alive.

Their escape tunnel didn't last long. They tumbled out through the shattered passageway where half the building had been torn away, opening them to the outside world. Lian searched about wildly, then pointed across the devastation to a hole showing beneath splintered floorboards.

The spine-scraping screech of a herrelspurn cut through the air and they dived into that dark hollow as a gust of fire caught the air behind them.

Everly skidded down a slope of loose bricks, hips and knuckles grazing as she tried to slow her descent. Her feet hit flat ground, and she wobbled upright in time to catch Harper tumbling after her. Rylan came through last, keeping his eyes on the gap above them, teeth flashing as he watched for any pursuers.

"I've never been down here before," Lian spoke into the dusty darkness. "But the garages are that general direction. I say we help ourselves to a vehicle and get the Everdark out of here."

Everly's entire body screamed with over-tired muscles, and her lungs burned. Harper kept her phone held up for both of them, and the light trembled as they ran.

"I've been here before." Rylan's pushed through to the lead and took a right when they hit an intersection. "This was where I first saw evidence of the Mesmans' work, in a small room up ahead. But they blindsided me and cleared everything out before I worked out who it was or could do anything about it."

Rylan passed a doorway, did a double take, then jogged back to it. Everyone stopped beside him, crowding to see what caught his attention.

Through the ancient cut-stone doorway lay a room too dark for Everly to see what made the others gasp. Harper shined her light in, and Everly glared at the array of skeletal figures standing before them. The carved-out room was so filled with bones it was like an ossuary. An army of misshapen undead standing at attention.

"Looks like they decided this space was safe to use again," Rylan muttered.

Denny stabbed at one of the bone effigies with his

machete. "A ghast-blighted storeroom for all their dark magic shitfuckery."

"Those are the lures?" Annabeth said, her words trembling.

"Yeah, but I don't think they are activated, or whatever. They aren't doing that horrible wiggly thing they do when they are," Everly said.

"Come on," Callan snapped, eyes locked on Tammy's marble white skin. "We have to keep moving. We don't have much time."

Everly's body groaned, but she drew every resource she had to keep up. The tunnel hit some stairs, which took them to an exit in an old brick toolshed.

Once outside again, Everly looked around, trying to get her bearings and track where the Infuscur was, but she'd never been in this part of the estate before. The sky was so dark now, she worried the Infuscur could be right above them, camouflaged by its aura of black around Mordan's body, and they wouldn't even see it.

Denny smacked the flat of his machete in his hand then pointed across a section of smaller cottages and training courts. "Garage is down that way. No more tunnels to take out here. Ya'll ready to hoof it?"

He didn't wait for a reply, just took off across the shadowed lawn.

Bursting from their cover, they ran fast after him,

keeping as close together as possible without elbows and feet clashing.

The manicured grass muffled the sound of their boots, and it felt unnaturally cold under Everly's bare foot. Down the hill, she could see where a long, low building met with a laneway that snaked around and joined the main drive.

They might actually make it. Get in, get a car or two, and get out.

But then what? How long could they hide from this? How far would this hellscape spread, as eidolghasts kept spilling through the enormous, unchecked shroudpool?

How much of the world would the Infuscur dissolve into nothingness?

Everly knew they had to get away, they had to regroup, save Tammy. But after that … after that might come nothing anyway. It felt like the end of the world.

Without warning, Denny veered off to the left, away from their target.

"Denny!" Rylan scream-whispered.

"What stupid thing is he doing to get us killed this time?" Harper rasped out. "He is going to be on the receiving end of some open palm cheek music if we survive this."

"I can't wait for him this time. I'm moving on." Callan slowed only enough to give them all a view of Tammy, her huddled mass a painting of black, white, and red.

Rylan nodded. "Anna, Jas, Cherry, stick with him, get some engines running. We'll go and get this jerk back in line."

With nods to acknowledge the order, they split off, leaving Rylan, Everly, Harper, and Lian to chase down Denny. Everly wondered how Rylan made the call on the split, but was grateful he didn't send her on without him.

She didn't want to leave his side, or Harper's, or Lian's. When apocalyptic sounds crashed and cried from every direction, all she wanted was her family close.

If this was the end, they were what would keep her fighting.

Denny kept ahead of them all the way to where one of the cottages had been split in half, one side standing nearly pristine, and the other lying in a jumble of red brick and torn upholstery.

By the time they reached him, he was lifting a slab of ceiling plaster with a grunt. A woman dragged her legs out from beneath, then moaned up onto her feet.

"Alexis?" Rylan gaped.

She didn't answer. She was too busy thanking Denny with a tongue-filled kiss.

"Okay," mumbled Harper, staring at the couple with more horror in her eyes than she'd shown before. "So this really is the end of the world."

"Alexis *Darkfrey*?" Everly blinked, struggling to take

in what she was seeing.

The woman's hourglass figure fit snuggly into a high-tech-looking black catsuit, and a fall of silky blond hair tumbled down her back.

Everly choked. "You mean ... it really was real?"

Denny lifted his head to the sky and crowed, "Told you so!"

"Keep it down!" Rylan said.

"Real enough maybe, but she still ratted us out on our way in, cost us the time we needed to stop all of this." Lian's top lip curled, revealing pointed teeth.

Alexis gasped, throwing a hand to her chest and pleading to Denny, "It wasn't me, I swear! Father was monitoring my phone. I didn't know until today."

"I believe you, babe," Denny crooned and leaned in for another kiss.

Rylan pushed them apart with a shove on Denny's shoulder. "You think that's where the Mesmans got their other info, about where Tammy and Everly were this morning? What else have you been texting?"

"Dick pics, mostly." He shrugged.

"Oh for ghast's sake." Harper dropped her face into her hands. "Can we just get out of here now?"

Alexis wrapped a hand tightly around one of Denny's. "I'm coming too. I should have gone with you sooner, I'm sorry."

Lian's eyes narrowed, shooting between the woman and the devastation of the estate behind them. "Don't you have kids out here somewhere?"

Alexis's pretty red lips twisted up. "Those clingy brats? Who cares? They're Darkfreys. Someone else will look after them."

"She's as awful as he is," Everly mumbled, finally seeing where the chemistry came from.

Alexis leaned into Denny, fawning. "They're not my family anymore. I'm done with it all. Everything is sorted. Screw that arranged marriage and the ugly little spawn it produced. It's just you and me now."

"I don't want to hear *anything else*," Rylan grunted, rubbing between his eyebrows. "Just ... get to the garage."

Everly and Harper silently communicated through woeful expressions of withheld bile, and then they were moving again. Their path passed the ruined cottage and brought them coming around to the garage from the lane leading in.

As they sprinted along the loose gravel, two cars whizzed past them, unfamiliar faces in the drivers' seats. At least some of the Darkfreys had enough sense to get themselves out of there, but so many more were staying, loyal to the end.

Everly wondered how many were dying. Whether the squads of younger, barely trained kids were rushing into battle, and being slaughtered.

Whether Alexis's kids were among them.

Another car raced toward them then peeled to a stop, skidding on the loose surface. The electric window rolled down and an older man with bulging eyes stuck his head out.

"Denny, boy! Whatcha doing here in all this mess?"

Denny reached out a hand, fist-bumping the man. "Uncle Teddy! We're here to save the world, of course. Might have been a little late though."

"Well come on then, jump in! I'm off to the bunker. Got a little bit of room for you if you want in." Teddy's eyes bulged even further, then squinted unevenly. "Only you though."

Oh, that *Uncle Teddy*, Everly remembered. Wait, wasn't that Tammy's Uncle Teddy with the bunker? Were they related?

Everly didn't care at this point. She held her breath, partly hoping Denny would go, partly wishing she had a bunker to hide out the end of the world in too.

"Aw, nah, that's all right, Teddy. I'm not going to go hide. Going to fight this thing out, 'cause I'm a damn good shadyr and I gotta show all these losers up."

Alexis leaned into him. "You are so fucking hot right now, I would do you in a chillifest portapotty."

Teddy's shoulders lifted and dropped, and he accelerated

away.

Rylan muttered a string of unintelligible curses, then took Everly's hand in the last dash to the open garage doors. "Almost there."

They hit the entrance as a large van pulled up from the shadows of the building, Cherry at the wheel. He called back, and Jasper slid the side door open. Inside, Callan and Annabeth squeezed around where Tammy lay on the end bench seat. They'd obtained a first aid kit from somewhere on the way and were focused on stemming blood loss.

About to climb in, Everly checked back for Harper and Lian, and — "Ugh, where's Denny?"

"Are you kidding me?" Rylan's teeth grinding were almost louder than his words.

Down in the middle of the lane where they had just been, Denny and Alexis stood together, making out with all the passion of love-sick teenagers.

And behind them, the void-black silhouette of the biggest weroth Everly had ever seen needled its way toward them. Its mouth opened in a jagged green grin.

CHAPTER SEVENTEEN

"Look out!" Everly screamed.

Denny and Alexis split apart, in time to not have the weroth's mouth close around both of their heads.

Instead, it just closed around Alexis's. The slurping crunch echoed across the air and turned Everly's guts to ice water. A range of curse words flew from the van behind her.

Alexis's body rag-dolled onto the gravel, spurts of blood arcing from her neck like a sick fountain.

Denny loosed a roar, already swinging at the creature with his machete.

Rylan and Lian were a few steps into a run when one of the weroth's pointed feet stabbed right through Denny's stomach from behind, and he froze statue-still with his machete mid-swing.

Everly tensed. If she glowed up now, she could get in and get the monster off him, kill it before the Infuscur noticed, if she was lucky. It was worth the try, even for Denny.

But everything happened so quickly, she didn't have a chance.

Denny surged into motion again, writhing and swearing, as the weroth lifted him like a skewered hors d'oeuvre toward its gaping maw. Lian, Harper, Everly, and Rylan charged forward again.

The pack on Denny's back swung loosely over one arm, and he dug a hand in, pulling out a long, gray brick.

Rylan skidded to a stop. "Is that C-4?"

"I thought I took it all off him!" Lian stared, wide-eyed.

The weroth swallowed Denny whole. There was a faint click.

Rylan screamed, "Get down!"

The four of them dropped onto the rough ground.

The force of the blast rushed through Everly's hair and over her back, and she was hit with a sound like lightning directly striking her eardrum.

Sharp pieces of gravel and chunks of acidic flesh flew over her head.

One hit Everly's bare foot, sizzling and stinging her skin. She gasped and kicked it off. Rylan maneuvered his body over hers as the bloody rain pattered over them.

A short moment that felt like an eternity later, the sound stopped, and Rylan rolled off to her side. "You okay?"

She nodded. Her ears rang and her vision blurred as she got onto all fours, checking the others.

Harper stared up at her, wide-eyed. "I died an hour ago, didn't I? None of this is even real anymore. That absolute, idiotic, jerk! He can't ... can't be *gone*?"

Everly's stomach clenched, and she swallowed back vomit.

He was gone? Of course he was, but her brain didn't want to comprehend the loss.

That anyone she knew could *be dead* was something she didn't want to face. That there was no body to look at and confirm made it harder to grasp the fact. Or maybe there was something left of him. Everly didn't want to examine the pieces of gore that had spattered all around them too closely.

She pulled Harper to her feet and then right into her arms. They broke away a second later, still wide-eyed and pale, but both knew they couldn't linger. The blast would attract attention.

Cherry brought the van to a halt right beside them, side door still open. Jasper grabbed Everly's arm and yanked her in, followed by Harper, Lian, and Rylan.

They burned out of the estate as fast as Cherry dared drive.

Cherry brought the Darkfrey van to a screaming stop at the steps to Howell House. Everly opened the sliding door and moved back so Callan could take Tammy out first.

Their arrival was met with a crowd of concerned faces and shouted questions. What was happening at the estate? Why had the sky gone dark?

"What happened to Lian's car and all my groceries?" Rushelle cried.

Then she took in their blood-stained, torn clothing and the bundle that was Tammy. She puffed up and cleared a path through the crowd of shadyrs awaiting answers.

Everly only knew Tammy was still alive by how fast Callan moved.

Lian climbed onto the porch and yelled to the expectant faces. "Everyone get inside. Get clear of the yard, and shelter in the house, lights off. Danger is coming."

"But what happened?" Lucas pushed to the front, his brace right behind him.

Molly stared at the darkened sky, her face pale and trembling.

"We told you the Mesmans wanted to open a shroudpool. Well, they did." Lian's shoulders slumped, and she pushed her way inside.

The crowd muttered among itself, then split off in a hurry, running to tents and makeshift homes to gather supplies before filing into the homestead.

Everly followed in after Lian, with Harper and Rylan close behind her.

"Neri?" Callan's voice cracked around her name.

She came galloping down the stairs, Birdie cuddled tight in one hand. She pushed straight through to Harper, throwing her free arm around her. Birdie yapped in the small gap between them.

"I was so worried! So worried! You were away so long, and the sky went black and I thought a sea storm was coming and you would be washed away from me!"

Harper's brown eyes filled with tears. Her un-made face was blood-spattered and worn.

She pressed her cheek to Neri's forehead for a moment then whispered, "Tammy needs you."

Neri broke away and looked around for her, finally realizing that she was what Callan carried. "Oh no. Oh no!"

Callan moved through to the living room. He lay Tammy onto a couch, turned a small side lamp on and the ceiling lights off, pulling curtains closed for good measure.

Neri dashed in after him, and a second later, her voice filled the house. The strength of it echoed through Everly's own aching bones. The Coruscare had healed the cuts and bruises she'd sustained already, but it didn't touch the deep, dull pain inside. She wasn't sure it was the sort of injury that Neri could repair, either.

It was loss, despair, hopelessness.

Still, the mermaid girl sang her mixed-up, yearning tune, and the beauty of it reminded Everly that she was still alive. And while ever she was still alive, she'd keep fighting for those she loved.

She could keep trying to fix things.

With a nod to Harper and Callan, who remained with Tammy and Neri, Everly continued to the kitchen, turned the lights off, and took a seat at the dining table. She placed her phone beside her, so that a little light remained for her to see by.

She wasn't sure whether keeping the house blacked out would keep them safe, but it might at least buy them some time before more eidolghasts or the Infuscur came barreling up to their door. Rylan sat close beside her, his shoulder pressed against hers. Cherry, Jasper, and Annabeth took seats across from them and stared down at the worn wood of the table.

Over in the kitchen, Rushelle clicked on the kettle then looked them over. "Where's Denny?"

Lian shook her head. She opened the pantry and rummaged around on a low shelf. Standing back up, she had an armful of beer cans, which she shared out around the table.

"They're warm, sorry, but I can't keep them in the fridge 'cause Denny steals them. Or did. But still. We have to toast the dumbass."

Rushelle took hers while her red lips wobbled and her head shook.

Everly accepted one, cracking the tab with a sigh. Around the table cans popped and hissed.

It was Cherry who stood up, raising his beer. "To Denny. He died the way he lived, doing something stupid."

Everly half-smiled, but her eyes drooped, heavy and sore. They all lifted their drinks in return. "To Denny."

"And to every shadyr who fought and died today, and will fight and die today." Rylan's eyes were hard and sparkled in the low light. "The dark must fall."

The three across the table nodded firmly, and Everly wondered how many of them saw bodies of people they knew back there. Friends they had grown up with, teachers they'd trained with. Family.

The shadyrs around the room murmured together, "So the sun may rise again."

Everly took a token sip of warm beer, the fizz sharp up the back of her nose. She put the can back on the table and tried not to cry.

The front door creaked and closed, creaked and closed, as the house filled up around them. Lucas and his brace joined them at the table, and more shadyrs stood throughout the room until they were shoulder to shoulder.

Hushed murmurs filled the space.

"They really opened a shroudpool? Impossible."

"I got a call from a friend up the hill. Things sound bad out there."

"But one shroudpool couldn't do all of this, could it?"

"My brother is still at the estate. I told him to get out of there, but he wouldn't listen."

Lian moved to the head of the table, taking a big swig of her beer then thumping it down.

"This is how things are," she said, her voice cutting across the whispers. "The Mesmans opened a shroudpool. A bloody massive one. Eidolghasts are coming through at a faster rate than I've ever seen. More than I've ever seen. Bigger than I've ever seen. The estate is a war zone. And to top that off, some other big nasty has come through and possessed Mordan."

"The Infuscur," Everly offered. "The Coruscare knows it."

Rylan's eyebrows furrowed. "Looks like it knew the Coruscare, too. What can you tell us about it?"

Everly nodded and opened her mouth, but Lian cut in. "Someone here at Howell House was passing info to the Darkfreys. That's how the Mesmans grabbed Everly and Tammy, how they knew where they'd be. None of this would be happening otherwise. Maybe we need to keep what we know in a tighter circle."

She glared around the room, catching the eye of every shadyr.

"It wasn't Jasper, if that's what you're thinking." Cherry kept his eyes forward on his beer, missing the split-second puppy dog look Jasper gave him.

"It could be anyone," Rylan said, casting his gaze over the crowd with a look of spite. "How many of you have we brought in, fed, shared this home with? All it took was one of you betraying us for the Darkfreys. For what? Did you think you were going to go back to them? To the ones who killed our families to make us better soldiers? They turned us against each other, when now more than ever it's clear we should all have been on the same side. One where we don't kill or betray our own kind."

Grumbles of agreement spread across the space.

"Whoever it was, what does it matter now?" Everly offered.

She didn't like the idea that someone there was the reason the Mesmans caught her and Tammy, almost killed them both, and started all of this. But there were bigger things to worry about. Neri still sang in the living room, and the tune raised hairs on Everly's neck the longer it went on.

Please pull through, Tammy.

"The Mesmans are gone. Mordan is gone. Half the

estate is gone. Who is anyone going to pass info on to now anyway?"

Lian dropped onto her chair with a huff. "That's a point."

Neri stopped singing, and the room went silent.

No more singing meant one of two outcomes.

Everly held her breath.

Shadyrs shuffled over, bunching up tighter to clear a path. Callan walked in, with Tammy at his side. He had an arm around her waist, and she looked woozy, but alive.

Lian pressed her hands to her chest and sniffed.

"You made it." With no spare seats at the table, Lian shot up fast and offered hers to Tammy.

With a weak smile, Tammy flopped down into it.

She muttered, "Yup, you managed to drag me away from death's sweet embrace yet again. I mean, thanks. I guess."

Everly sniffled out a cross between a giggle and a sob. She reached across to place her hand close to Tammy's, but not quite touching.

"I know you're happier here with us, and we're all happy you're here too."

"Maybe. Whatever. Shut up."

Behind them, Neri beamed. Harper's dusty cheeks had tracks cleared by tears. Callan leaned on the wall behind Tammy, breathing like he'd run a marathon.

Tammy's eyes widened. She sat straighter and leaned toward Everly. "Did you get it? What happened to the orb?"

"We got it," Rylan said, bringing the green crystalline sphere up and placing it on the table in front of him. "What is it?"

Tammy sighed. "It's, ugh, I can't say its proper name, but it translates roughly to Swallower."

Harper rubbed a hand down her face. "Aw man, Denny would have loved that."

Tammy's face fell, but she continued, "The Mesmans had it, and Blaise, he snuck peeks at their work, and he thought ... He thought he could close shroudpools with it. It was supposed to somehow absorb the shroudpool."

Timid before the crowd of shadyrs hanging on her words, she licked her lips. "It didn't work. At least not for us. We mucked around with it for a while out at Dark Corner and got no results. But then, his parents showed up, caught us out. And then, then that thing activated. It pulsed, just a bit—"

Visions from the dream of the Coruscare's past, with the orb pulsing, expanding and contracting and crushing the lives of thousands of eidolghasts into tiny drops of blood, flooded over Everly. The Coruscare stirred within her, riled up. She could hear its thoughts overlaying into hers.

We can beat our dark twin. We need to beat it. We just

need to be stronger. She didn't sip any more beer, but she squeezed the can tight in her hand, dinting the metal.

Everly refocused on Tammy's voice. "The orb ripped through the shroudpool and knocked Blaise down with it. I used to think it was all ... I don't know. Bad timing. My fault. My curse."

Around the table, everyone shook their heads.

Tammy shook hers too. "It wasn't. We saw today how Kole is using old shadyr magic. He's got bones, ancient shadyr bones, embedded all through his skin. It was Blaise and me trying to say the old spell words, but the Swallower reacted to Kole. And despite everything terrible that happened, we did sort of close that shroudpool. It's not gone, but it's dormant. And if we could use this thing again to close the one at the estate, we might have a chance."

Everly could almost feel the threads of hope spreading across the room. Backs straightened. Eyes widened.

She exhaled softly then lifted her voice. "I've seen that before too. In the Coruscare's memories. It was used by the Infuscur to make the Bane, or at least, fill the Bane with energy, the condensed blood of thousands of eidolghasts. It looks ... Dangerous is an understatement. And we don't even know if we can activate it without Kole's magic."

"It's still something." Standing behind Tammy, Lian folded her arms. "A chance to close the portal. Maybe you've got the power to use the orb? If the Coruscare was powerful enough to open a portal, maybe it can close one too?"

We could. We could close it. Everly frowned at the sickening sphere. "Maybe? I could try."

Lian pointed to Everly. "Okay. Everly keeps the orb with her."

Then she jabbed her finger to their close group around the table. "And we get Everly to the shroudpool safely."

"How do we do that, with that Infuscur thing zooming around, turning people into nothing?" Cherry asked.

"And especially hunting the Coruscare," Rylan added.

"Don't suppose you saw a weak spot on it with that fancy sword of yours?" Lian asked Harper with a lift of her chin.

"No, sorry. Same as with Everly. No result on them for an easy kill point."

We can beat it. We can ... if we were whole.

The final word echoed down into Everly's toes, tingling and cold. Whole.

Then we beat the Infuscur. Then we close the shroudpool.

Everly squeezed her temple, trying to block out her dragon's voice. It had never spoken so much while she was awake before, never so clearly. Never so loudly. What it was saying gave her hope, but also terrified her.

Could she really trust the thing inside her? Could she continue keeping it under control if it were stronger? Did she have a choice not to try when this could be the end of Shroudhaven, maybe the end of the world?

"What do you know about this Infuscur being?" Lian asked her.

Everly blinked, trying to gather her thoughts. "It … it's the yin to the Coruscare's yang. It possessed Mordan because it and the Coruscare are more energy-based creatures. They can't exist in this dimension for long without a host. The Coruscare is power and light and essence …"

A few shadyrs around the room, including Annabeth, looked at her with awe-filled eyes.

"*Not* to be confused with goodness though. It exists to consume. The Infuscur exists to destroy. It is null, void, nothingness. The Coruscare can't beat it by taking its soul because it has none. These two beings, they've spent forever fighting each other. But when they're both at full power they are basically equals and cancel each other out. The Infuscur only broke apart the Coruscare last time by using the Bane."

Rylan slammed his hands on the table. "Shit, where is the Bane now?"

A swell of sickness rose in Everly's mouth, and she choked it back. "I don't know, it was on me before the portal opened, but I didn't see it after that."

Or feel it.

Rylan held her gaze with eyes darkened by heavy brows. "We need to make sure the Infuscur doesn't get it and use it against you."

"It doesn't need it, not really." Everly looked away from him. "I'm only holding two-thirds of the Coruscare in me. It's not at full power. The Infuscur thrashed us out there."

She was leading her friends down the line of reasoning to a conclusion she wasn't sure she wanted. As though it would be easier if they made the decision for her.

"So we power you up again!" Harper clapped her hands, hope glittering in her eyes. "And we already know where the third piece is. Then you'll be safe and could even kick the Mordanfuscur's butt."

And there it was. The idea. The hope. Laid out like a noose around her throat.

Yes. We will win.

Everly tried to smile in a reassuring way, but her lips twisted and curled. The Coruscare was being so loud, and she didn't understand why it had such confidence. If both it and the Infuscur were at full power, they would just be back to their endless, futile clash of equal opposites.

Rylan grabbed Everly's hand where it trembled under the table. "That doesn't sound safe. Look what happened to Mordan. The thing in him has total control. It was like it burned Mordan out of his own body."

"It is a lot of power for a human body to contain,"

Lian murmured.

"Ev's got this." Harper put her hands on hips lost under the old shirt of Everly's she still wore. "Mordan had no idea what hit him, but Everly's been keeping a crazy extradimensional deity locked down almost her whole life. She's got the experience and the strength. If anything, she's been more in control since getting the second piece."

Everly turned her face to her friend, drinking in the words. She almost made it sound possible. *Maybe I can do it. We can do it.*

Lian paced, moving closer to Everly. "Do you agree?"

Everly's words scratched out over a dry throat. "Making the Coruscare whole would give us a fighting chance, and I'll do my best to keep it under control."

Lian assessed each of the team for a long moment with narrowed eyes.

She closed them briefly, then let her words out in a long breath. "Okay then. We go for the third piece of the Coruscare, then head to the shroudpool fully powered and try to shut it down."

Bringing her gaze to the other shadyrs who stood around the room, she added, "And you lot, get ready. We'll gather up as many of the scattered Darkfreys as we can, and let you know when it's time to move."

The room started to clear out, hushed murmurs following the crowd. They couldn't go very far with every room and hallway packed, so word of the plan spread like a game of whispers out to those farthest away.

Neri thumped one fist on the table, startling Everly. "I'm coming too this time. I'm not going to sit on my own all scared and waiting. If you're all going out and getting hurt, I want to be there and sing to you then, not when you come back almost dead."

She wrapped a hand tightly around Harper's wrist, in a way that suggested she wasn't going to let go without a fight, and stared at the others with eyes rimmed in red.

"I'm in, too," Rushelle said.

"Neither of you have to. You don't have to be fighters. No one would mind if you stayed here," Lian told them.

"Ma'am, you've let me sit out plenty." Rushelle pressed a blond curl back into her high do. "And I'm more than grateful for that. You've let me be me. But today, I want to do more."

"You do enough. More than enough. You all do." Lian tugged her gray cardigan tight around her beanpole body. "I don't want to lose any of you. Even Denny, that stupid, stupid man ... was a loss I don't want to bear. But right now, I'm not sure we have any other options but to fight."

Callan peeled himself off the wall and stood tall beside his mother. "And we'll all fight together."

Everyone moved then, going to find supplies or to do whatever they felt they needed before what was likely a suicide mission. Only Everly stayed at the table, alone among a crowd of strangers, staring blindly into the space that had so long been her truest home.

Rylan returned to her side. He'd swapped his torn shirt for body armor, and he placed a pair of replacement boots in Everly's size in front of her, then drew his chair so close to hers that she was straddled between his thighs.

He whispered, "You don't have to do this. If you don't want to."

She half-turned her face, and found it nose to nose with his. "It might be our only chance to save the world."

"I'm not sure that's worth losing you. You are my world. I'm done with being the loyal soldier, giving away my life and everything *I* want for the cause. For a war we didn't start. Why does that have to be your responsibility? Why does it have to be your risk, your sacrifice? It's your choice, and you don't have to if you don't want to."

Everly shifted away, catching her breath. She didn't want to risk losing herself. She didn't want this to be the end. And a sharp feeling in her gut still didn't trust the Coruscare, no matter how pliantly it behaved. But what else could they do?

"We'll go and get the third crystal, but we won't use it unless we absolutely have to, okay?"

Rylan bent down and pressed his forehead against hers, exhaling a sigh. "I've been doing my best to be okay with you being in danger, but I can't lose you now. I would fight every beast from the Everdark with my bare human hands if it meant keeping you safe. I would die for you. *YOU.* Not the thing inside you. I'm just scared that what I do isn't going to make a difference."

Everly closed her eyes to the warmth of his touch, bringing a hand to his cheek. He leaned into her palm. Everly wondered whether she was the only one who *could* make a difference, and the thought left her shivering.

The creature inside her had enslaved part of Rylan, had killed her dad, had killed and consumed so many.

Deep in her bones she knew it was a threat to everyone she loved, but now, the only way to save them was to make that creature *stronger*.

Chapter Eighteen

A lone siren wailed in the distance, blending with faraway thundering crashes and the wind that howled down the main street.

At midafternoon, Shroudhaven gave the distinct impression that it was the early hours of the morning. The streets were dark, their emptiness broken by teams of shadyrs rushing by, chasing, or being chased by creatures of the Everdark.

The building beside Everly had a long, jagged gash carved into the side. Granite blocks had crumbled away as though slicing through a sandcastle.

She turned her face up, and found the Infuscur, high in the ashen sky above the town. Its black-hole silhouette hovered and stalked over the streets, long dark ribbons dragging behind it like a jellyfish, tangling and obliterating all in its wake.

At times, it would lash out, attention drawn by movement, and there would be screams that silenced too quickly.

It was looking for her. Hunting the Coruscare.

"Cover," hissed Rylan from the front.

Everly, Harper, Neri, Rushelle, Callan, Tammy, Lucas, Molly, Benson, and Parker pressed themselves into the shadows of the wall at their backs as a herrelspurn swooped through the street.

Everly glanced over those with her, those who volunteered to go with her to get the third Coruscare piece. There had been others, but Lian needed assistance as well, and they figured a smaller group would be more likely to go unnoticed.

Everly was both glad and terrified to have her friends there with her. Harper had a battle-ready gleam in her eyes and moved with almost the same military precision as Rylan and Callan.

Everly didn't know Lucas's brace very well, but having their extra support was appreciated. Even from the youngest of their group, Molly, whose attempt at a brave face was ruined by trembles and twitches.

The poor thing looked terrified. Tammy had pulled up well from her brush with death, now suited in body armor like the rest of the shadyrs. They even found a spare suit for Neri, although it was too large for her boney chest, and hung crookedly.

With her being the least experienced of them all in situations of mortal peril, it was good she had something. She still clung to Harper's wrist, her hand like a shackle, but she kept up and kept quiet. Rushelle held the back of the line, bright-eyed and alert.

Rylan leaned to the side, checking the glass door behind him.

With a quick crack of his elbow, he split the glass, reached in, and flicked the lock. "Let's go through. We can get to the next block under cover, then look for Barry again from there."

Everly pressed her lips together tightly. Finding the third piece wasn't proving as easy as they'd hoped. They knew Cardboard Box Barry had it, but they still had to find him.

They'd circled around five blocks of Shroudhaven main streets already without any sign of him or his underground cardboard world.

With Rylan at the lead, they shuffled through the lawyer's office, heads down and silent. Inside, the sounds of wind and wailing beasts dulled, and a different sound drifted through the space. A lilting tune came from an old-fashioned radio on the reception desk.

There's a mermaid in my lighthouse, and her heart

belongs to me.

There's a mermaid in my lighthouse, to her I own—

A crash of shattered plastic and static fizzle burst from the radio, which now had the pointy end of Harper's whip sword lodged into it. The length of it hung between the radio and her hand, then with a tug and a click, she reeled it back into a rigid blade.

Rylan put his finger to his lips and glared, but no one said anything. They crept through to the back corridor past private offices. Within one, a couple of people huddled together, tucked under a desk.

Lucas patted the doorframe and flashed them a smile. "We're with emergency services. Nothing to worry about. Just having some issues with, a, um—"

"Town-wide gas leak," Callan offered.

"Escaped dangerous animals," Rylan said at the same time.

"Both?" Lucas shrugged. It was pretty clear their excuses were only going to cover so much this time. "Please stay inside and keep quiet as best you can."

The older woman and man nodded and ducked down farther. Everly wondered how much they knew of what really went on in this town.

In Shroudhaven, everyone had at least one strange story that others pretended not to believe. Everyone had someone they'd lost to unexplained circumstances. Gone missing in the woods. Drowned in the lake. Mauled by wild animals.

Everyone knew that when the sun went down, when the lights were out, you stayed inside, or you might never make it home. People joked that the estate on the hill was run by vampires.

Maybe nobody said the word 'monster.' Maybe they didn't know about shadyrs, or understand that despite their vampire, werewolf, or ghost forms, they were the ones fighting to protect the world. But Everly was sure that people knew.

Deep in their gut, they knew. Shroudhaven wasn't a normal town.

They reached the end of the building, and Rylan pulled the floor bolt and flicked the lock of the back door. It opened to a narrow alleyway around the corner from where they'd started.

At the mouth of the lane, a group in Darkfrey uniforms had the remains of a vasmire under their boots, wrenching the last of its life from its tentacles. It flopped wetly to the ground, and they dashed off toward another target.

All except for one, who glared down the alley.

Everly knew that square-edged, action-figure silhouette. His blond crew cut was gray and gritty in the low light.

"You runts. This is all your fault!" Nilson Darkfrey bellowed at them, approaching in heavy strides.

"How is this our fault? You think we asked to be kidnapped and tortured by the Mesmans?" Tammy stepped to the front.

The top of her head barely reached the man's shoulders, and she was a third his weight, but she held her ground as he approached. "And it was your dumbass daddy who gave them the go-ahead! He could have stopped this!"

Rylan spoke softly. "Come on, Nils. We've all lost a lot already. We don't need to be against each other. Come with us, help us, we might be able to stop things getting worse."

Nilson spat on the filthy pavement in front of them. "I'd never fight beside traitors. Only one of you remained loyal."

He lifted his chin, offering Molly a nod.

Her face froze in a look of horror.

"What does he mean, Molly?" Lucas asked in a deep, low tone.

Her head snapped toward him, and she gaped, her young eyes round as a full moon. Her feet worked their way slowly backward. Then she ran, bolting off around the corner.

"Ghast dammit," Lucas hissed, slamming a fist against the wall.

He took a step as though about to make chase but swung his attention back to the Darkfrey looming over them.

Nilson's meaty face split in a humorless grin, glaring between Tammy and Everly. "You, and her, that bliv, running around full of cursed magic like it's not a problem, not a threat to all of us. I should have put you down out in the woods with the other animals when I had the chance."

His hand shot out, wrapping around Everly's neck and crushing hard.

Everly's eyes bulged, and she swatted at his tree trunk arm. She could free herself with the dragon's light, but it would call the Infuscur that stalked the skies above right to them.

Shouts went up around her as Rylan and Harper lunged onto Nilson, dragging at his arms. He stumbled sideways with their weight but didn't loosen his grip around Everly's throat.

Panic swelled in her as her lungs screamed, and with it, the dragon rose too. If she lost enough control of her own body, it would take over for self-preservation and the Infuscur would come for her and her friends.

Through the pounding in her eardrums, Everly heard a spitting growl from above. She turned her gaze to the roof's edge, and saw two gleaming blue eyes staring back.

Rylan jabbed punches into Nilson's ribcage. Harper pressed the edge of her sword to Nilson's throat. They were both thrown back by the sleek, furred body that smashed down onto Nilson's face.

Nilson screamed, letting go of Everly. She reeled back, gasping for air through her crushed windpipe. Her vision wavered over Nilson, who stumbled backward, swatting at the creature that clung to him with deeply buried claws, hissing and yowling.

"Zozo?" Everly croaked.

The cougar's paw slid from where it had dug in to Nilson's scalp, down the full length of his face, carving four lines of ruby gore in their wake.

Nilson swore and thrashed, but Zozo readjusted around his swinging body, climbing him like a tree, puncturing his flesh with every step. The undead cat snapped its wide muzzle around Nilson's throat, sharp teeth glinting in the low light as they sunk into his flesh.

Nilson's screams turned to gurgles.

He stared at the sky, arms hanging limp and feet marching on the spot as though of their own accord. Then he toppled flat onto his back.

Zozo went down with him, never loosening the vise grip of his jaws.

Everly and the others remained still as Zozo kept his teeth in Nilson's neck for a long moment after the man had stopped twitching. When he finally detached, the white fur around his muzzle dripped red, and the low growl rumbling from his throat sounded satisfied.

This was the man who had killed the old lady that

tended Zozo back to life. The one who slaughtered so many other animals that Nell had rescued. Zozo had taken his revenge.

Everly expected the big cat to turn tail and run, but instead, he padded silently up the alleyway toward her.

Harper and Rylan shot her concerned glances as she took a step forward herself, then crouched down to Zozo's level.

The tan fur across his forehead sat unevenly between thick scarring, and his eyes glowed an eerie, milky blue. When Everly reached out a hand, Zozo bumped his forehead into her palm. She brushed over his fur and rubbed behind one ear.

"What are you doing here? You're not tied to me anymore."

Zozo snuffled, then vaulted himself up the wall and onto the roof, taking a guarding position like a gargoyle on the edge.

"Was that ... *a cat*?" Neri gasped out the words, her eyes locked onto Zozo.

Everly figured it must have been her first time seeing a cat of any kind, and she looked *very* impressed.

"That was Zozo. I ... don't know why he came back."

"Of course he came to help you." Harper stepped forward, lifting Everly's chin so she could inspect the rapidly fading bruises around her neck. "It's because of who *you* are, how *you* were kind to him. Not because of the Coruscare's soul bond. I mean, how many people would see a zombie cougar stalking around their home and think, 'I'd better put some food out for it'?"

"You've been *feeding a zombie cougar*?" Rushelle scolded.

Tammy shook her head, pinching the bridge of her nose. "How you've stayed alive this long, I have no idea."

Everly's cheeks burned hot.

Callan tilted his head, grinning. "Maybe we should all be following her lead. I mean, zombie cougar feeding paid off."

Lucas and his remaining brace shuffled at the edges of their group, muttering between each other, then Lucas spoke up. "We're going after Molly. I'm sorry to be cutting out on you guys, but ..."

"Molly's one of your brace," Callan said softly.

Lucas winced and nodded. "I'm sorry she screwed up, hurt you guys. But she's just a kid. We all know how Darkfrey indoctrination messes with your priorities."

Rylan grunted.

Rushelle patted Lucas on the back. "Go get the little duck. No one should be out there alone. We'll be just fine."

With one last look back at them, Lucas, Benson, and Parker split off, running the way Molly had gone.

"Come on," Rushelle said. "In amongst all the animal

attack excitement, I think I saw something box-shaped down thataway."

She took off, and the others followed. Everly avoided Nilson's body as they jogged by.

Rylan moved up beside her. "Harper's right. It's who you are that drew me to you. It's always been that. Your kindness, your caring. Even after everything you've been through, you still reach out to comfort others. You make the world brighter than all the Coruscare's light."

Breath caught in Everly's hard-working lungs. She found hard to keep her eyes on where her feet fell rather than only on him. She wanted to be everything that he seemed to see in her. To be her best and do everything she could for those she loved. They deserved that and more.

Her backpack, which held the Swallower orb, thumped as she ran, and soon that bag would also hold the third piece of the Coruscare, waiting on the moment they needed to fight back and end this. "I wouldn't be who I am without you, Lian, your family. Your love. I wouldn't have even known love without you."

"I'm sorry I took that away from you for so long." Rylan's eyes narrowed as he looked ahead. "It's him, Barry. Up on the corner!"

The older couple from the law office hadn't taken their advice. Barry had them in tow, ushering them toward his blanket-draped cardboard box as a herrelspurn circled above.

They nodded to him with familiarity then crawled in and didn't reemerge.

"Barry," Callan called out as the old man moved to follow them in.

Barry straightened, arching his back in a way that exaggerated his pot belly, and he tugged on his braided beard. "Ah, it's you lot. You need somewhere to lay low?"

"We actually need something more," Harper said. "We need the crystal heart of your maze."

Barry grinned crookedly, guffawing at the joke. But as nobody else joined in the laughter, his face fell.

He gave a swift shake of his head. "Oh no. No, you can't have that. I mean, my house is yours, but without the heart, there is no house. I got people in there I'm keeping safe from all this."

He waved his hands, pointing in every direction.

"All of this isn't going to end any time soon unless we have the crystal," Everly said, her voice lacking confidence even to her own ears.

Barry was out here saving people. Maybe that was what they should be doing. Helping him get everyone into shelter to wait it out. Come up with some other solution. There were too many 'what ifs' circling in Everly's head and getting tangled on each other.

No. We have a plan, and we should stick to it.

Barry's head swung side to side, his beard following it like a pendulum. "What do you think you're going to do with it, anyway?"

Harper said, "We need to break it to release the thir—"

"BREAK IT?" Barry howled into the empty street.

Less human howls echoed back.

Everly held up her hands in a gesture of peace. "We won't break it yet. Only if we need to. We've got a plan to make everybody safe again, to close the portal that's flooding the town with monsters. I can stop all of this chaos. But I need to get that piece of crystal."

"She's right." Rushelle quirked her red lips, out of place on the dim street in her sunny yellow halter top. "None of us have more of a chance than Everly here to bring an end to this destruction. I know we're asking a real big sacrifice from you, but we're all going to lose everything anyway if we don't do something. She can do it. The kid seems about able to do anything."

Barry pressed a hand to his chest as though he was having a heart attack. "Oh child. I hope you're right. I hope you are. If you think you can stop all of this, I'll give you the heart of my world. 'Cause someone has to stop this."

He didn't say the other part, but Everly felt it. That if she destroyed his sanctuary and couldn't stop the Infuscur or close the shroudpool, there'd be nowhere left to hide.

"Come on then, let's get to it," Barry said, his voice

clogged with grief.

Harper, Neri, Tammy, and Callan followed him into the box maze. The hairs on Everly's neck rose, as she bent down to crawl in after Rylan.

Rushelle held back the blanket doorway for them, waving them along like herding sheep.

"Thanks," Everly smiled at her.

"No problem, duck." Rushelle's last word caught, and she stilled.

Pieces of skin peeled and floated from her pretty pinup face. A black ribbon whipped away as her body crumbled into nothing before Everly's eyes.

Chapter Nineteen

Rushelle's typewriter-shaped necklace hung in midair for a moment, miraculously untouched as the rest of her faded away. It jangled to the ground. Then all Everly could hear were her own screams.

Hands grabbed at her, dragging her along the smooth cardboard tunnel. Everly stared at where Rushelle had been. Where she had smiled back with friendly eyes an instant before she was erased from existence.

Blackness rushed at her, diving from the sky and swooping like a wave of shadows toward the cardboard box entrance. As the Infuscur shot more dark strands out from Mordan's body, the corrugated boards folded closed by themselves, shutting the flaps like a barricade.

Everly's screams cut out, and she held her breath, waiting for the box to crumble and fade away like Rushelle had. Nothing happened.

The magic that ran the strange cardboard maze had closed them off and removed them entirely from the outside world.

The hands around her waist and shoulders pulled her through to where the tunnel was tall enough to stand. She met Rylan's eyes as he pulled her to her feet.

A hot sting punched her nose and her tears spilled freely.

He pulled her in close, pressing her face to his chest. "I know. I'm sorry."

Neri let out a harsh wail, muffled quickly to a stark silence by the cardboard walls. There were no echoes, except for Rushelle's last words, looping nonstop in Everly's head.

No problem, duck.

She couldn't be gone. It didn't make any sense that someone so full of life and love could be there one moment then wiped clean from the world the next.

Tammy muttered strings of denial and sobbed out curses against Callan's shoulder. Harper pulled Neri close and whispered comforts into her tangle of curls. Barry stared at the ground, whispering something that sounded like his own version of last rites.

Everly watched them all as Rylan stroked her hair, and her insides seemed to fill with cement. Which of them would be next? Which loss would crush her world to pieces next? Would she be able to endure it?

Make me whole. Then we can save them all.

Everly nodded to the voice in her head, her cheek moving against the firm material of Rylan's chest armor. *I have to be strong enough to save them. And I'll do whatever I have to do to make that happen.*

"We need to get to the final piece of the Coruscare." Everly's words feeling sticky and heavy.

We need to make it all worth it.

Barry shuffled to the lead. His hand gestures suggested he was following some strange process of navigation along the straight tunnel. Everly took in the bizarre space. She'd never seen inside Barry's kraft-colored world herself, but Harper had described it to her.

Being inside it was different though. She felt like a child, playing in a massive box fort, like the time Lian had bought a new fridge and she and Rylan made a cubby of the leftover packaging, staying in it all day.

Rushelle would have loved this. Everly imagined her buddying up to Barry, telling him about her books.

How many of her stories will now remain unwritten? Everly's eyes felt flayed raw, and she struggled to keep them open. They followed along without speaking, footsteps scuffing against the soft cardboard. Shoulders slumped, but they all kept a fast pace toward their last hope for salvation against further loss.

When Barry pushed through into the central hub space, he called out, "Okay folks, plans have changed and you can't stay here."

At least a dozen heads popped up from around the room where they had clustered together in small groups beside the makeshift beds and mismatched lampshades, gossiping and sharing stories of what they couldn't possibly have seen outside.

"I don't want to go back out there!" one man cried.

"S'all right, I'm going to send you out a special way." Barry strode over to a sidewall, gave it a bump with his hip, and then dug his fingernails into the cardboard. With a tug, he peeled open a door-sized flap.

"Head straight through, don't take any turns, and you'll end up down by the river at the far end of town. Should keep you out of reach of the danger, at least for a little while. And here's hoping this lot will have everything fixed up before then."

There were grumbles and whimpers of shock, but the civilians gathered their bags and coats and shuffled their way over to him. As they did, the view through to the middle of the room cleared, and Everly caught her first sight of the Coruscare crystal hanging there like a twisted modern art chandelier.

It glowed, calling to her.

And she glowed in return.

Her heart was wrapped in chains, dragging her forward.

"Evie, what are you doing?" Rylan growled.

Everly stared at her shining hands, then cried out as her feet lifted from the ground. "I'm not! I'm not doing this."

Stop it. STOP IT. I'm in control! she roared into her own mind.

The Coruscare remained silent, apart from a rising sense of victory.

Glittery tendrils appeared and stepped her across the large space, floating her over stacks of canned food, furniture pulled from trash collections, and crates of water bottles, then over cardboard dividers that screened the wide hall into smaller rooms.

Everly turned back to the others, gaping.

The civilians had paused in their exit to see why the lighting had just brightened, and stared at her in wonder.

"Get them out of here!" she screamed, and Barry pushed them out through the doorway.

"What's happening? Ev?" Harper yelled.

She chased after her, running zigzag through the maze of cardboard screens and supplies. The others were right behind her, trying to keep up.

"I'm not in control. The Coruscare is doing this."

Her body turned icy, as though she'd had her major arteries cut and the blood drained from her.

She had never been in control.

The Coruscare seemed to chuckle from within her, rattling her chest.

What were you doing? Playing dead? Telling me what I wanted to hear? Pretending I had you leashed?

Everly clenched her teeth and tensed her whole body with effort. She must have *some* power over the dragon still, or it wouldn't have bothered with games.

She focused all her being onto taking the reins. Her eyes ached and her fingers tingled. The movements of the scintillating tendrils slowed, becoming a grating mechanical motion. But she continued moving forward.

Everly cried out. It was strong, so much stronger than she'd ever realized.

I've been feeding. Sneaking. Building energy to defy you.

What? When? She had noticed it take in souls during the chaos of fleeing the Everdark, but also ... also bodies kept being found in the morning.

Shadyr, human, and eidolghast bodies, all around Shroudhaven. Lian's old friend, Candace. So many others. Dead in their sleep. No wounds. No explanations ... No soul left after it had been consumed.

Her dreams had been so strange, with a sensation of movement she'd never experienced before, because she *had* been moving.

The Coruscare had been hijacking her body and taking it out to feed every night. That's why she was never overcome by its hunger. It had taken over when she was weakest against it, when she hadn't known what it was doing, until it could take over entirely.

"Fight back!" Rylan broke free of the others and plowed straight as an arrow toward her, crashing through low cardboard walls and vaulting over beds.

"I'm trying!" With a roar of strength, she pulled back on the Coruscare again, dragging it to a complete stop.

But it already had one tendril around the hanging piece of crystal.

Glittering light around shining glass, the Coruscare squeezed. The crystal cracked.

"Run! Get out of here! All of you, now!" Everly screamed.

The room filled with light. It swirled across Everly's flesh, rushing like a blast of molten metal up her nose and down her throat.

We.

Are.

Whole.

The words thrummed through her.

We will take back our realm. Take this realm too, maybe. But first, first we take revenge.

Everly wanted to whimper like an infant, to thrash and whine. It said it would help them, that it would close the shroudpool, but it was clear that the Coruscare didn't intend in any way to do so.

It used her, and now she could feel it using her up.

She couldn't see where anyone else was in the blinding glow, but she worked her jaw, trying to push out words through an uncooperative mouth. She could feel herself fading and needed the others to know the creature's plans.

"It's going ... revenge on Infuscur ... but doesn't ... won't close shroudpool. Wants ... Everdark back."

Did she even speak? Existence felt like a dream that slipped away so fast she couldn't be sure she'd ever held it.

She was light. She was power. *We are whole.*

Creatures moved around beneath them.

Nothing but motes of dust, specks of life beneath her attention.

Everly grunted at the thought, trying to steal back focus to her own eyes.

Not specks. Friends. Family. Love.

So much she hadn't said. So much she hadn't done. So much she wanted to do to save them. She wanted to reach for them, but her body was so numb she might as well not have had a body at all. Her head felt like it filled with tepid water, drowning her from within.

She tried to hold onto her vision, her consciousness, but it washed away like a sandcastle in a storm.

With her final scrap of self, she cried, "Rylan! Rylan, I love—"

Chapter Twenty

Light streamed from Everly's mouth and eyes like a beam from a lighthouse, cutting off her words. Rylan smashed right through a low wall of cardboard, fingertips reaching for her as though his touch could pull her back, could wrench that creature of light right out of her body. But as his hand grasped out, there was nothing left in the space where Everly had been.

Rylan blinked, the brightness burning globs of color into his vision. He whirled around to track her.

Pieces of broken crystal crunched under his feet, and through partial blindness he glimpsed Everly, disappearing through an exit like a shooting star.

If it was still Everly at all.

If she hadn't been forced out of herself entirely by the Coruscare's full might.

No. I can't think like that. She's strong. She's still in there, fighting.

"Ev! Everly!" Harper screamed.

A piece of cardboard the size of a flap from a box floated from the ceiling. Rylan swatted it away, heaved in a deep breath, and ran. He had to catch up, if he could just *reach* her, maybe he could get her back.

"Oh no, oh no, oh no. It's all falling apart!" Barry cried from behind him.

Rylan glanced back for a fraction of a second but didn't slow his pace. Barry had moved over with the others, running with Harper and Neri.

Callan and Tammy were ahead of them, trying to catch up with Rylan. All of them were yelling. Rylan's name, Everly's name, other things—Rylan couldn't hear exactly what over the roar in his ears, and the smashing, scrunching sounds around them, and his desperate mind screaming *get her back.*

A sheet of ragged cardboard as big as Rylan flopped down in his path. He dodged to the side and leaped over a stack of water bottles. Unable to control his frantic momentum, he collided with the corner of the exit passage. The cardboard tore like wet tissue against his shoulder. A howling sound pushed through the hole left behind, echoing from a vortex of darkness.

"This place is coming down around us!" Harper yelled.

A high-pitched scream that was probably Neri followed.

"Rylan!" Callan called. "We have to stick together!"

Rylan kept going, pounding his feet against the tunnel floor that grew uneven and soft beneath his boots. He just had to reach her. She was already out of sight.

The exit came up quickly. The passageway lurched, shifting sideways. The walls crumpled and compressed, crushing in on him. Dark gaps split between the cardboard and a nightmarish cacophony of yowling wind sounded through them, though the air remained still, stifling.

The scratchy cry of an old man's voice came from behind him. The strained voices of Harper and Neri followed. Rylan burst out through the ratty floral sheets into fresh air, his gaze shooting left and right.

Where is she?

Callan and Tammy appeared at his shoulders, bumping into him in their haste. They breathed hard, gasping breaths.

"No, no!" Callan bellowed, dropping down out of Rylan's field of view.

There was no sign of Everly, no glow or flash of light in the streets around them. Every nerve in his body itched to keep running, keep chasing after Everly, but he didn't know which way to go.

Rylan tore himself away from his search to check on his brother.

Tammy joined Callan with a cry, landing on her knees. The box they had just emerged from lay flat on the ground. "Harper, Neri?"

Callan dragged back the crumpled tarp, flinging it away.

Rylan crouched beside him, grabbing at the loose sheets of cardboard. They came away freely, revealing nothing but dirty pavement beneath.

A muffled squeal came from Tammy as she scraped at the concrete with her black fingertips, as though she could dig through. "Where are they? *Where are they?*"

"They were right behind us, but they stopped to help Barry ..." Callan reached over and put a hand onto Tammy's, stilling her as she fingerpainted the ground red.

She gulped, then flung herself into his arms, pressing her face into his shoulder to muffle her sobs.

Rylan stared at the concrete, disbelief clouding his eyes. He squeezed the cardboard in his grip, flipping it over, checking both sides as though there could be a magic portal hidden under one of the moldering scraps.

They had been right behind him. And he'd lost them. He lost Everly's best friend.

"What do we do now?" Tammy's words wheezed out through harsh breaths.

Callan caught Rylan's gaze and his usually bright, smiling eyes were so dull that it made Rylan's chest convulse.

Brightness flashed in the distance. Rylan turned his face upward, seeking Everly. High in the sky, above the estate, light and darkness clashed. Living lightning and sentient shadow tangled together and blasted apart, as dueling gods waged war.

"No, keep going!" Barry grumbled and reeled back from Harper's outstretched hand. One of his feet had plunged straight through the decaying cardboard, suctioned into the void beyond.

Harper shook her head and reached for him again. Neri whimpered at her side, wide-eyed, and reached out as well. They both clasped their hands around one of Barry's arms. His wrist felt like soft crepe paper wrapped around bone.

"Don't worry about me, there's no time," he pleaded with round eyes under bushy brows.

"No way. You're coming with us." Harper tightened her grip and pulled.

There wasn't a chance she was leaving him behind. Not this kind man who had come to see if she needed help when she was having an argument with Everly on the street. Who had helped them run from the police. Who had saved potentially countless citizens of Shroudhaven

from the things that prowled in the dark.

With the sound of a vacuum coming unclogged, Barry's foot slid free, and the three of them tumbled onto the worryingly soft floor.

When Harper turned around, the exit closed over with a patchwork of card and brown paper. Everly had sped out through there before them.

Not Everly, the Coruscare. It seemed to have taken control entirely. At least for now. Harper still hoped Everly could regain control. She'd pushed her friend to this, and if she'd pressed Everly into something that destroyed her, how could she ever forgive herself?

She may not have to feel the heavy lump of guilt in her throat for long though. Harper swung around and she scrunched her face when she saw the other end of the tunnel collapsing in toward them.

"No, there has to be another way out." Hers and Neri's hands were still grasped tight around Barry's.

He shook his head and pulled away, groaning as he brought up his foot. His shoe was gone, and the top layer of skin had been scraped clean, as though someone had hit him with a sandblaster.

Barry's wide eyes watered. "I'm sorry. You shouldn't have stopped for me."

"It's okay, I can heal you so you can run again, then you can tell us which way to go." Neri raised her voice in song, and it sounded strangely muffled, interrupted by the howling and crumpling board sounds.

Barry's skin smoothed over, and he stared open-mouthed at Neri. "Just when I thought I'd seen everything in this wild town."

Harper had her eyes on the tunnel they'd run through, where the cardboard warped and folded like twisted origami toward them. Harsh, ripping sounds followed. She stood and pressed her hands against the closed exit.

"Barry, how can we get out?"

"I can't see any other exits, no other routes. Normally the direction is clear to me but it's like it's all gone, the whole cardboard system just isn't there. This is all that's left." Barry shook his head and brushed his fingers over the healed skin of his foot, as though only touch could make him believe his eyes.

Harper put a long, shining fingernail between her teeth, chewing it roughly in a sudden return of a habit she'd kicked before she'd hit puberty.

"Neri, she got her powers from being close to a piece of that crystal for so long. You've been near your crystal heart of the maze for ages, right? Maybe you have something too, some special power of your own, even without the crystal."

Barry's wrinkled face creased into heavier lines across his forehead. "Like healing?"

"I don't know, hopefully something that gets us out of

here. Like finding the right way ... like you normally do." Harper's voice grew quiet as she went on.

She was clutching onto a hope that didn't make sense. That probably *was* Barry's power. His ability of navigating the strange cardboard tunnel system. But the tunnels were gone, and he'd already said he couldn't sense any other directions to go.

That was it. There were no other options, and their single remaining passageway was contracting upon them fast. The cardboard pressed against the top of Harper's head, and she ducked.

Barry's eyes tilted downward, heartbreakingly. "I'm sorry. I'll try ... if there's anything I can do, but ..."

But they were trapped. They'd run out of time. The world was closing in on them, becoming nothing, and they were about to be crushed or shredded or lost into that howling void.

Not Neri. Harper couldn't bear to imagine Neri's life ending there. Not Neri, so full of wonder and enthusiasm for a world she'd been locked away from. So kind, despite all she'd suffered. Not Neri, who filled Harper's heart with warmth and longing in a way she'd never felt.

Why did she have to come along? And why did I have to be so arrogant, thinking I could keep her safe?

Harper threw her arms around Neri. "I didn't want this for you. I wanted you to have a good, long life to make up for everything you missed out on so far. I don't want this to be the end for you."

The scrunching, tearing, yowling sounds grew louder, and the ceiling bowed in above them. They dropped onto their knees, still holding each other.

"I'm okay," Neri replied, her voice trembling. "I'm okay because I'm with you."

"But I don't know how to save you from this!" Harper's whip sword hung heavy from her belt, but not it, nor any skill she'd pushed herself to be the best at during her life, could stop a magical dimension from crushing them within its implosion.

"You don't have to save me from everything. I just wanted to be with you."

Harper tangled her fingers into Neri's thick, curled hair and pressed it to her face as though it could stem her tears. "I didn't want to say anything, because I didn't want you to feel any sort of pressure ... but if this is the end, I want you to know that I like you, more than as friends. I like you in a romantic way, in the way that I want to be beside you every moment."

Neri pulled away enough to look into Harper's eyes. "I feel like that about you too. Like, you're my Prince Charming."

Harper scoffed gently. She had introduced Neri to fairy tales in a subtle attempt to explain some of the hazards of the world, including the risks of 'love at first sight,' or anyone who would lock a princess away in a tower.

Neri shook her head fiercely. "But in a good way! You saved me, and looked after me, but never asked or expected anything from me. You've let me have time to learn who *I* am. And *I* like you."

A hysterical laugh shuddered from Harper.

There she was, in one of Everly's old T-shirts, makeup undone, hair untamed, eyes untinted, and Neri looked at her as though she was *everything*.

In careful, tentative, questioning motions, Harper moved her mouth closer to Neri's. Neri met her in the middle, her lips plump and soft and tasting of the sea.

The cardboard moved beneath them like they were on a waterbed. They clung to each other for stability as pieces of shredded board rained around them. The roof caved in lower, and they had to lie down, curled on their sides to stay face-to-face.

Neri stared wide-eyed at a hole above them, then turned back to Harper, offering a wobbly smile. "Having the time I've had with you, it almost makes me forget everything else before. I wish we could have had more, but it's been enough."

Of all the ways Harper thought she might go out—even with adding a slew of new and terrifying options since coming to Shroudhaven—she never thought it would be in a collapsing dimension made from cardboard, clinging to a mermaid she loved.

She wouldn't be able to help her best friend, if there was any chance of still saving Everly. She hoped Rylan would do that for her. The guy was okay. She could almost see what Everly saw in him these days, and she was certain he would do anything to save her.

She had to hold onto that thought, hoping for everyone else out in the world to go on without her, Neri, and Barry.

Harper looked at him through the small gap between sheets of pressed cardboard, tearing apart before her eyes. He had tears filling his smile lines, and he rubbed his forehead, muttering to himself as though still trying to muster up some magical way to save them all. She released one hand from Neri and reached to hold onto Barry's.

His fingers felt leathery in hers, and he gave her a tight-lipped smile. "I'm sorry you got stuck here for me. You two, you're some of the good ones. You thought about me before yourselves. You know love in the most selfless way. It's always been how I've tried to be. I always tried to act out of love, trying to save people. I think that's why I always thought of the crystal as a heart, too."

Harper's body was pressed and pulled between strange, opposing forces, crushed and suctioned as their tiny pocket of space closed even farther and tore apart at the same time.

She squeezed Barry's hand. "I think it was you who

was the true heart of this place all along."

One of her legs slipped through a hole, and she cried out as her skin peeled and flayed. Barry lurched sideways, falling into the same hole.

Neri sung to them, as the last scrap of cardboard life raft fell away.

Chapter Twenty-One

Rylan's entire body was a raging tornado of sensations as he ran with Callan and Tammy to the arranged meeting point.

His eyes burned from unshed tears. The icy chill of beshadowed mist stung as it swirled around his feet. The screams of dying humans and unearthly shrieks of hunting monsters echoing through the unnaturally dark streets would haunt him for the rest of his life, no matter how short that might be.

But all he could think about was Everly. Everly, gone, taken over by the being inside her. Rushelle, Harper, Neri, Barry, all lost. *Everly ...*

The Boutique All came into view as they rounded a corner. It had seemed like a good place to regroup, back when they'd had the audacity to make plans, the naivety to think they could take some action against the overwhelming hellscape that was engulfing the town.

Seeing the ridiculous name and aging facade of the budget store now, Rylan swallowed back sickness in his throat.

We should have been here, regrouping before making our move to win this. But now ... Now what can we do?

The front windows had blown out at some point and glass glittered across the ground like scattered diamonds, reflecting the blasts of light that flashed from above. The three of them checked the street was clear, then dashed across and vaulted in through the open frontage.

In the darkness of the store, scores of shadyr eyes stared back at them.

When he saw Lian's face, Rylan thought his heart might stop completely, that his body would simply give up and shut down. She stared at the three of them, open mouth shaking as her eyes counted over them, again and again, as though their missing numbers would magically reappear.

"What happened?" Her normally stoic tone was absent, her words strained and cracking. "Where are the others?"

It was Tammy who answered, but not in words. A sob escaped from her, and she ran into Lian's arms, clinging tight as her body heaved with sorrow.

Tears filled Rylan's eyes with a suddenness that made

him inhale sharply. He clenched his jaw and wiped quickly with the heel of his hand.

There was a not-small part of him that wanted to run into his mother's arms and weep, too. He wanted to hold her for all of the years he grew up without being able to, for all the pains and the lies and the times he'd tried to be so strong, all for nothing.

He was lost, untethered, his whole world flipped upside down then dropped from an immense height so that it shattered on a hard, unyielding ground.

And he didn't know how to put himself back together. Not without Everly. Not if she was gone.

The hope that she still existed was the only thing that kept Rylan on his feet.

Lian's eyes were wide and panicked as she looked over Tammy's shoulder to Rylan.

She repeated in a whisper, "What happened?"

"The Coruscare took over." Rylan's husky voice scraped to a rattly whisper. "As soon as it got near its final piece, it ... took over. It's gone to fight the Infuscur, but from what Everly said, it's not going to close the shroudpool."

She'd said more, with her last words before the light overwhelmed her.

Rylan, I love—

Her voice still echoed inside him to the beat of his heart. "Everly tried to fight it ..."

"I'm sure she's still trying," Lian said vehemently.

"Rush? Harper? Neri?" Cherry stepped forward, and Rylan blinked at him as though he'd appeared in a puff of smoke.

Cherry, Annabeth, and Jasper stood beside Lian in front of the crowd of other shadyrs they'd gathered from Howell House and anywhere else they could find them. They all listened in, soft mutters of conversation passing between them as they made sense of news that to them wasn't personal. To them, wasn't a hole in the chest the size of a cannon ball.

"The Infuscur got Rushelle," Callan said softly. "She's gone."

Lian put a hand over her mouth as though stifling a scream.

Rylan swiped the wet from his eyes again. He had to hold it together. "Harper and Neri—and Barry—they didn't make it out of the cardboard tunnels. I ... don't know what that means for them."

"FUCK!" Cherry hollered.

A chorus of shushes replied.

He repeated himself in a softer whisper. Running his hands into his red hair, he leaned face-first against a nearby shelf of greeting cards. Jasper moved closer to him, putting a hand on his back and murmuring in his ear.

"Lucas's brace?" Lian asked with a small shake of her

head, as though she couldn't bear another answer.

Rylan shared a knowing glance with Callan then said, "Got separated out on the streets. They might be okay."

Lian's shoulders slumped, and she kept turning her face left and right in small, repetitive denials.

Annabeth rolled her head around and stared at the ceiling, fidgeting with the piece of bone on her necklace. "So, what now? We've lost the Coruscare. Did Everly still have the Swallower, too?"

Rylan had forgotten about it, but for all he knew it was still with Everly. He nodded.

Annabeth grunted in frustration. "With what we learned about how Kole was using magic, I thought maybe I had an idea for closing the shroudpool at the estate. But I need the Swallower."

Rylan stared blindly for a moment at Annabeth, and out over the crowd of shadyrs behind her who waited to be told the plan, now that Plan A had crumbled out from under them.

The shroudpool still needed to be closed. The shadyrs trapped by eidolghasts and dueling gods at the estate needed to be rescued. That was what everyone else was there for, what they were all prepared to risk their lives for.

But Rylan could only think of Everly, and her last words, and whether she would ever forgive him for losing Harper and Neri if he could even get her back. He'd gone colder inside than when he held Everly's body in icy seawater as she cracked apart from the Bane.

Rylan clenched his fists. *The Bane.*

He locked his gaze with Annabeth. "If you think we can close the shroudpool, we will get the Swallower back. The Bane is still out there, somewhere. If I can find it, maybe it can subdue the Coruscare enough to help Everly take over again. We get her back, and get the Coruscare under control, and finish this."

And if finishing this means using the Bane to break the Coruscare apart again, break Everly apart, could I do that?

Rylan didn't want to consider that outcome.

Tammy turned within Lian's embrace, her face red and splotchy. "The Bane was on Everly right up until the shroudpool opened. But I didn't see it in the Everdark. It must still be somewhere near the shroudpool. There was a lot of rubble, it's probably buried under there."

Lian nodded in slow motion, her voice flat. "That's something. If we could get it, it might turn the tide in our favor again."

Lian raised her voice to the watching crowd. "We've lost a lot, too much. But we have to keep going. They would want us to see this through. We've got our mission."

She caught Rylan's gaze and nodded to him. "The rest of you, split into groups and work on extracting any shadyrs or civilians trapped at the estate or nearby, then fall back. Do not engage with either Mordan or Everly—or the things controlling them."

A man in the crowd called out, "What about the estate? How do we get it back?"

Rylan knew many of the shadyrs there, most of them recent defectors from the Darkfreys. But through the blur in his eyes, he couldn't work out who the man was. It didn't really matter. There was a rise of murmurings in support of his question and Rylan understood why, because he felt the same. The estate itself was their home, or had been, for so long.

Lian rubbed her eyes. "Look, I'm not your leader or your boss. You're welcome to do whatever the Everdark you want to do. I'm just telling you that there are two gods of destruction laying each other out near a massive shroudpool that's spilling eidolghasts like a gushing wound."

Low whispers reverberated in the space as her words sank in.

Lian raised her chin, her gaze hard. "I think it's best that you keep things to a strictly 'save who you can and get out alive' plan. Because we're all shadyrs, which means in a way we're all family, and I don't want to lose any more family."

The man stared them down silently for a long moment, then nodded. The crowd broke up into smaller groups, conversing, sometimes arguing, before leaving the cover of the store. Rylan trusted that they would do some good.

That's what they'd been trained to do.

The problem was, they'd been trained to put the good of the world and the fight against the darkness above everything, even their own lives. What was the point of winning if they lost everything they were fighting for along the way? The touch of Lian's hand against his arm made Rylan twitch, his whole body tense and on edge.

"We'll do anything we have to do to get her back." Her brown eyes were hard and sparkling, and she had her other hand on Callan's shoulder. "But please be careful with yourselves. For me."

Rylan gave a thin-lipped smile and nodded numbly. He wasn't sure any amount of care could save them from what they were about to face.

The crowd cleared, leaving just them, Tammy, Cherry, Jasper, and Annabeth.

"Since we barely got out of that Everdark-blighted place alive last time, how are we supposed to get ourselves right back up to that shroudpool again?" Cherry asked, his voice flat despite the sardonic tone of his words.

"Could we find some kind of distraction?" Annabeth asked.

"Oh no ..." Lian's eyes widened.

Rylan tensed, ready for danger. "What?"

His mother's mouth twisted wryly. "I have a terrible, terrible idea."

Despite their efforts to sneak their way back into the estate and avoid the worst of the fighting, Rylan's arms were already covered in eidolghast blood.

"Pin its wings! I'll go for the weak spot," Rylan yelled over the herrelspurn's roar.

The eidolghast ambushed them as they crept around the corner of a dorm building, trying to get inside. It lashed out a leathery wing, catching the hooked claw around the shoulder strap of Rylan's body armor.

Ripping back, it pulled Rylan tumbling toward it, until the straps gave, tearing through.

He came to a rolling stop directly beneath the creatures hideous face, and the glow of flame rose up its neck.

Woah no. He wasn't prepared for fire, not shifted into the heat proof form being near a herrelspurn provided. With so many creatures around, he'd stayed shifted into a more manageable mix of vampire and werewolf form.

A figure body-slammed the monster's long, twisting mass of necks from the side, redirecting the jet of fire away from Rylan.

"Thanks."

Callan smiled as he gave him a hand up. "Do I look like the kind of guy who lets his brother get cooked?"

Rylan tugged on Callan's hand, pulling him away as the monster swung a wing at them again.

Jasper and Annabeth leapt in unison, landing on top of that wing and holding it still beneath them.

Rylan grinned viciously. Having Callan, Jasper, and Annabeth fighting by his side made Rylan feel at home, as though he had a solid brace at his back that could overcome anything together.

"We've got the other one," Cherry called out.

He and Tammy were the least experienced of the lot. Rylan was worried they'd hold the team back when hit with the influx of eidolghast energy, considering how Tammy hadn't been able to control her mermaid form not long ago.

He'd even whispered to Lian that they should be left out of this mission, but Lian wanted them kept close by.

In the thick of it, Rylan noted that they were handling the influx of eidolghast energy well. They both managed to hold a stable form, and both chose vampire. The easiest and one of the earliest forms shadyrs learned, but with its regeneration powers, a good pick.

They launched themselves together at the herrelspurn's other wing, catching it less elegantly and efficiently as the others had with theirs, but still effective.

Callan and Rylan grappled the creature from each side. They each ripped into the tangle of flesh that formed its multi-strand neck, but it kept moving, lifting them from the ground as it thrashed, shaking them like ragdolls and throwing them off.

"Where's this weakspot?" Lian appeared beside the two boys, legs wide in a martial stance and hand on her sword in its hilt.

Rylan had never known the warrior side of his mom. Seeing her so brave and at ease in front of a roaring, flame-breathing monster gave him a newfound respect for her.

"I don't know exactly. Harper and her sword aren't here ..." Rylan pushed down his guilt and grief, they wouldn't serve him now. "But it's one of the necks."

"Right." Lian nodded once, and as the creature thrashed around against those pinning its wings, she drew her sword.

With feet placed firmly, and head turned away, Lian stilled, waited, and then slashed the black shadyr sword through the air in front of her. The screeching eidolghast stilled, its masklike face and needle filled mouth hanging limp for one moment, before dropping away clean from its tangle of spaghetti-like necks.

With a *sshckt* Lian sheathed the sword again and inspected her work. "Beheading pretty much always does the job too."

"That it does," Rylan replied, eyes wide and grin growing. Turns out his mom was kind of amazing.

Mixing with the turmoil of all his other emotions was the sadness that he hadn't known that sooner, that he'd abandoned her for so long. He had no time for that now though. They had a mission.

The herrelspurn was dead, its body twitching slightly but no longer a threat.

"Everyone good?" he checked around the team as they came back together.

They nodded silently in reply. Each of them carried a heavy pack they'd loaded up back at Howell House, and even with shadyr powers, Rylan's body rebelled with fatigue. He'd been fighting so hard, so long. They all had.

But nobody complained.

Then Tammy's face turned upwards and pulled long in horror. She let loose a whimpering scream.

Chapter Twenty-Two

Rylan followed Tammy's terrified stare, expecting to see another herrelspurn flying down towards them. But something darker moved, crawling along the side of the building.

A weroth, bigger than any he'd ever seen before clambered like a spider along the wall their way, its pointed legs stabbing through the stonework with each step, crumbling debris down upon them.

How did that thing even fit through the shroudpool?

"No, no, no." Tammy shook her head, backing toward the building entrance.

Still breathing hard from the previous fight, Rylan didn't particularly want to try to take that giant down either.

"Go, get inside, quick!" He herded the others before him, racing towards the main doors as the weroth raced down the walls to block their path.

Rylan pushed through the doors last, tumbling across the marble floors as the weroth jabbed limbs like rapiers toward them. One caught the back of Rylan's arm, leaving a thin puncture wound. He hissed at the sting and rolled further away.

The weroth roared through the doorway, too large to fit. The ancient wooden beams of the doorframe splintered and cracked.

"Keep moving, fast!"

Back on their feet, they dashed down the hall as the building shook, plaster raining over them from the cracking ceiling. Lian led them down into the system of tunnels and they ran single file through darkness.

Close to their destination, they had to leave the shelter of the underground tunnel and make a break across clear ground, giving a view of the battlefield in the sky. The clash between Coruscare and Infuscur above was a spectacle that unwillingly drew the eye like a gory car crash.

Light tangled and tore into darkness against the backdrop of gloomy gray. They would part, circling far out across the town, then rocket back toward each other with an impact that made the earth shake.

At times, they would swoop low enough that the tiny

human bodies suspended within those massive energies were visible, then they'd shoot back into the sky, so fast and far that Rylan worried they would leave the planet entirely.

Can Everly's body survive this?

He had to hope that the Coruscare would make sure of that. He knew it had done what it could to protect her in the past. If she died, it seemed to fear it would, too.

The Infuscur caught the Coruscare's glow tightly in a wrap of void-dark tendrils. The light flickered, faded, then burst free. Diminished, the Coruscare dipped and bobbed away, shooting long, glittering strands downward.

Rylan saw where they hit—a group of shadyrs mid-combat with a weroth. The Coruscare latched onto every one of them, shadyr and ghast, consuming their souls to renew itself. Their bodies dropped, empty and used up, and the Coruscare returned to the fray, glowing as bright as ever.

It will just keep eating souls to keep going. It could keep fighting the Infuscur like that forever. It has to be stopped.

The Infuscur too seemed to draw some kind of negative sustenance from what it destroyed, as though annihilation renewed it.

Rylan reached the entry to the next building and ushered the team in ahead of him. He caught their glances of concern as they passed, having seen the same as he had.

They all knew the Coruscare had to be stopped. But

could it? And what about the Infuscur?

Even if they got the Bane, brought the Coruscare down, closed the shroudpool, they'd still have a god of void and annihilation to deal with and no idea how. Part of Rylan hoped that Everly—the Coruscare—would defeat it and take the revenge it clearly wanted, but for all Rylan could tell as he looked back one last time, they seemed at a stalemate.

Turning away, Rylan ran after the others through the building and into the deep, older tunnels. They reached the room they'd found on their way out before, which held the Mesman's collection of inactive lures.

A corner of the ceiling had broken through since they'd last been in there. The gaping hole revealed the sky above. The room that had been on top of them was mostly gone, vanished to nothing as if it never existed.

Flashes of light from the warring gods flickered through. The intricately combined black bones stood like an ominous army in the dim illumination.

Lian and the others already had their packs off, unloading blocks of C-4 and rolls of fuse. Rylan joined them, wondering again at how Denny had ever managed to accumulate such a massive stash of explosives. Lian supposedly confiscated it all from him, but even then, he'd still kept enough to go out in a spectacularly messy way.

"Just how big is this explosion going to be?" Tammy

asked, eyeing the stacks of pale putty and blasting caps.

Lian pulled a crumpled wad of papers out of her pack and unfolded them, grunting at the printed diagrams and notes. "Do I look like a munitions expert? I'm just hoping they go off at all."

"I almost wish Denny was here. Almost." Cherry leaned over Lian, squinting at the instructions.

Tammy sighed. "Yeah, the dumb bastard would have loved this."

Rylan knew as much about rigging C-4 as the rest of them, which wasn't much, so he left them working on it and checked on Annabeth. She had moved closer to the boney effigies and shifted back into human form.

"You good?" Rylan eyed the sharp blade she held to the back of her forearm.

She gave him a trembly smile. "Give me a weroth bite any day. Somehow cutting myself is so much worse."

"Want me to do it?"

She jerked away as though he'd snatch the knife. "I've got it. Just need to get my head together. This is, well, if it works, this is kind of huge."

"Don't go getting those horrible things activated until we've worked this out!" Lian called over, her hands busy laying out a length of fuse.

Rylan squeezed past a couple of lures then climbed the wall near the hole. Sticking his head out, he saw half-crumbled walls and remaining building standing on one side, and an open view over a large section of the grounds on the other.

Splintered timber chairs lay pushed up against one wall and a large painting of Mordan Darkfrey had fallen on top of them. It was once a classroom Rylan had studied in.

"Can we get the fuse up through here?" he called to the others. "We've got a good vantage to watch incoming ghasts, and some walls to take cover behind."

Lian eyed the roll of fuse. "Looks like it's pretty long. I think we're done setting these. Let's get this unrolled and see how far we get."

Cherry nodded and took a step away from the stacked C-4. "I don't know what's scarier. Thinking that we got it wrong, and it won't work, or that we did it right and it's ready to blow."

Jasper moved closer to him. "I believe we have followed the diagrams accurately. But there's no indication as to the explosion size."

"Death by a swarm of eidolghasts, death by explosion, death by disintegration, or death by having our souls eaten. We have so many exciting options now," Tammy replied.

"How about we aim for not dying?" Callan took the detonator, pulling it across the room as Lian stayed to help unroll the fuse.

"I mean, I suppose that's an option, too," Tammy

grumbled as she followed behind him.

Rylan gave Callan a boost through the hole and watched him disappear around the corner of a crumbled brick wall. He helped Tammy up as well, and Cherry and Jasper lined up to join them.

"How's it going, Anna? You're on."

"Okay, okay!" With a deep breath and set face, Annabeth plunged the knife into her skin.

Her lips twitched and twisted but she made no sound. She cut a straight, one-inch gash, nice and deep, then dropped the knife. Reaching to her throat, she grabbed her necklace and tore it free. She took the small piece of bone from it—ancient, original shadyr bone—and closed her eyes as she pushed it into the bloody wound she'd made.

Lian appeared by her side with gauze and a bandage and wrapped the injury. With her other hand, Annabeth extracted from her jacket pocket the spell notes Jasper had stolen.

"Okay, let's see if this shadyr bone does what it's supposed to do." Annabeth stared at the page, her eyes moving over the text a few times before she opened her mouth again.

She nodded as though to herself, then spoke. Her words were incomprehensible, guttural, and eerie in a way that made Rylan's bones shiver and his eyesight blur. He could hear a pattern in her words, a melody, as she repeated a verse over and over.

When she stopped, his heart was pounding, and a sheen of sweat prickled all over his skin. Annabeth looked about the same, the color drained from her face.

She leaned weakly against Lian. "Did it work? How do we know if it worked?"

In the gloomy room, the bones of the effigies seemed to wriggle.

Above Rylan, Cherry called out. "It worked! It definitely worked!"

Rylan pounced up the corner of the room again to look out through the hole. Across the estate grounds, there was movement. Eidolghasts, dozens of them, prowling their way.

"Come on, out of there, quick!"

He dropped back onto the stone floor with a thud and gestured Lian and Annabeth to him, then got into position to boost them up. Annabeth grabbed his shoulders and stepped onto his entwined hands, and with a push, he threw her up and out. He bent down again for Lian.

"Hurry!" Annabeth called back.

With a strain of his muscles, Lian too disappeared up through the hole.

Rylan stretched his wolf-like arms and used his long claws to scrabble out of the hole himself. He rolled onto the floor of the room above to see flames gusting in the air over his face. Two herrelspurn swooped low, wrestling with each other midair as they rushed for the lures.

Getting to his feet, Rylan bolted after Lian and Annabeth, following the line of the fuse across the long classroom toward the still-standing walls.

A glance over his shoulder as he ducked beside Callan wasn't enough for him to count the approaching beasts. Easily a dozen, two dozen, maybe more. They squabbled and fought among themselves, driven into a frenzy by the mass of activated lures in the underground room.

The herrelspurn were already there, clawing at the hole in the ground.

Rylan frowned at the detonator in his brother's hands. They were a decent distance away from the explosives, but if the blast was going to be big enough to take out that many ghasts, were they really far enough away?

"Did you use all the bricks?" he asked.

"Yup," Callan replied. "I mean, what were we going to save them for?"

Tammy popped her head over the wall then ducked down again. "That's a fuckton of ghasts. I hope this is going to be enough to take them out."

"Even if we just get a bit of a boom, it should be enough to draw more attention over here while we go and get the Bane. That's what we're after, right?" Cherry said with a shrug.

Rylan checked over the wall again. The area above the underground room was now a writhing mass of creatures. "Either way, I think it's boom time now."

Callan's eyes were on Tammy as he nodded and held up the detonator. With a push of his thumb, it clicked.

The shockwave hit the wall at their backs, blasting right through. It cracked against Rylan's bones, smashing through him like a ghost train as bricks and mortar flew.

He didn't even hear it, his head drowning in a numb, pounding hum of its own.

The force of the explosion left him flat on his back, and the sky above him was filled with a hailstorm of black bones, flooring timber, and bloody chunks of eidolghasts. He groaned, his lungs too flattened to cry out in the pain that hit his every muscle.

Blinking eyes that were filled with patches of darkness and floating spots, Rylan was sure that the regeneration from the part-vampire form was the only thing keeping him alive. He could only hope through a pain-deadened mind that the others were still alive too.

Fucking Denny and his fucking C-4. We should have known he'd have way, way too much.

At least it had cleared out a lot of eidolghasts, but it had knocked him down too, for too long. Rylan could barely drag air into his chest, let alone make a dash for the Bane as planned.

He could only lie, paralyzed, staring at the sky as his head spun in dizzy nausea.

At the edges of his vision, silhouettes of more eidolghasts lumbered their way, drawn by the explosion. Above them, the Infuscur had the Coruscare grappled again, held tight in a web of darkness.

The Coruscare faded fast, and twisted around, moving strangely. It seemed to be folding on itself, reaching for something at its core.

Something small fell from it. The bag that Everly had carried. It drifted, empty, to the ground.

Even from the great distance, Rylan could hear what seemed to be Everly laughing, but a twisted version of it, tainted with the sound of a being not from this reality.

The Coruscare held the small orb shaped artifact above it with glowing tendrils.

The Infuscur writhed, letting go of the Coruscare and backing away, but too slow.

The Swallower expanded, exploding out to a massive green sphere across the space where the Infuscur had been. The Coruscare reared back, trying to keep clear, but strands of its light were sucked inward, caught in the web-like orb as well. The world shuddered as the Swallower crushed back down again into a tiny ball. The darkness was gone. The light went out.

Two bodies tumbled from the sky.

Rylan wheezed, pushing himself onto his elbows. His eyes locked on the falling figures.

No, no, no. If the Coruscare is gone, Everly can't take that fall.

It was a moment of both relief and heartbreak when a dim glow sputtered back to life around Everly before she hit the ground nearby.

With a grunt of effort, Rylan rolled to the side and onto all fours.

He had to move. This might be his only chance. Ghasts were still heading their way, the Infuscur might be down, and the Coruscare too, at least for now.

He had no doubt it would be finding its next meal to repower itself as quickly as it could. If he could get to the Bane and back to Everly before then, they might have a chance to take control.

He lifted his head, ears still ringing, and cast a gaze across the bloodied rubble.

He counted out his team. Lian and Annabeth, Callan and Tammy, Jasper and Cherry, lay sprawled throughout the debris. Groans and sobs came from twisted and reddened bodies, but they all moved.

They were all alive.

Rylan gritted his teeth. He didn't have time to do more for them. If he was going to help anyone, he had to get to the Bane.

As he stood up, his ankles threatened to crumple beneath him. His body stitched itself back together, but not fast enough. In a swirl of black mist and red sparks, he let go of the partial werewolf form he'd been holding and drew entirely on vampire essence to increase his healing.

Before the magical smoke had faded away, he broke into a staggering run down the rubble-strewn corridor.

He wasn't far from the old ballroom that housed the shroudpool, just the next building along.

Struggling to run in a straight line, he ricocheted from wall to wall along the corridor, then barged open the door at the end. He almost lost his footing down the few steps outside and staggered drunkenly onto the lawn.

Light flashed in the distance. The Coruscare, gaining strength. Rylan paused for a single moment to catch his breath and the sharp leg of a weroth pierced down beside him. He snatched it in two strong hands. Wrenching in opposite directions, he tore the pointed end free.

The weroth's glowing maw snapped at him as it tripped over its amputated limb and fell flat onto the ground. Rylan leaped onto it, driving its own sharp leg into the soft spot at the top of its head.

Without the fur of werewolf form, the weroth's acid burned his pale, vampire-like flesh. He cried out, eyes stinging, as he rolled back onto the grass and pushed forward to the shroudpool. His whole body was racked with more pain than he'd ever known.

His bones stabbed him from within. His skin sizzled. His heart was squeezed in a vise.

It would all be worth it if he could get to the Bane, save Everly. He just had to push forward. A light flashed again at his back, casting his shadow in front of him, driving him faster.

He climbed in over the broken wall of the ballroom and half-ran, half-crawled across the tangle of timbers and bricks toward the shroudpool.

As he drew closer, another herrelspurn burst through the massive portal, swooping out and into the sky. Rylan ducked low, rolling toward the base of the shroudpool.

In among the rubble there were pieces of bone in all shapes and sizes, smashed from the blast of the spell coming into being. Wishing he still had his werewolf claws, but not daring to take the time to shift again, Rylan plunged his hands into the sharp mess, digging down through the knee-deep wreckage.

Splinters pricked deep into his fingers and when his hands came away wet in a red so dark it edged on black, at first, he stared, confused. With a blink of understanding, he dug faster. It was the blood of the Bane.

A large sheet of roof plaster, drowned in blood, lay in the space he cleared. He lifted it with both hands, tossing it aside.

Beneath it lay the Bane.

Crushed, torn into two battered pieces by a sharp edge of stone beneath it, floating in a deep pool of blood.

A wild, animal-like sound burst from Rylan's throat, and he fell onto his hands and knees.

It was gone. His last hope to save Everly was gone.

Chapter Twenty-Three

The blast still rung in Lian's ears as she dashed across grass stained with blood. She'd seen Rylan head off toward the Bane.

Hopefully he would have it soon and be able to save Everly—or at least stop the Coruscare. Lian didn't want to think that way, but her reserves of hope were running perilously low.

Each flicker of light that came from behind the main building where Everly had fallen, growing in strength each time, scared her more. She almost turned that way, to try to get Everly back herself, but figured she'd be nothing more than another snack to rebuild the Coruscare's strength if she did.

She had decided on a different mission for herself.

She'd tracked where Mordan's body had tumbled from the sky—somewhere around the back of the palatial main building.

Around the corner, the manicured gardens were roughed up. Neat hedges were bent and torn through, and a couple of statues toppled onto the marble paths. A white-eyed stone head lay decapitated at Lian's feet as she searched with her gaze. More bodies scattered the ground than she wanted to see, eidolghast and shadyr.

Things were calmer now, with many of the shadyrs having fled and eidolghasts taken out in the explosion. Some of the bodies around the estate were probably still alive, or could be saved, if they got medical attention soon enough.

But that couldn't happen until the omnipotent creatures inside Mordan and Everly were stopped, and the shroudpool closed.

The twilight dimness confused Lian. She couldn't comprehend what the time was, how much time had passed since the shroudpool's opening blocked out the sun that should be shining above.

Maybe it was nighttime already. Maybe years had passed as they battled. Her body sure hurt like it had been that long. Even with full-vampire form regeneration going, it was barely keeping up with her injuries and strain.

A deeper darkness caught her eye, and she scurried down the pathway as silently as she could, one hand on the hilt of her slim sword that hung from her belt.

Mordan lay against the round rim of a grand fountain. His body was twisted at an odd angle, with his head on the ground and legs up over the edge, dangling in the water. His chest heaved with sharp breaths.

"Mordan?" Lian could see it was his body, but that didn't mean it was him.

He groaned as he tilted his head back to see her. "You? Where is everyone else? What happened?"

It certainly seemed to be Mordan in control. Did that mean the Infuscur was gone?

Lian stepped forward cautiously. "You've been under the control of something real nasty. I guess that's what you get for opening a portal to the Everdark in your backyard."

With a grunt and stomach-curdling crack of bones, Mordan lurched to the side, bringing his legs down onto the ground with his torso and rolling onto his front. "If my shadyrs followed my orders, this wouldn't … you put doubt into them. You turned them … mutinous."

"Oh, so this is all my fault, is it? See, here's the thing you never understood. They aren't *your* shadyrs. Using them as you pleased for your war. If you ever understood that, maybe half of them would still be alive." Lian crouched to his level, scrutinizing his broken body.

A haze of darkness surged outwards from him. A black ribbon shot toward Lian, and she rolled backward. On instinct, she unsheathed her sword and swiped it blindly in front of her as she got back onto her feet.

There was a hiss and a crack as she quickly sheathed the blade again, desperate to have the use of her eyes in case she had to dodge more of the destructive strands.

The Infuscur withdrew, the ribbon jittering and broken.

Well, that's interesting.

Mordan let out a gurgling roar, and the darkness slurped back into him. Obsidian eyes cleared into a sparkling shadyr gaze.

"The thing ... it's trying to take control again. Getting stronger ..." He coughed, and a thick ichor dripped from his mouth.

He shuffled into a sitting position, leaning against the rim of the fountain. Lifting his hands in front of him, he stared as though trying to make sense of his own body parts. A couple of fingers hung limp the wrong way.

"So much power ..."

"Oh no, don't you even think about it."

Lian half drew her sword from its sheath. It would only blind her once fully drawn, but halfway was enough to send Mordan a message.

Mordan glared at it, then her, and spat a wad of clumpy blood from his mouth. "Thief."

Lian nodded. "It's quite the bounty, too. You never

knew what its power was. Just thought it was cursed to blind its user."

"Enlighten me then, what does it—" darkness shimmered around Mordan, and he clenched his teeth as his eyes blackened again, then cleared— "do?"

Lian couldn't be sure it had made contact with the Infuscur before. She hadn't seen exactly what happened. But if it didn't cut the ribbon of darkness, why did it withdraw?

She found a final glimmer of hope to hold onto. "It can cut into creatures that aren't there. It can cut into nothingness, and destroy it."

Mordan's reddened lips twisted into a mocking grin, but when Lian kept her expression firm, his smile dropped, and fear flashed across his eyes.

"You wouldn't. You couldn't. No, Lian, don't do this. Help me. I ... I can control it."

Lian shook her head and pulled her sword an inch higher from its sheath.

Mordan tried to back up, blocked by the marble fountain edge behind him. "Come now, you're not a murderer."

"Aren't I? Isn't that what the Darkfreys create? Isn't that what we shadyrs do? We kill monsters. I tried to be different. I tried to live a life without being a killer, but you dragged me back into it. You dragged my sons into it.

I have lost so much to this world of death and darkness."

The sharp tip of the blade traced the lip of the sheath, steady in Lian's grip. Her words blew out through clenched teeth.

"But maybe, maybe if I kill just a couple more monsters, my sons and all the rest of my family can live a better life, without being killers. Without becoming monsters themselves. I can do that for them."

Mordan bared his blood-stained teeth at her, and the darkness of the Infuscur surged out from him again.

Lian adjusted her stance. "I don't like having to kill you, Mordan. But luckily, I don't even have to see it happen."

Her vision went dark as she whipped her sword out, then down.

She aimed right for where she knew Mordan's chest to be. It struck, meeting the resistance of flesh, ribcage. Lian leaned into the hilt, pushing through.

Mordan's cry of pain was short, cutting out into a sputter as she twisted the blade. The hilt tingled beneath her palms.

A shudder of disgust rattled her bones as she wrenched the sword back and sheathed it.

But she kept her eyes closed a few moments longer.

Taking in a shaky breath, she opened them.

Mordan sat deathly-still before her, facing up to the sky, his mouth hanging open. His chest around the wound was black rather than red, spidering out in cracks. The cracks spread rapidly, running over his flesh and clothing alike, turning them gray and ashy as they went.

Before Lian's eyes, Mordan's body crumbled away into dust. It spread over the path in the light wind.

"What in the Everdark ...?" Lian whispered, staring at what was left behind.

Where Mordan's chest had been lay a twisted crystal of matte black. As large as her arm, it was so dark it looked more like a hole in space than a real object.

Despite every instinct inside her screaming not to, she reached out to touch it. She couldn't leave the thing there, unguarded. If it was what she thought it was, she worried what would happen if it broke.

The crystal was smooth as room-temperature oil under her fingers, and when she touched it, she heard a crackle of energy from her side.

Putting a hand on the hilt of her sword, it zinged with the same tingle she'd noticed before. It flickered with the opposite of sparkling—shimmers of blackness, imbued with dark power.

"Okay then," Lian muttered.

She took a deep breath, then drew the sword briefly, but it didn't react in a way out of the ordinary. She'd have to work out what that meant later.

She hmphed as she crouched down and picked up the

dark crystal carefully with two hands.

Bringing it near her face, she tapped on the glassy surface with a broken fingernail. "Got you."

One god-like monster down.

Lian drew a long breath, filling her lungs with air that tasted like hope. As long as Rylan got the Bane, maybe, just maybe, they would be okay.

Rylan knelt in the thick blood, hunched over, staring blankly at his hands. In a moment of panic, he tried to put the Bane back together.

The ornately etched metallic material that formed the artifact was thin and had torn right down the middle. A messy, twisted tear. Each half was crushed and bent in on itself, so it didn't even line up cleanly.

He tried reshaping them, his fingers sliced by the jagged edges. He tried holding the pieces back together, but it didn't miraculously reform. Not that he thought it had any reason too, but he needed something to happen. He needed something to work.

The warped pieces didn't even bleed anymore. Once the residual blood had dripped off, there was no constant oozing as the Bane used to do when not wrapped in its parchment. All power had ebbed from it, spilled onto the floor.

What do I do? What do I do now?

He firmed his jaw and brought his shoulders back. He'd do whatever he could. He would never stop fighting for Everly.

The beams of light in the distance were slowly moving his way. What had Everly said? The Coruscare wanted revenge, and it wanted the Everdark back. The realm it once ruled before it was broken.

If the Infuscur was down, then the Coruscare would be headed to the shroudpool next. If it went through, if it took Everly with it, he might lose her forever.

He wouldn't let that happen. No matter what.

But how? The defeated voice in his head asked. *The Bane is gone.*

Rylan wouldn't let himself think that Everly was gone though. She was still in there, even if the Coruscare was at the wheel, she must still exist. And as long as she did, she'd still be fighting. So he would too.

"Did you find it?" Lian's voice reached him, followed by footsteps crunching through the rubble.

Rylan turned from the pool of blood to her. He stood up, and almost threw himself into Lian's arms as Tammy had done before, needing that comfort that only his mother could provide, a comfort he'd been missing most of this life. It was only the sight of the thing she cradled like a baby in her arms that stopped him.

Rylan blinked a few times to clear away the tears that washed over his vision. "Is that ...?"

Lian nodded, readjusting her hold to give him a clearer view of the matte-black crystal. It twisted around on itself, creating hollows and overlapping threads of intricate, delicate patterns.

"The Infuscur, trapped in whatever stasis this is. Must have the same near-death defenses as the Coruscare."

A wave of relief buoyed Rylan. He'd seen it and Mordan's body fall, and the Coruscare had given up its chase too, but it was good to know for certain the destructive creature was gone. One less threat to worry about, locked in that crystal prison.

"It was down, and Mordan is gone, too," Lian continued.

She stared at the pool of blood, a frown exaggerating the wrinkles across her forehead. "The Bane?"

Rylan shook his head, his teeth and mouth clamping shut as though trying to hold back his voice, as though saying it made it reality.

He forced the word out. "Broken."

Lian's eyes met his with the full comprehension of that word and it almost broke him too.

Light glowed from over the other side of the shattered

ballroom wall. So close now.

Rylan spoke desperately, "It's going to go back into the Everdark. The Coruscare is going to take Everly away with it."

Lian glowered at the crystal in her arms as though she were about to smash it in anger. "If the Infuscur was still out there, at least it would keep the Coruscare busy, keep it here."

They could free the creature again, let it infect someone else. But at what cost? The battle between the opposites of light and dark was destroying all around it. Without additional weapons to take advantage of, the two of them just canceled each other out in an endless war.

If only they could cancel each other out for good, without obliterating and consuming everything between them ...

A thought formed in Rylan's mind, too scary to put into words. But he tried anyway.

"What if ... we release the Infuscur again, but into Everly? Put it in there *with* the Coruscare. No two separate bodies for them to fight with. The two of them might battle it out inside her rather than across our world."

"That's ..." Lian blew out a long breath. "That's an idea, but it has to be a huge risk. What if Everly isn't strong enough to withstand that?"

Rylan had an answer for that, and it was the part of his idea that didn't scare him. He'd considered the huge strain it would have on Everly, on her body and psyche.

"She'll be strong enough. Because I'm going to let her know what is happening. I'm going to be there for her, to help her."

Lian's nose wrinkled. "How?"

The light of the Coruscare crested the broken wall of the ballroom, lifting over the open roof like a sunrise. Everly's body hung within that bright glow, the Swallower held between her hands.

Rylan stared, burning trails into his eyesight. "I'm going to get it to consume me."

Lian put the black crystal down in a nest of broken roof tiles, then snatched his shoulder in one hand, shaking him until he looked back to her. "What good will having your soul eaten do?"

Rylan grew calm as the light drifted closer. "She's going to catch me, like she did before. She did it last time on instinct, and she understands so much more now. I trust her."

"We don't have the Bane! There'll be no way to get you back, even if—"

"It doesn't matter. I'll be with her, and we'll do what needs to be done." Rylan brought his arms around Lian, holding her tightly. "Break the Infuscur crystal over Everly as soon as I'm gone. If it works, hopefully it will lessen the Coruscare's control. Try to get the Swallower off her then.

We'll do what we can from the inside."

He stepped back out of their embrace. Lian stared at him for a breathless second.

Her voice was small and scratchy. "It's a good plan."

Rylan wasn't sure he'd call it good. There were so many ifs, so many ways it could go wrong.

But it was something, and that was more than he had a moment ago. If having the Infuscur and Coruscare housed together in the same physical form worked how he hoped, with the two of them destroying each other from the inside, then the powers that let Everly hold onto souls might not last long.

He would only be with her for the end, one way or another. But if that meant she pulled through on the other side without those ghast-blighted deities possessing her, he'd do that for her, and so there'd be a world for her to live in afterward.

And if the Infuscur couldn't inhabit Everly too, if the Coruscare kept control, and took itself back into the Everdark, at least he'd still be with Everly, in her dreams. At least the others might be able to close the shroudpool behind them and save this world.

The Coruscare floated lazily, triumphantly toward the shroudpool, dragging the tips of Everly's feet over the rubble. Rylan faced it, blocking its path.

"You're not leaving here without me," he yelled at it.

Everly's eyes turned to him, burning white as stars.

"Come on, damn you! You remember me, right?" He put his arms out to the sides, palms turned upward. "I know you want to eat me again. Do it!"

Scintillating threads shot out from the Coruscare at him.

This is it.

"Rylan, I love you. I never stopped," Lian said from beside him. "Callan too. All the rest. Just ... hold this for me?"

Lian pressed something cold into Rylan's open palm.

On instinct, he closed his hand around it, and the world vanished.

Chapter Twenty-Four

Confused ghosts surrounded Everly.

The space around her was like a shimmering cage of crystal, as though she'd been trapped inside a massive, pure white geode. She knew she was annoying the Coruscare. A thorn in its side that refused to blink out of existence and let it have its way.

At times, it would try again to assert its influence over her, like a heavy pressure squeezing her from all sides, making her want to disappear and become nothing. But she would push back. And remain.

She was still there, still herself, and still trying to regain control.

Then the first of the souls hurtled past.

She could sense their essence, and then the crunch

and slurp of the Coruscare's ethereal consumption. The satisfaction. The boost to the soul eater's power.

That was when Everly knew she had to change tack.

She might never gain control of her body again. Even with two pieces of the Coruscare in her, it had only lulled her into thinking she had control. It was always too powerful for her, and now it was whole.

But somewhere, out in the real world, there was the Bane. The others could get it back, use it against her. Break her, if they had to. She knew it would be hard for them. Harper would fight it, Rylan too. But maybe Lian would be strong enough to do what had to be done.

If it was between her life and stopping the Beast of Teeth and Stars from ruling over two dimensions, Everly knew what she'd choose.

And if she could save as many souls as possible in the process, maybe they would be spilled back into their bodies when the Bane broke the Coruscare. Even if there was a chance that could be the outcome, Everly wanted to try for it.

The spirits now surrounded her. She didn't know any of them. Darkfrey shadyrs mostly. Eidolghasts had been consumed, too. Everly could sense the difference between their energy and shadyr energy.

She let the ghasts go through. The idea that they were also keeping the Coruscare fed wasn't something she liked, but she had no idea what having spirits of those monsters roaming around in this space would mean.

The shadyr spirits wandered, shocked and distraught. Many seemed to think they were dead, that they were now trapped in some kind of purgatory. Some cried.

Everly tried to explain but had to keep most of her attention on task.

Sometimes souls would fly so fast and thick, she'd miss one, and feel a surge of guilt as someone's essence was consumed and lost for good.

Everly had no idea what was happening outside, or how much time had passed. It felt like an eternity.

Maybe this was purgatory, after all. If she could control the world with the sheer need of her wishes, she'd be back in control of her body, with her friends and family. With Rylan.

She missed them all so much, and despite being surrounded by a crowd of bewildered ghosts, she felt utterly alone.

Then a new essence streamed inward. And it felt different to the others. It felt familiar.

Straining her will, whatever part of her power she held in this unearthly space, she reached out and caught them before the Coruscare could devour their soul.

A figure materialized in her outstretched hands.

"Lian?" Everly choked out her name.

Oh no.

Lian's shoulders dropped, and she smiled wanly back. She didn't seem confused at all about where she was or finding herself there with Everly.

Reaching out a hand, she patted Everly's cheek. "Good catch, kid. Looks like you've been busy."

"I ... I've been trying. But ... it got you. No, it got you ..." Stifled sobs interrupted Everly.

She stood frozen, gaping at Lian, not wanting to believe it.

Lian waved a hand as though it were nothing. "Shh, it's okay. We have to be quick now, so listen. The Infuscur has been subdued, and we have its crystal. We're going to break it, on you, okay? It's going to be happening any moment now."

"What? Why?"

"We're hoping the two bloody beasts take each other out while trapped together in you. Maybe they will at least keep each other busy enough that you can take control again. Or something that helps."

Everly shook her head, lips twisting. "If the Infuscur is down, you should have used the Bane on me. Take out the Coruscare too. Who knows what having the two of them together will do?"

Lian's eyes glittered, and she cupped Everly's cheek in her palm. "We ... didn't want to do that to you. We're hoping you'll survive this. That's why I'm here. To help you, any way that I can."

"You came here on purpose?" Everly winced at the high whine of her voice. Her bottom lip trembled.

"Of course. You know I'd do anything for my kids."

Everly pulled Lian close and squeezed her in a crushing embrace. "I'll get you out again, okay? When this works, and I'm in control, I'll use the Bane to put you back into your body. I'd do anything for you, too."

Lian sniffed and patted the back of Everly's white hair. "I know."

With a heavy sigh, Lian pulled back, but kept Everly's hands in hers.

There were so many other questions Everly needed to ask.

Had anyone else been lost? How was the Infuscur beaten? What was happening with the shroudpool?

But the glimmering crystal ball around them dimmed suddenly as shadows spilled over the world. Ghosts of shadyrs cried out.

Lian squeezed Everly's fingers. "Get ready. Things are about to get crazy. But you can do this."

Everly centered herself, drawing strength from the love in Lian's eyes, the reassurance of her touch.

Lian, who had never been bonded to her by the Coruscare, but had been there for her as much as Rylan had. Who showed Everly kindness and caring where her own mother had failed.

Any strength she had, she owed to Lian.

"*We* can do this."

A prickle of energy zapped through Rylan's hand, and the blindness confused him for a moment too long. Then the rush of denial and grief came with realization.

No, no! It wasn't meant to be this way.

He roared a painful howl and dropped the sword. Vision returned with a brightness that blinded in its own way.

His mother stood in front of him, wrapped in pulsating strings of light.

Rylan's breath caught in his throat as he stared through watering eyes. His knees wobbled, thighs ached, body wanting to fold in on itself.

You can't stop. You can't grieve. You have to do what has to be done.

The Coruscare was distracted. He had to act now, or Lian's sacrifice would be for nothing.

He spun wildly, searching for where Lian had put the Infuscur crystal. There, a couple of steps away, hidden behind a tumble of roof tiles, nested in a puff of torn insulation.

She didn't have to do this. It should have been me.

Lian's body went limp. The tendrils unwound themselves, and she flopped loosely to the ground, lying on her side as though asleep. Rylan picked up the obsidian-like stone.

I only just got my family back.

The Infuscur was disturbing to touch. Slick and smooth, yet matte and sharp. It was transparent emptiness and solid blackness at the same time, making him dizzy to look into it.

He clenched his teeth, fighting back the rattle of sobs that trembled up his spine. His face burned with the effort to hold back tears enough to see.

The blood from the Bane, the broken, useless Bane that couldn't get his mother back, oozed into his boots.

Keep moving. Follow the plan.

The Coruscare had stilled, hovering where it had paused to lash out at them. It reeled its tendrils back in, and through the eye-stinging glow, it seemed as though Everly's face twitched.

Something was happening inside her. He had to act now.

Mom ... please save Everly.

Rylan hefted the heavy crystal up, and with a howl of

effort, threw it, javelin like, at Everly's feet.

It shattered spectacularly. Thousands of dark shards burst from the point of impact like a swarm of insects, and a cloud of darkness exploded out.

The force knocked Rylan onto his back.

It engulfed the light of the Coruscare entirely. Inky swirls spun like a miniature tornado, then rushed into Everly's body.

The darkness disappeared. The light went out. Everly floated down into a kneeling position, staring blankly through her own clear blue eyes.

"Evie?" Rylan rolled forward off his back and scrambled on hands and feet across the rubble to her.

She sat upright, expression empty, hands hanging limp at her sides.

Lying beside her was the spherical artifact.

Rylan's chest contracted when he got close. There were dark and light cracks running like veins across her chest, up her neck, over her cheeks, splitting her skin. Flickering energy shone and shadowed from within.

But the gods of the Everdark weren't showing themselves.

Is that it? Did it work?

Rylan put a hand against her cheek with a feather touch. "Evie, are you there?"

With a gasp, she blinked and looked right at him.

"Rylan?"

Her mouth trembled and a single tear spilled down her cheek, tracing the lines that marred her flesh. A swirl of darkness moved across one eye as though someone had splashed a drop of ink into it, then it was burned away with a flash of light.

Everly pitched forward and cried out painfully.

It wasn't over.

He gathered her hands into his, squeezing them gently. "Is ... is Lian with you? Do you know what's happening?"

Her face crumpled, and she nodded.

"I'm sorry. I'm so sorry." Rylan choked out the words, for Everly, and for Lian, if there was any chance she could hear them.

Everly's chest heaved, and she screwed her eyes shut. "I can feel them. Fighting."

"Let them. Keep them stuck inside so they can't renew themselves by eating or destroying. Let them use each other up until they are gone. Just stay strong so we don't lose you, too."

Everly's head tilted. "I'm trying. Lian ... she's helping. Her strength is helping me stay aware. But it's too much. It feels like the universe is being ripped apart inside of me."

She shook her head in a tumble of messy, white hair.

Through the corners of his eyes, Rylan saw movement. A quick glance confirmed it wasn't a threat, but Callan and the others joining them.

His brother moved closer. "What's—"

"Keep back. It's not over," Rylan called out.

He didn't have time to communicate to them everything that had happened, was still happening, but they accepted his order and took positions around the ballroom and in front of the shroudpool, guarding them.

Rylan returned his attention to Everly. "You have to stay strong, okay? You always were the strongest of us all. No matter what happened, you'd always keep going, keep trying. I know you can get through this. You have to, because I'm not strong enough to lose you."

"I—" Everly's eyes went entirely round, and she reeled back in a panic.

She threw one hand out as though reaching for Rylan, but at the same time she scrambled away.

She cried, raggedly, "Lian said ... if you have to stop this, stop us ... use her sword. It might ..."

Her back arched so forcefully it threw her off her feet, and she hovered there, tipped backward in midair. Arms and legs jerked and twitched, bones cracking with the unnatural bends. Her hands balled into fists and her teeth bared.

"Fight it, Evie. Fight it!"

Shafts of light and darkness shot out from the cracks in her skin, and she bellowed. Jet black painted the lengths of her flying hair, streaking between the white.

Her cries pitched low then high, moans of pain that made Rylan want to throw himself forward into that maelstrom and hold her.

Then ribbons of night and day struck out. The owner of each reached for sustenance, any power that could give them an advantage.

Rylan flipped backward, splashing into the pool of Bane blood. Something sharp scraped his leg—a long blade, crackling with energy.

Lian's sword.

The tendrils were almost on him. He snatched the blade out of the pool in a stream of flying red droplets, and his vision blanked out.

Rylan swung the sword blindly, body thrumming with adrenaline. It made contact, passing slower for a moment, as though cutting through a stream of sand.

There was a glassy tinkling of small objects smashing near his feet.

What? He threw the sword high into the air, gaining brief seconds of clarity.

The tendrils of the Infuscur and Coruscare had backed off but approached again. Two small crystals in opposite shades lay smashed at his feet, and a tiny swirl of each energy clung around his legs. He tried to stumble back from the broken essences of the creatures, but they slid in through his pores in a sensation that rattled his spine.

The sword arched and came back down, and he caught it. His heart raced, and blacked-out vision turned gray, streaked through with dark and light streamers, rushing toward him.

With a cry, he lashed the sword out again, swinging it like a bat. It hit those streams, slicing through again.

Sparkles of light and shadow spun across his grayed-out sight, landed a long distance away, smashed again.

Rylan screamed through gritted teeth. The Infuscur and Coruscare kept reaching for him, relentless in their efforts to strengthen themselves.

He could see them now. That's all he could see, with the sword hilt clenched in his fist. And every time he cut them, he was spreading them farther. Some had already absorbed into him.

Is that what's letting me see them?

He didn't know what the other consequences might be. The pieces were tiny. Much smaller fragments than the pieces that Everly had taken in one at a time.

The attacks kept coming, and Rylan swiped and slashed, chipping away. More pieces fell at his feet. Some lay unbroken. Others flew far out of his field of view.

He had no idea this sword had the power to cut through those tendrils. He wondered how Lian seemed to know.

Sweat poured down Rylan's neck and chest. His arms

burned, shoulders aching from fighting back the never-ending assault. He went onto one knee, unable to stand as he put all his strength into keeping the creature's whipping strikes at bay.

And then, the light and dark that filled his vision withdrew.

The strands were so much thinner now, and tangled in on each other, wrenching and wrestling. They zoomed away, and Rylan dared to let the sword's hilt roll out of his hand onto the ground.

The tendrils of the beings slurped back into Everly's body, fighting each other all the way. A burst of solid darkness expanded around her, then shrunk away. Then a glow of pure white, in and out, like a heartbeat.

Thu-thump. Darkness.

Thu-thump. Light.

Between each, the cracks on Everly's skin split wider. She raised higher and higher into the air.

Darkness. Light. Darkness. Light.

Then nothing. And she fell.

On stiff, aching legs, Rylan pushed into a run. Ankles twisted over the uneven ground. He stumbled, righted himself, and reached out. Everly slammed into his arms.

The weight from the fall brought Rylan cracking down onto his knees, but he held her up.

He wouldn't let her fall. He wouldn't let her hit the

ground.

Sparkling pieces of the opposing gods littered the rubble, and he couldn't let her body break the shards and absorb them again.

She let out a soft, breathy grunt.

Rylan shifted his hold on her to tilt her head toward him, resting it against his chest. "Hey, hey, you still with me?"

"Uh-hm." Her eyelids fluttered, and strained open.

The cracks across her skin that flickered with white and black changed before Rylan's eyes. The glow of energies faded, stuttered out. But the cracks remained. A flush of red tinged their edges, and blood oozed in to fill the space.

"I can't ... can't feel anything," Everly said, sounding like she spoke around a swollen tongue. "Does it mean they're gone?"

Rylan nodded, even though he didn't know. He had no way of knowing for sure, but he wanted to comfort her. There was no sign of the beings in her, and he hoped with every goosebump that spread over his skin that they were gone.

They are *gone*.

And Everly had been strong enough to pull through on the other side without them.

"You're amazing. You did it," he whispered and placed a soft kiss against her forehead. She turned away from him.

He pulled back to see why, but her head wobbled limply to the side, eyes blank and mouth parted.

"Evie?" He shook her gently, but she didn't respond. "Everly? Please, come on, wake up. Wake up!"

The cracks that dripped blood over her skin ... what if they were inside, too? He pulled her closer to his chest, holding her tight.

"Help! She needs help!"

She'd pulled through in spirit. She'd kept her *self*, her consciousness intact as gods warred within her, but now her body was giving in.

They had beaten two otherworldly deities of destruction only to have her die from mundane injuries. It wasn't fair. It wasn't right. If they only had Neri, something ... They had all given everything they had.

And now there was nothing left.

Chapter Twenty-Five

Everly was alone.

She opened her eyes to an endless field of flowers that changed from roses to daisies to tulips as she observed them.

I'm dreaming, she thought. Rain fell around her, but she remained dry. No clouds filled the sky, which shone a startling bright cyan.

The crowd of confused ghosts she'd gathered were gone.

"Lian?" Everly called, turning her eyes to every horizon. She narrowed her gaze to scan for signs of her dragon, or its dark twin.

No reply. No sign of the creatures.

They were gone, all of them. She'd finally rid herself of

the soul eater, and that made her feel as though she could float as effortlessly as its powers had allowed her to do.

They had beaten it. The Coruscare, the Infuscur, were defeated. She trusted the others to find a way to close the shroudpool. And it would be over.

The flowers around Everly were velvety and warm. Comforting. She wanted to curl up among them and sleep. Even in this bodyless existence inside her mind, she felt tired. As though falling asleep in a dream was all she wanted to do.

I'm fading away. That thought should have panicked her, but it only drifted slowly to her awareness, with a tinge of sadness. Rylan, Harper, Neri, Callan, Tammy, Cherry, and all the others, they would live, and go on without her. Out there, in the real world.

The very edges of her world, her self, seemed to be turning off. It wasn't light, or darkness that swallowed those places, but a sense of peace, gentle and cozy.

This is the end.

Part of her wished she could turn around and find Rylan there, or Lian, or even Zozo. That some fragment of their beings was still with her. She wanted to be with someone, have their support, as her life shut down around her. But also, in being so starkly alone, she felt a lightness she'd never known.

Still, she knew she wasn't *truly* alone. She knew out

in the real world, Rylan was right there with her, holding her. That if he could hold her body together with the sheer strength of his will, he would.

So that's what she had to do for him. She had to hold on.

But Everly could feel that her body was too far gone.

Maybe, maybe she could be healed.

Where was Neri? Everly hadn't seen her among the group of shadyrs who had guarded around her and Rylan. Maybe she was safe back at Howell House, or somewhere with Harper. A cold worry wormed through Everly. She hoped they were okay.

All she could do now was try to stay okay herself, and hold onto life for a second longer, then another second, and another. As long as she could.

Ripping of flesh, sharp cries, an inhuman wail—the sounds of fighting came from behind Rylan.

Another eidolghast had emerged from the shroudpool. His friends worked to keep it away.

Rylan could barely lift his head to acknowledge the battle.

Everly lay deathly still in his arms.

That was all he could understand and couldn't

understand at the same time. His whole life he'd just wanted to keep her safe. Whether that desire came from him or the Coruscare's bond with him, he wasn't sure. He didn't care. But even if she was far away, as long as she was safe, he could survive.

He'd only just allowed himself to want more. He still wanted her to be safe, but he also wanted *her*. To be near her, to love her.

He would have done anything to save her, but it wasn't enough.

The others yelled nearby. He couldn't make out their words. An anger stirred that they were doing anything other than mourning. He knew it wasn't logical. He knew they were protecting him as he was paralyzed by grief. He knew there wasn't anything any of them could do to change the outcome.

Callan, Tammy, Cherry, Jasper, and Annabeth were among the voices he heard.

There are so few of us now ...

Had Callan noticed Lian's body lying crumpled nearby? What about Tammy, who had already suffered so much? Would this break her? Rylan squeezed Everly into him, pressing his forehead to hers as his tears dripped between them.

The ground shook in sympathy with his anguish, as though the very earth sobbed for those lost. Then a louder rumble caused the broken roof beams in front of Rylan to slide around on top of each other.

What's happening?

Rylan looked up, checking the horizon in case some gigantic eidolghast was about to crush them underfoot.

But the source of the shaking and grumbling earth seemed to come from across the room. A pile of broken bricks bulged from beneath. Like a lava bubble it grew, grew, and then burst in a spray of torn paper and cardboard. It rained across the destroyed ballroom like confetti.

A hole appeared, and from it, Rylan heard a voice.

"They're here! This is it!"

Harper? It couldn't be, could it? Rylan swallowed hard and his hands shook with a fresh flush of adrenaline.

The hole was large enough to drive a small car into. It angled at a smooth decline into the earth, lined with layers of brown corrugated board.

Bent low, Harper jogged out, with Neri and Barry right behind.

Rylan's throat closed up in disbelief.

Then he dragged in a breath and bellowed, "Here! Over here. We need you, now!"

Standing back up to full height, Harper saw him and Everly first. "Oh no!"

She crashed across the debris at a perilous pace, sliding and scrambling on her hands and knees when loose rubble knocked her feet out from under her. She reached them in seconds and turned her head between where Lian lay nearby, and where Rylan held Everly. Then she knelt close, casting her eyes over the bleeding cracks on Everly's skin.

Running her hand over Everly's forehead, then down to a pulse point on her neck, she said, "I think she's still holding on. That's my girl. Neri? Please, we need—"

Neri was already there. She didn't even wait for Harper to finish the request.

She started to sing. Her face furrowed in a frown that her wide-open mouth exaggerated as low, mourning notes emerged. The force of her voice vibrated through Rylan's body, right to his bones with a frisson that left him renewed.

Barry stepped up behind them, offering an awkward half-smile under worried eyes.

Rylan gaped at them in awe. "How? I thought we'd lost you."

Harper shuffled across the ground to Lian. "I thought so too. But we worked out that Barry has powers, like Neri, from being so close to the Coruscare crystal for so long."

She checked over Lian's crumpled body, moving the lifeless arms and head into a more comfortable position, frowning deeply all the while. She caught Rylan's eye for a second but didn't say anything more.

Barry shrugged bashfully, tilting his head to Harper. "T'was this lady here who helped me work it out, saying

I was the heart of the maze and all. Figured I'd have a go making a new maze on my own. I couldn't do exactly that, but we got enough space to keep ourselves safe, then started working out how to make an exit."

Harper crawled back. Deep lines were etched into her forehead and her eyes shone, glossy with tears.

"Is it working?"

Rylan checked the cracks in Everly's skin, but they didn't seem to be closing. He imagined them running deep into Everly's body, down through her organs, into her bones.

The reverberation of Neri's song ran through Rylan, and he only hoped it worked the same for Everly, that those healing notes hummed through her, finding every break, every pain, and knitted her back together.

"They're back?" Tammy cried as she stumbled over to them. Callan followed, both of them with clothing shredded and spattered in gore. Tammy gasped at the sight of Everly and Lian, and Callan pulled her into a hug which she didn't fight.

Callan gave Rylan a smile that seemed confident. "Neri fixed me up when I was cut down the middle. She's got this. It's going to be okay."

Rylan wasn't sure it was exactly the same, but he nodded in thanks. He was also far too aware of how Harper chewed her lips and sniffled away tears at regular intervals ever since checking on Lian.

She wrapped a hand around one of Everly's and leaned her head onto Neri's shoulder, humming in harmony to her tune.

Barry watched over the scene, running his hands down his long beard. "Sorry it was a while getting back to you all. Took me a bit to get the hang of how to go where we wanted to go, and even after that, took us a while to find where you were. Harper here was clear that was where we needed to be."

"I knew you guys would be getting into all kinds of danger without us." Harper half-smiled, then her body shook in a silent sob. "If only ..."

Neri's voice lilted and lifted, strumming notes in Rylan's heart as the fractures in Everly's flesh sealed.

He huffed a laugh of relief. "It's working, she's healing."

As though zipping closed, the bleeding gashes turned into fine, cobweb-like scars across her skin. Her pupils moved beneath closed eyelids, then peeled open in a burst of light.

Her whole body glowed a warm, golden glow of a sunny day, and she lifted weightlessly from Rylan's cradling arms.

Gasping a deep breath, she turned upright, black-and-white-streaked hair hovering around her face as she took them all in with wide-awake eyes. Then she lowered back to the ground beside Rylan and the light dulled away again.

"Are you ...? Was that ...?" Rylan reached for Everly, wanting to know with his hands that she was real, back together, that she was herself.

Had he missed one of the crystals? Had the Coruscare survived and taken over again? Why was she still glowing?

She caught his hands in hers and smiled, though her eyes remained sad. "I'm okay. I'm me, just me. Everything ... everyone else is gone."

Her voice cracked over the word 'everyone.' "I guess not all the powers went with them though."

Rylan's voice was barely a whisper, as though his question could break the illusion of a reality he could barely believe. "How do we know it's really you?"

Everly smirked. "On a scale from one to smuggling me your uneaten lunch in third grade because you were too scared to let your mom know you didn't like her sandwiches, how embarrassing of an anecdote do you want?"

Rylan laughed as relief and wonder burst from his lungs. "I'd forgotten that. But that wasn't really why I did it. I just wanted to make sure you were eating properly."

Everly's eyebrows lifted. She pouted and squeezed his fingers in hers.

"Of course you did."

"You probably still have powers like Neri and Barry still have powers." Harper pushed in over their clasped hands, throwing her arms around Everly's shoulders.

"Seriously though, you've got to stop scaring me like this. I missed a bunch, so I have no idea what you've just gone through, but as long as you're here, and whole, and still my goddess of a best friend, we'll work it out."

"I'm good," Everly murmured through Harper's hair. "It's like, for the first time in my life I'm not carrying the weight of that monster. I feel ... light."

"Told you all she'd be all right," Callan said.

Tammy play-punched him in the side. "Insufferable optimist."

"Adorable pessimist," he countered.

Behind them, Neri still sang. Her voice grew ragged and racked with sobs.

She paused to draw in a long breath, and whispered, "Why isn't Lian waking up? She should have woken up too."

Then she returned right back to her song, louder again.

Harper pulled away from Everly, her bronze skin paling, lips moving but words not coming through.

Rylan knew what she was trying to say but couldn't.

There was no coming back for Lian.

Harper had no way of knowing why, what Lian had done, why her body lay prone. Yet when Harper had checked her for life, it was clear she'd found none.

Everly understand too. Her face crumpled as she looked

to him.

Rylan shook his head. "The Bane was destroyed. I'm sorry."

Everly stuttered in a breath. "The Coruscare is gone. Even if we had the Bane, I don't think she's ... I don't think there's any way to get her back, if she even still exists at all."

Harper frowned at their conversation, then moved closer to Neri, wrapping her arms around her and shushing her softly.

"What happened? What do you mean?" Callan asked, his voice hard.

"Lian's gone," Harper said gently.

Tammy's eyes widened. "*Gone* gone? There's got to be something we can do, she can do."

She pointed at the still singing mermaid girl.

Harper shook her head, pulling Neri in tight. "It's too late. I'm sorry."

Neri's song cut off with a guttural sob.

Callan ran his hands back through his hair then folded over, crouched down with his head on his knees. Tammy stood stock-still, but her body flickered, phasing in and out.

Rylan and Everly's hands were still wrapped around each other, and Everly squeezed tight. He should offer some words of comfort, for her, for the others, but he didn't have the strength left in him.

Would it have been better if it had been him instead

of Lian? It should have been that way. Everyone else here would mourn him less than her. She had been a protector and mentor to so many who had no one else.

Rylan had missed too many years of her courage and care due to his stubbornness, blaming her for something that was never her fault. And even still, when it came to it, Lian had put his life before hers. Even when he had abandoned her, she had remained his mother to the very end.

Getting Everly back, and Harper and Neri, was a win greater than he'd dared hope, but loosing Lian was a loss he couldn't fathom, one full of shame and regret.

Rylan wasn't sure how such conflicting feelings could exist within him at the same time. Relief and joy clashed against sorrow, and he wondered if this was how Everly had felt when gods of light and darkness fought within her. As though the riot of emotions swirling at his core could eat him away from the inside out.

"I'm so sorry. This is my fault," he murmured.

"No. I'm done with that. This isn't your fault, or mine, or anyone here. You can't pick through a sequence of events full of moments out of your control to find the one time your action might have changed things *if* you had known the future." Everly sat back, snorting a breath.

"You can't think like that. You can't live like that. It's not that moment that matters, it's your intentions in every other moment. You *try*. Isn't that what you told me once? You try to fix things. You try to make things better. You are the light in this world." Everly held his gaze with the intensity of eternity before addressing the others. "All of you are."

Harper nodded firmly, smiling through streaming tears.

At a distance, Annabeth stepped closer, awkwardly. She was breathing heavily and wiped sweat from her temples. "Um. I know this isn't a good time, I'm sorry. But we still have a massive shroudpool over here, and there are still ghasts spilling through."

She gestured behind her, where Cherry and Jasper, along with a dozen other shadyrs, finished off a vasmire.

Rylan nodded slowly. He had to keep moving. They had to finish this. For Lian, for everyone they had lost. He had to try.

He got to his feet, pulling Everly up with him as though their hands were fused together. Annabeth watched them, then scuttled closer over the debris.

"Is that? It is!" She reached down near Everly's feet and pulled the Swallower out from a hole between splintered timber.

Everly shook her head. "The Coruscare is gone. I don't know if the power I still have will get that to work."

Rylan squeezed her hands. "You can try."

Everly bit her lip and nodded.

Annabeth examined the orb, rolling it like a basketball between her palms. "I've got a little something to put into it now too. If Tammy remembers enough of the ritual, if she can guide us, we might have a chance."

Tammy remained where she'd been standing before, unmoving, but solid. She blinked at them as though just taking in the conversation.

Then her expression firmed into a snarl. "Let's shut this ghast-forsaken portal down."

Chapter Twenty-Six

Every moment of the day when Blaise had fallen into the shroudpool was burned into Tammy's memory.

Like a hot brand on her consciousness, she remembered every word, every action, from having relived the moments over and over internally for years. As though that could somehow have changed the outcome. She never thought those painful visages would be good for anything other than fueling the guilt she thought she deserved.

As she crouched beside Annabeth, sounding out the words of the spell Blaise had tried, her heart beat strong and fierce with purpose. They *would* close this shroudpool.

She only wished Blaise could be there to see it.

Annabeth translated the words Tammy only knew by sound into words she knew from her studies of ancient shadyr linguistics. She scrawled them down with a pen and scrap of paper she'd scrounged from somewhere, while the rest of the team fought back monsters around them.

Clothing and armor hung shredded from the shadyrs and the range of forms they took. All were spattered with blood in dark reds, greens, and black. Neri sat with Tammy and Annabeth too, safe within the ring of shadyrs.

Neri's singing had attracted some eidolghasts back to where they'd entered this world, and still more came through the portal.

Neri's singing didn't bring back Lian.

Lian had been such a solid, ever-present support for Tammy in recent years that she couldn't believe she was gone. She couldn't imagine going back to a home without her, without Rush, even damned Denny.

Would Birdie miss them all too? The thought of the old pup searching the house for them in confusion almost toppled Tammy into a pit of despair.

Was Callan hurting as much as her? Or more? Tammy screwed her eyes closed, pushing the grief away. There would be time to grieve later. Lian's wasn't the only body on that battlefield, and there would only be more if they didn't get the damned shroudpool closed.

With the piece of true shadyr bone embedded into her arm, Annabeth thought she'd be able to make the ritual work. Tammy's heart ached to know that even if things hadn't gone terribly wrong, the spell would never have worked for her and Blaise.

They just didn't have the magic. They had repeated the spell and ritual over and over and over that day to no effect. It was only when Blaise's parents arrived that anything happened.

It was Kole's presence that activated the Swallower, knocked Blaise into the portal, and left that shroudpool dormant from the half-completed ritual. Tammy knew why now—Kole's dark magic, which had caused so much pain and loss.

At least they could use what they'd learned to try to end this.

The smashing, scrabbling sounds of fighting eased. The current wave of eidolghasts were defeated. More shadyrs had joined them around the shroudpool.

Many had ignored Lian's orders to clear out to somewhere safe. Now that the gods of the Everdark were no longer clashing in the sky, the shadyrs were coming together with a glint of hope in their eyes.

Everly glowed, unwrapping a tendril from a defeated weroth.

Harper yanked her sword free. "Really glad you got to keep some powers."

Everly snorted softly. "Feels like a decent consolation prize for having to host a soul eating deity most of my life."

Callan stretched out his back, wolfish snout wrinkling. "If this isn't over soon, I think my bones are going to grind themselves to dust with overuse."

Everly floated back to the ground, and they came over to Tammy, Annabeth, and Neri.

"Watch out," Rylan said, pulling Everly to the side by her arm.

Tammy followed his gaze to see a piece of unbroken crystal there.

Callan watched with a funny expression on his face. "Sooo, aah, if some of those bits of crystal did break on or near you, should that be a concern? Asking for a friend."

Tammy eyed him with a frown. Did he get hit, too? A bright, sparkling chunk had smashed against her shoulder earlier. It was a worry, but on the scale of all the current worries, she'd ranked it fairly low for now.

"Yeah, I have a friend who'd like to know too," Cherry said.

"Is that me? Am I the friend?" Jasper said.

Annabeth put her hand up without looking away from the words she had written. "I got done as well."

Rylan sighed and rubbed his forehead. "So, everyone then? At least a few of each kind broke near me. I don't know what it means, but so far I'm not feeling the urge to either eat or obliterate any souls."

Still catching her breath, Harper put her hands on

her hips. "Are you guys telling me that magic powers were raining from the sky and I missed out?"

Everly looked to her feet as she stepped over another piece. "Personally, I don't want even a little bit of those things in me again. But they're small. The Coruscare and Infuscur are so broken up and spread out, hopefully they won't have any influence over you. Be careful though, just in case."

"Aw, I was kind of hoping I'd get some of those cool light whips." Cherry flung his hands out as though slinging a rope. He flicked one, then the other, then a bright spark glittered across his fingertips.

"Holy shit." He plunged his hands into his pockets and froze in place.

"What didn't you understand about being careful?" Everly scolded.

"All right, I think I'm ready to try this," Annabeth said, standing up, her eyes still going over the words of the spell. "Swallower in the middle, right at the base of the Shroudpool. Then get clear, I guess."

"Want me to try anything? I'm not sure whether the powers I have left will work now they aren't from the Coruscare itself," Everly offered.

Annabeth shrugged. "Let me try the spell first and we'll see how we go."

Rylan scooped up the orb and put it into place. They

all moved back and watched as Annabeth began chanting the words.

The hairs up the back of Tammy's neck stood on end and a warm hum filled the air as though the words lay thick throughout it.

Tammy mouthed along to the spell silently. The Swallower wobbled on the ground, shuddering on its own. Shadows danced across the surface of the portal. Annabeth reached the end of the incantation, and nothing else happened.

"Ugh. I can feel it. I can feel it almost working, but I don't have enough power. That one little bone from my necklace isn't cutting it." She rubbed a hand over the bandage on her arm, frowning. "It also feels like, I don't know, the spell is trying to draw from something else inside me. But it's still not enough."

"The Coruscare," Rylan said, his eyes on Everly. "It managed to activate the Swallower, to use it against the Infuscur."

She nodded. "And it was the Infuscur that made it in the first place. I'd guess either of them would have the power for this. They're gone now though, at least from me."

Everly chewed her lips for a moment. "But maybe all the smaller bits combined could be enough to give the spell the boost it needs."

"Okay, anyone that got hit with a crystal, gather

in," Rylan hollered and waved them together, close to Annabeth. Callan moved beside Tammy.

With questioning eyes, he laced his fingers into hers. She squeezed back in reply. Cherry and Jasper moved in as well. A few other shadyrs from around the ruined ballroom joined them, confusion twisting their faces, but willing to follow orders.

Everly, Harper, and Neri stood at their backs, keeping guard.

The group linked hands, and Annabeth spoke the words again. This time, when Tammy mouthed along, she did so with a loud, strong voice.

The ground trembled, and the air grew stifling, heavy in Tammy's throat. Her vision wavered and something inside her ignited. A hot spark of power, flaring into flame.

The Swallower shifted, rolled, righted itself, and flew into the air.

It hovered there for a moment, right in the middle of the shroudpool.

With a cacophony of booms, the small orb exploded outward. It grew larger and larger, engulfing the shroudpool entirely in a green web. Pressure sent air blasting around them. Tammy and Annabeth shouted the words over the deafening rush of wind and flying debris. And the Swallower grew larger.

It expanded out, right toward where Tammy and the

others stood, rushing toward her face.

On instinct, Tammy thrust her hands forward as though to hold it back. Her blackened fingers met the intricate webbing of the artifact. Reality flickered in and out. With a thunderous crack, the crystalline web stopped.

The beats of a million broken hearts pulsed beneath Tammy's touch. A throbbing, slurping sensation. The inky blackness that stained her skin flowed into the orb, absorbing into it, and darkening its surface.

Tammy cried out the final words of the incantation. The Swallower shuddered, rippled, and rushed back in on itself. The implosion pulled Tammy forward, onto her hands and knees, and the others fell around her.

As the sphere grew smaller, the place where the shroudpool had been became clear again. And it was gone.

We did it. We did it! Oh, Blaise ... Tammy huffed a soundless, teary laugh as she stared at her pale, normal hands.

The Swallower retracted back to its original size, warping and twisting crookedly where black lines marred it. A howl of screaming monsters emerged as it split down the middle and fell, cracking into two halves.

Callan flopped over on his back across the rubble and gazed up at Tammy with tired eyes and a laughing mouth. "I thought for a second we were going to be taken out along with the shroudpool. You ... you are so fucking amazing."

Tammy huffed, and wiped her eyes with pale, peachy fingers. She couldn't stop staring at them. Her tainted, Everdark-cursed hands were gone.

She was no longer cursed. Maybe she never had been. Maybe she could finally accept that. She broke her gaze away from her fingers to smile back at Callan.

At those lips that had *kissed* her. *He had kissed her.* Maybe she could even start accepting *more*.

Above them, the sky seemed to melt. The unnatural darkness that clung there dripped down like rain, revealing bright beams of a flaming sunset.

"It's done. It's over. It's really over." Everly sat sprawled on the ground, arms wrapped around Harper and Neri on either side.

"And we won. Can you even believe it?" Cherry laughed.

Tammy giggled along with him, and sobbed, and smiled, and sniffed. Callan reached up and pulled her down beside him.

She stared at the lightening sky that showed off all its best colors in defiance of the nearing night.

They had won, and yet they'd lost so much. The surviving victors sat, tangled and wrapped together in a messy bundle of laughter and tears, amid the broken pieces of those who didn't last to see victory.

Tammy scrapped a handful of crumbled brick into

her hands. This place that had once been her home lay in ruins. "For a win, there's not much left."

Callan's chest rose and fell in a sigh. "As bad as the Darkfreys could be, they were a large part of what protected the world from darkness overtaking it. A lot of that protection is now gone."

"Looks like that Swallower thingy is busted too," Cherry sighed.

"But we're still here," Tammy said.

"We are still here," Everly replied.

Her face was smeared with dust and streaked with tears, and her now black and white hair hung in a tangle. Her smile spoke of a deep inner peace that sent a surge of longing through Tammy. She wanted that peace, too. She could almost taste it, on the horizon.

Everly turned her face to the sky, and orange light set her aglow. "And you don't have to be a Darkfrey, to fight against the darkness. You just have to try."

CHAPTER TWENTY-SEVEN

"Neri's lost her voice," Harper called out over the makeshift triage field.

The moon hung full and bright, stalked by the shadows of clouds across the night sky.

Everly straightened, cracking her back, strained from hours bent over carrying stretchers. Hours spent sorting the bodies of those who could be saved from those who couldn't. Their faces would haunt her nightmares, but the work had to be done.

Neri's song lilting across the blood-spattered lawns of the estate grounds was all that had kept Everly going, all that had revived so many of the shadyrs who were too close to joining the list of couldn't-be-saved.

The silence snuck up on Everly. She'd noticed Neri's

voice growing hoarse, quieter, as the night went on, but she'd had so much to focus on herself that she missed the moment the singing stopped.

Beside her, Rylan shifted from the strong, werewolf-cross-dragon form he'd been using to free survivors from under fallen rubble back to his normal self.

There weren't many eidolghasts around anymore. Any surviving ghasts had fled the battle to terrorize another day. Although a few monstrous corpses lay scattered nearby, Rylan said it was as though the small pieces of Coruscare energy in him let him still choose his forms as he pleased. That was going to be interesting for the other shadyrs who got a dose of the soul eater as well.

"Come on, let's go check in with the others," he said to Everly, pushing a strand of hair back from her face.

She nodded numbly. If Neri was out of action, that was going to slow things down. They needed to work out what was next.

Sitting on a low garden wall, Neri took small sips from a water bottle as Harper knelt beside her and rubbed her back.

"You did so, so well. It's okay," Harper cooed.

"I ... I want to ..." Neri's voice was like the soft scratch of fingernails over bark.

Harper leaned in and pressed her forehead to Neri's. "I know. You've done so much already. You've saved so many lives."

To the side, a team of shadyrs had already begun taking over the triage and treatment. One looked up from his patient. He wore a Darkfrey hoodie and had the all-boney-joints appearance of a boy in his late teens.

"We can take over from here. I mean, we don't exactly have musical healing magic, but if that option isn't available anymore, we'll make do with sutures if we have to."

An older woman frowned at Everly and Rylan. "You guys are still here? Go and take a break. Consider that doctor's orders. You're relieved."

With a grunt of frustration, she returned to flashing a light into the eyes of a boy that was way too young to have been involved in the fight.

With another huff she said, "Thank you, for everything. But also get the Everdark out of here."

Everly stared at their surroundings. There was still so much to be done, but she knew she couldn't push on any longer without her body giving in entirely.

With a nod to Rylan, they followed Harper and Neri away. Somewhere along the path through the grounds, Callan and Tammy joined them, then Cherry, Jasper, and Annabeth.

Getting from the estate to Crowea's bar went by in a blur.

Exhaustion made the edges of Everly's sight hazy, and

often when she blinked, she was surprised she had the energy to open her eyes again.

She wanted to find a bed and sleep for a million years, to dream dreams unhaunted by any other soul.

She wanted to find a place to sleep beside Rylan, holding him in the real world instead of her sleeping mine.

But Rylan told her they had to go and toast those they'd lost.

"It's shadyr tradition. It's what we do. Even after the longest of nights."

On the way, they saw shadyrs busy trying to put the Humpty-Dumptyed town back together. News had gotten out of the shroudpool closing. Now everyone was working together on damage control.

The cleaning crews had done a surprisingly efficient job of clearing the broken monster bodies off sidewalks. Everly didn't think there was much they could do about the townsfolk though. For many, it would have been confirmation of what they always suspected. Others would continue to live on in denial.

It was a strange weather event, escaped dangerous animals, gas leak, anything to avoid knowing that monsters truly crept in the shadows of their home.

When they reached The Crow's Nest, Everly was glad to see the establishment still standing, although there were streaks of blood marring the heavy door. As they stumbled into that warm space filled with jangly clutter, eyes turned to them, and a silence fell.

Almost every table and seat was filled. Battle-bloodied and bent, shadyrs clung to their drinks and watched as Everly, Rylan, Harper, Neri, Callan, Tammy, Cherry, Jasper, and Annabeth stepped inside. The Howell team. The runts. The outcasts. The blivs and freaks.

A chair scraped the floor as a man lunged to his feet, raising his glass. Then an avalanche of sound hit them as the rest of the room followed.

At the bar, Crowea beat her fist on the bar twice.

Her voice boomed out, "The dark must fall!"

Thump thump, feet and hands across the room beat a reply.

"So the sun may rise again," all chorused.

Only Everly, Harper, and Neri didn't answer the call. She'd heard those words before, when they toasted Denny with warm beer a lifetime ago.

Rylan bowed his head to Everly. "This is what we say when a brace loses someone in battle. We will fight to hold back the darkness, in hope of a better day."

Tammy sniffled and pressed a hand to her chest. "Both outside, and in."

Everly nodded, and echoed the reply, "So the sun may rise again."

They approached the bar as the other patrons returned

to their seats.

Crowea had a row of shot glasses lined up, filled with clear alcohol. She pulled another bottle and dripped a single drop of thick, black liquid into each. With a swipe of a lighter she caught them all aflame.

"Drink your sorrows, babies. Take them in and know them well. They will grow lighter with time."

Rylan took one and blew out the flame. "To Lian. The best mother and leader any of us could have asked for, even if it took me too long to realize it."

Everly reached hesitantly for a shot, and Crowea slid a glass with all clear contents her way with a wink. Everly took it, and when she tipped it back, found it to be water.

She returned a confused, thankful smile to Crowea, unsure when the barkeeper learned she wasn't much of an alcohol fan. The old witch smiled back knowingly, beneath wrinkled skin and the ghast-tooth embedded in her eye.

The others tipped their drinks back too, then placed the glasses on the counter for a refill. Crowea repoured them again as before.

Tammy lifted hers, staring at her pale fingers holding that glass.

"To Rush. She had more love, joy, and kindness in her than anyone in this world. She ... she ..." Tammy choked up.

"She wrote one heck of a spicey story," Harper added.

A man with a Viking's stature and well-groomed red

beard appeared next to them. His eyes were as red as his hair, tears streaming from them.

"She was too perfect for this world." He took a long mouthful from a pint-glass as they all drank.

"You knew her too?" Cherry asked.

His shoulders slumped forward as he nodded, then he walked away, sobbing into his cup.

Crowea moved along the bar to pour the same darkness-tinted shots for a group of three shadyrs who had just stumbled in. Everly squinted, and recognized Lucas. Him, Molly, and Benson. No Parker. Their faces were gray and drawn, especially Molly's, as she shook with silent tears under Lucas's arm.

Everly's sympathy swelled for the girl. She must have been a few years younger than Everly, trained her whole life as a Darkfrey.

She'd passed info back to them, info that kicked all of this off, but she no doubt thought she was doing the right thing. Told she was doing the right thing, along with all the other lies the Darkfreys had fed her through her entire life.

Everly couldn't find it in her to place blame. Punishing mistakes, casting people out, that was the Darkfrey way. If they wanted the sun to rise bright again tomorrow, things had to change. Everly's shot glass of water was empty, but when she caught Lucas's eye, she raised it to him as they drank their sorrows. He nodded solemnly in return.

A table cleared and Cherry shooed them toward it. "Go grab some seats, I'll get some more drinks."

Everly dropped into the low lounge. Her muscles ached from scalp to heels. Harper sank in beside her with a dramatic sigh. Her shirt—Everly's shirt—was pockmarked with tears and spotted in blood.

"I let you wear my clothes for one day and you've gone and ruined them," Everly said, half-smiling.

Harper's eyelashes fluttered in confusion as she looked at herself. "I put this on today? How was that this morning? Also, that's the last time I'm going to let you guys dress me."

She put on a mocking voice. "What's the worst that can happen if you don't put on your makeup? The end of the world?"

"I mean, technically it didn't end," Callan said.

Harper dismissed him with a wave. "Only 'cause we saved it. Still, every time I get dressed now, I have to consider, are these the clothes I'm going to be facing apocalyptic disaster in?"

The lounge was a two-seater, but Neri squeezed in next to Harper, bringing them all close together. Rylan took an ottoman to Everly's other side, and Callan and Tammy took armchairs across from them. Annabeth pulled over a couple more chairs for herself, Cherry, and Jasper, who were still at the bar. Groans of relief sounded all around.

"Let's not have any more end of the world situations

any time soon, okay?" Callan sighed.

Tammy tsked. "Spoilsport."

There was a life, a smile in Tammy's eyes that Everly hadn't seen before. Like a sun rising strong from the darkness within the girl. Everly desperately wished Lian could have been there to see it. To see that they were okay, and would be okay.

Her voice sounded quiet against the clinking glasses and mournful toasts around the room. "I wish I could have kept Lian with me. That I didn't lose her along with the Coruscare. It would have been nice to have her there in my dreams, to be able to tell her that everything turned out, that we're all here. Thanks to her."

Rylan leaned with his elbows on his knees, head hanging, bouncing in small nods.

Then he looked up, mouth twisted in the barest of smiles. "Maybe she is still out there. A little piece of her in everybody who now has a piece of the Coruscare in them."

Tammy lifted her hands to cover her mouth as tears flushed her eyes. "Do you think so?"

Callan held Rylan's gaze, jaw clenched. "I like the sound of that. I'll look for her, in my dreams."

Tammy nodded enthusiastically. "Me too. Even if she's just a feeling. Even the smallest essence, I'd be honored to carry her. She carried all of us, gave us so much, and accepted us when no one else did."

Everly reached for Rylan's hand and squeezed it hard. He tangled his fingers in hers and didn't let go.

Cherry and Jasper stood by the table, carrying glasses and two jugs filled with colorful liquid, leaves, and flowers.

Cherry stood solemnly, staring at Tammy.

"I like the sound of that, too. That Lian is still with us. It's a comfort," he said softly as he shared out cups. "I found my parents tonight."

Callan sat up straight. "Found them, how?"

Cherry shook his head. "They didn't make it."

"Oh no, I'm so sorry," Harper said, reaching out to him as he took a seat.

He held her hand for a moment, then shrugged. "Yeah, it's ... rough. But it also made me realize how long I'd been hung up on hoping for their approval. Even after I'd scolded Jasper for seeking approval from the wrong people."

He twisted a wry smile at Jasper as he took the seat beside him, still somehow looking neater than all the rest of them in his beige cardigan. "All the love and acceptance I needed was here already, and damned if I ever needed anyone's approval to be myself anyway."

Jasper side-eyed him. "The audacity of fitting so much wisdom into such a handsome body."

"Like you can talk." Cherry leaned in until their shoulders pressed together.

"Here, cheers to love and acceptance," Harper said,

pouring a drink and handing it to Cherry.

"The pinker one is a mocktail. For the kids," Cherry said, passing the cup along to Tammy.

"How very dare," she hissed, and passed it along to Everly.

Everly chuckled and sniffled as she took the drink happily. Harper poured from the other jug for everyone else except Neri, who chose non-alcoholic as well.

Mostly through short whispers, pointing, and meaningful looks, since her voice still hadn't returned. Harper handed Neri the glass with a smile, and their fingers entwined for a moment, causing a blush across Harper's cheeks that Everly didn't miss.

Everly raised her eyebrows when Harper turned her way.

Harper bit her lip and leaned in close to whisper to Everly. "She likes me. Like, *likes* me."

Everly put an arm around Harper and pressed her head against hers, cheek to cheek, whispering back, "Of course she does. Who wouldn't?"

A slim man in an expensive business suit approached their table. "Um, hi, I'm not sure if I'm in the right place. I'm here for Rushelle. I'm her partner, and was told this was where to be, since ..."

He pulled a silk handkerchief from a pocket and dabbed his nose.

Cherry's eyes grew wide, and he looked across the room then back at the man. "Aah …"

The man followed his gaze. With a nod of recognition, he walked over to where the red-bearded man sat.

"Oookay, so while we were at the bar, this other dude said he was Rush's partner too," Cherry said, pointing across at a big guy in a leather biker's jacket, sitting beside the Viking man.

They both stood up to their imposing heights as the businessman approached them.

"Are we about to have a situation here?" Rylan asked.

The three men moved closer together, then arms went out and wrapped around each other in a sobbing huddle.

"Holy shit," Harper hissed, staring shamelessly.

"You don't think …" Tammy said.

Harper nodded. "That our Rush was living her own real-life reverse harem? I am definitely thinking that right now."

"Complete with all the spicey scenes," Tammy laughed.

"Can I imagine you imagining all those spicy scenes?" Callan asked from behind his drink.

Tammy gave him a withering look. "Someone call an exorcist, because I think Callan's channeling Denny."

"Dick pics!" Harper exclaimed suddenly and broke down into hysterics.

She laughed so hard the couch shook.

"Um, are you okay?" Everly asked.

Harper gasped in breaths between her laughter. "Denny said ... that's what he sent ... Alexis ... and Mordan was monitoring ... Can you imagine?"

She wheezed, tears of mirth pooling under her eyes.

Everly put a hand over her mouth, frozen as she tried to process that thought and the various levels of disgust, absurdity, and tragedy that came with it.

"I really *don't* want to imagine," Tammy groaned.

"I'm with you. Team 'Let's not imagine things more horrifying than the Everdark'." Everly snorted and leaned forward from the lounge with her hand up to high-five Tammy.

Tammy hesitated for a moment, then lifted a pale hand to slap against Everly. As their palms met, a flash of light glowed around them.

Tammy gasped back, folding her hands against her chest.

Everly snorted again. "Kidding. Sorry. Couldn't resist."

"Oh my ghast! My hands mightn't be cursed anymore but they can still strangle people just fine!" Tammy huffed, but a smile broke across her lips. "You're lucky I can't teleport away anymore, or I would have made you do pickup."

Callan leaned across onto the arm of his chair, smiling at Tammy. "I'm happy you don't vanish anymore. I like it much better when you're right here with me."

"Gross," Tammy grumbled, rolling her eyes, but she leaned across onto the arm of her chair too and planted a kiss on his cheek.

"I knew it!" Harper let out a hoot so loud someone across the bar dropped their drink. Cherry and Everly joined in, whistling and cheering.

Tammy sank back into her armchair, pulling her hood over her head. "Kill me now."

Laughter spilled across every lip as free as the tears from their eyes.

A round of drinks came over with thanks from Lucas, and then another round came from a group of Darkfreys at the bar, and then another.

Callan threw back a shot, then slumped, giggling hysterically. "I'm not sure if they are thanking us or trying to murder us with alcohol."

Everly went to pour herself another glass from the mocktail jug and found it empty. "And that's my cue to call it. I'm so exhausted."

"How exhausted are you?" Cherry hollered back like it was a pantomime.

Everly twisted her lips and put on an old-timey comic accent. "I'm so exhausted I feel like I've been to the Everdark and back and all I got for it was a lousy dark twin to the soul-eating god that possessed me."

Callan pointed a finger at her enthusiastically. "Oh! That happened! We did that! We went to the Everdark and back again!"

"To the Everdark and back again!" Tammy echoed, raising her drink.

Everly groaned melodramatically, resting her head on the lounge. "We're never getting out of here. I just want to go home."

Rylan scooched closer until they were sharing an armrest. He stared at the drink in his hands—one from earlier in the night, mostly untouched. "Where is home going to be for you now?"

Everly gaped at the question. She hadn't even started to think about what would be next.

She was free. Free of the Coruscare, and any obligations that came from hosting a dangerous supernatural creature from shadyr mythology. She could go home to her and Harper's apartment in the city. But *home* didn't feel like the right word for it anymore.

In Rylan's low-cast gaze, with long lashes lying over his high cheekbones, she could see so much of the boy she'd spent her whole life loving. His feelings were his own now, and so were hers, and she still loved him. With a yearning that she'd cross the Everdark again to satisfy.

"Home is wherever my family is. It's with the people I love," she said.

He looked at her from the side of his eyes.

"It's with you." She reached over the armrest, grabbing the torn body armor on his chest and turning him to face her.

Rylan's Darkfrey crest tattoo that lay over his heart was visible where the ripped armor hung loose, spattered with dust and blood. When Everly had first seen that tattoo in her dreams, she worried that Rylan had become nothing but a Darkfrey soldier.

Now, she could see it was a symbol of the best parts of him. His loyalty, his devotion to helping others, and his desire to make the world safer for those he loved.

"All the world is filled with monsters, of one kind or another. It's the good people you surround yourself with, the people you love that make it bright. That's you. It's always been you. I love you."

Rylan closed the gap between them, wrapping his hands into her black-and-white-streaked hair as their lips met.

They kissed each other with a hunger even the soul eater couldn't match. With a love that had held on, unrequited, all their lives.

And Everly glowed.

EPILOGUE

Nails slipped satisfyingly into the timber, and Everly smiled. Her new nail gun was making short work of framing up the replacement wall and window for her kitchen. It also felt good being able to buy the new things she needed, knowing that she wasn't going to be moving them all again somewhere else. This was home. For good.

And although she did break down crying when they gave her the 'family discount' at Pimey's Hardware, it was as much happiness as sorrow.

The rebuild was a big job, but she had the tools, and could do the work. Building supplies were in high demand for a while after *the incident*, as most Shroudhaven residents vaguely referred to it as.

Everly, Neri, and Harper had lived for a few weeks with the gaping hole tarped over, surviving on takeaway alone without a functioning kitchen. Everly loved every moment of it, sharing that home with them, even if the walls were broken.

They had cleared enough of the antiques store by then to create a living area in there, and the upstairs loungeroom she'd been camping on the couch in became a real bedroom for her. She'd even splurged on a brand-new king-sized bed, which she and Rylan had been putting to a lot of use.

She blushed at her own thoughts. If younger Everly could ever have known ...

A movement in the corner of her eye brought a low rise of anxiety washing over her. She inhaled slowly as she turned to see what it was. Even under the sparkling light of a rare, sunny day, Shroudhaven could still be dangerous. Not that her anxiety needed true danger to set it off.

The caramel flanks of the cougar she knew so well slunk around the corner of the fence and down the side path to the back of Everly's home.

"In broad daylight? You're getting bold." Everly returned to her work, punching in a couple more nails.

Zozo would find the food where she'd left it for him. Not that he needed it. He was looking noticeably rounder, and Everly knew that Neri—utterly obsessed with the cat—had been putting out extra food on top of his regular feedings.

Everly exhaled deeply as the spike in her anxiety settled.

Stepping back to check her build, she smiled. Anxiety was still a constant for her, but for now, she had it under control. Now that it wasn't tangled in the spirit of what she used to think of as her dragon.

Now she never had to worry about consuming souls again. Now she had a better understanding of events around and inside her. It would never be gone, but she had the tools, and could do the work.

Some days were harder than others as she healed through her trauma, but she found that she loved herself regardless. And she knew that the family she'd found accepted her too.

Her phone pinged, and Everly pulled it from the back pocket of her jeans.

Rylan: *I know you wanted to get lots done on the house today, but can you come up to the estate early? Got big news. Real big.*

Checking the time, she saw it was a couple of hours until she was expected there for training. She still struggled to get her head around the concept of being a teacher.

There wasn't a whole lot she felt she could teach, but then again, there wasn't exactly anyone more qualified. No one else had hosted the Coruscare except for her. Now that a few dozen shadyrs found themselves with at least a fragment of that being inside them, Everly had agreed to do what she could to share her experience with them.

Days had been spent combing the area around the final showdown to gather any unbroken pieces of the Coruscare and Infuscur.

One particularly large piece went to Barry, in hopes he could get his tunnel system back together again. Another was sent to the Crybel's Cove shadyrs for the lighthouse rebuild. The rest were locked away for safety. The full implications of hosting even small parts weren't known yet. Especially for the Infuscur.

Everly tapped out a reply: *OMW, <3 U*

Everly wondered what the big news could be, but it wasn't curiosity that had her downing her tools for the day. Any excuse to spend more time with Rylan was a good excuse.

Everly poked her head into the living room-slash-antiques-store area. "Hey, can I take the van for a bit?"

Harper emerged from the side room, dressed in a lacey Lolita dress, skin deathly pale, with a perfectly placed line of blood dripping from her mouth. "Sure, we'll be busy here for a while."

Some antiques Everly's dad had left her turned out to be surprisingly valuable, but nobody wanted anything from the 'room of cursed toys,' as Harper had dubbed it.

She and Neri decided to work on her haunted doll photoshoot she'd imagined when they first explored the untouched old rooms. Then they'd hire a skip bin and send the creepy playthings off for good.

Neri stepped out, camera hanging from a strap around her neck, brown curls bundled on her head. She wore the long cotton dress Lian had given her the night they'd brought her home from the lighthouse.

She wore it at least once a week. When Everly speculated that it was going to fall apart at the seams soon, Neri proclaimed she was going to learn how to sew. She had taken to learning new skills with a near-Harper-level of enthusiasm and dedication. Taking on being the photographer for Harper's shoots was her current mission.

"Do you think the lighting is working on these?"

Harper leaned in close to look at the camera screen and gasped.

"You have such a good eye." She pecked a kiss to Neri's cheek, and Neri's nose wrinkled happily as she turned and kissed Harper back.

"I'm going to get tooth decay around you two with these high sweetness levels."

Harper blew Everly a kiss. "Bye-eeeee! Don't get kidnapped and kick off an apocalypse again, kay?"

Everly chuckled. "I'll do my best."

Harper waved over her shoulder as she returned to looking at the camera. The tips of her fingers seemed to sparkle for a moment.

Everly did a double take and Neri let off another flash

from the camera, testing the reflections. Laughing at herself, Everly grabbed the campervan keys and headed out.

Managing to not get kidnapped and kick off an apocalypse, Everly drove in through the Darkfrey gates and up to the main building.

Only half the structures at the estate remained standing after the incident. A few more were so damaged they had been cordoned off, deemed unstable and requiring demolition at a later stage, but much of the other debris had been cleared.

All activities and dorms had been scaled back into the buildings that remained largely untouched. The shadyr community worked together to keep essential functions running. Things like patrols, cleaning crews, training, and schooling for the younger, far too frequently orphaned shadyrs.

All those who had defected to Howell House returned, including Annabeth, Cherry, and Jasper. Only Rylan, Callan, and Tammy remained at Howell House now, although they spent a large amount of time at the broken estate.

Callan had told Everly that Lian managed to start again from a broken place, to become something more when she'd lost almost everything, and he and Rylan intended to try to do the same. They took on leading roles in getting the estate and shadyr community back on track.

Everly knew Lian would be proud. Maybe she was, somewhere in her sons' dreams.

Although with Mordan gone and legalities a mess, there wasn't much they could do on a larger scale until questions of funding were answered.

Alexis Darkfrey's children, the only line surviving from Mordan, weren't even in their teens yet. Only a few hardcore Darkfrey fanatics treated them as heirs to the shadyr throne. Most others had been either directly or indirectly hurt by the Mesmans' dark magics and Mordan's choices, and were happy to work toward a new way of life for the shadyrs of Shroudhaven.

As Everly strode the long hall, she could feel the eyes of the portraits of famous shadyrs watching her.

It didn't surprise her to see their gaze shifting, actually following her with eerie accuracy as she passed by.

The estate wasn't the place it used to be, in more ways than one.

When the Bane had broken, it spilled tons of mixed, ancient eidolghast blood that had flowed, soaking into the ground and setting off a permanent, low-level beshadowing throughout the estate.

There were some early calls for evacuation, but the side effects seemed to have limited themselves to mild haunted house vibes.

It still sent a shiver down Everly's back.

Callan walked the hall toward her, shaking his head and laughing to himself.

"This is going to set off some risen hackles, big time," he said, chuckling some more. "You're not going to believe it. I can barely believe it myself."

"Should my hackles be rising? Are you going to clue me in or what?"

Callan smirked and shook his head. "I'll let Rylan have the honors. He's up in the meeting room to the right. I've got to go tell Tammy."

Everly found the room mostly from the stream of flustered men and women in suits filing out of it, sorting papers and gossiping between themselves. She waited for them to pass, then stuck her head through the doorway.

Rylan stood near a polished boardroom table, sorting a thick wad of papers into sections. He wore a similar bemused smile to his brother's.

"What in the Everdark is going on?" Everly moved forward, trying to catch a glimpse of meaning from the documents.

Rylan scooped them out of her view.

He came around to the front of the desk, leaning against it and patting the spot beside him for Everly to join him.

Everly rested her hip against the table and Rylan handed her a collection of clipped together papers off the top of the stack.

A wall of legalese met her eyes. "What is this?"

"A copy of the last will and testament of Mordan Darkfrey," Rylan explained. "Leaving his estate to his children Nilson and Alexis."

Everly nodded. That's what had been expected all along.

"So Nilson," Rylan handed her the next sheets, "he didn't have any kids, so they had a setup where his portion of the estate would go to Alexis and her children, to keep things in the Darkfrey line, of course."

"Okay, so Alexis's kids are the sole beneficiaries, we figured that already."

Rylan sighed and chuckled with the same breath. "Except then we get hit with the kind of chaos that only one special person was able to bring to the party. Denny."

Everly's face scrunched back in shock. "What?"

Rylan handed her another document, pointing at a date and entry down the page.

His body shook with contained laughter. "Alexis had her will changed in secret. She left everything to Denny."

"Nooo, what? I mean, she had that real ride-or-die thing going on with him in the end ... but *Denny*?" Everly stared at the name on the page as though the fleet of lawyers had somehow made a mistake.

She flipped the pages back and forth, but they were clear. "What ... what does that mean though, with Denny gone?"

Rylan's bemused mirth eased, and his chest stilled. A softer smile curled his lips as he handed her the next document.

"I was worried at first they were going to say it went back to Alexis. But as big of a jerk as the guy could be, he clearly knew who had his back at the end of the day. Not that he had much to leave, as far as he knew. I reckon he thought he'd only be leaving his RV ..."

Rylan pointed at the papers, and Everly gasped.

"Lian? But then—" Everly snatched the final document from Rylan's hands, leafing through for confirmation.

Rylan grew solemn and nodded. "Callan and me. She only added us on once we'd come home. Once she trusted us enough to continue the home she created at Howell House and not clear her family out in some twisted service to the Darkfreys. If all of this had happened a few weeks earlier, Callan would have got the lot."

Rylan huffed a bewildered laugh.

"The lot, as in, *the lot*?" Everly jumped to her feet and waved the papers at their surroundings.

"Yup."

Everly froze, hands still midair and papers crinkling.

Rylan winced. "Yeah. It's ... a lot. There you go. That's the big news. Honestly? Still in shock myself."

Everly lowered slowly back onto the desk and put the

wills down.

That *was* big news.

Plunging her hands into the pockets of her red bomber jacket, Everly tried to comprehend what it would all mean.

She couldn't imagine either Rylan or Callan ruling from on high as Mordan had, from his gilded office, commanding the army of shadyrs he thought he owned.

Just because the brothers owned the estate now, didn't mean they ruled it.

And that could make all the difference.

Looking up at Rylan, she smiled. "I think you are going to do wonders for the estate and all the shadyrs here."

Rylan shrugged. "I don't know. I mean, I know I want to help rebuild a home for shadyrs. There's so much work to do. And I want to help keep fighting back the darkness. That's such a huge part of me. But also, maybe I want to take a break from being a full-time soldier for a while. Find out what other parts of me there are."

"I am so on board for exploring your parts." Everly smirked. "But seriously, I think that sounds like a really good idea, finding yourself."

Rylan swept an arm around her waist and dragged her over in front of him, between his legs. "As long as I can find myself with you. Because I have a feeling that the me I find just wants to focus on making the most beautiful woman in at least two realms happy."

"Not being my protector?" Everly wrapped her arms around his shoulders.

"Like you need one," Rylan scoffed then leaned in close. "I'm happy just soaking in every bit of your light that I can, for every moment that I can."

Rylan buried his face into her neck, pressing warm lips into the dip of her collarbone and then running a trail of kisses to her ear.

A thrill of goosebumps chased after his touch, and Everly melted under his warm hands.

Before she lost all sense to his touch, she said, "You know I used to wish that we were soul mates, fated to be together. I'm glad that wasn't the case."

Rylan pulled back. "Ouch. Thanks?"

"Because it means we could *choose* each other. We didn't get here because of some unfightable destiny, but we're here because we fought *for* each other. Because we wanted it." Everly ran her fingers down Rylan's cheeks, staring into his warm, olive-green eyes that looked like home. "And I want you, more than anything."

Rylan's gaze sparkled. He picked her up around the waist, carrying her over to kick the door closed, then kissed her in a way that made her head spin with a rush of pleasure.

Of all the monsters and mysteries that had bombarded Everly since returning to Shroudhaven, nothing surprised her more than how she'd been able to find herself a home in that place.

That a house of tormented memories could grow warm again.

That abandoned fantasies of love could blossom into something better than she ever dreamed.

That with so much darkness, so too came a glorious light.

THE END

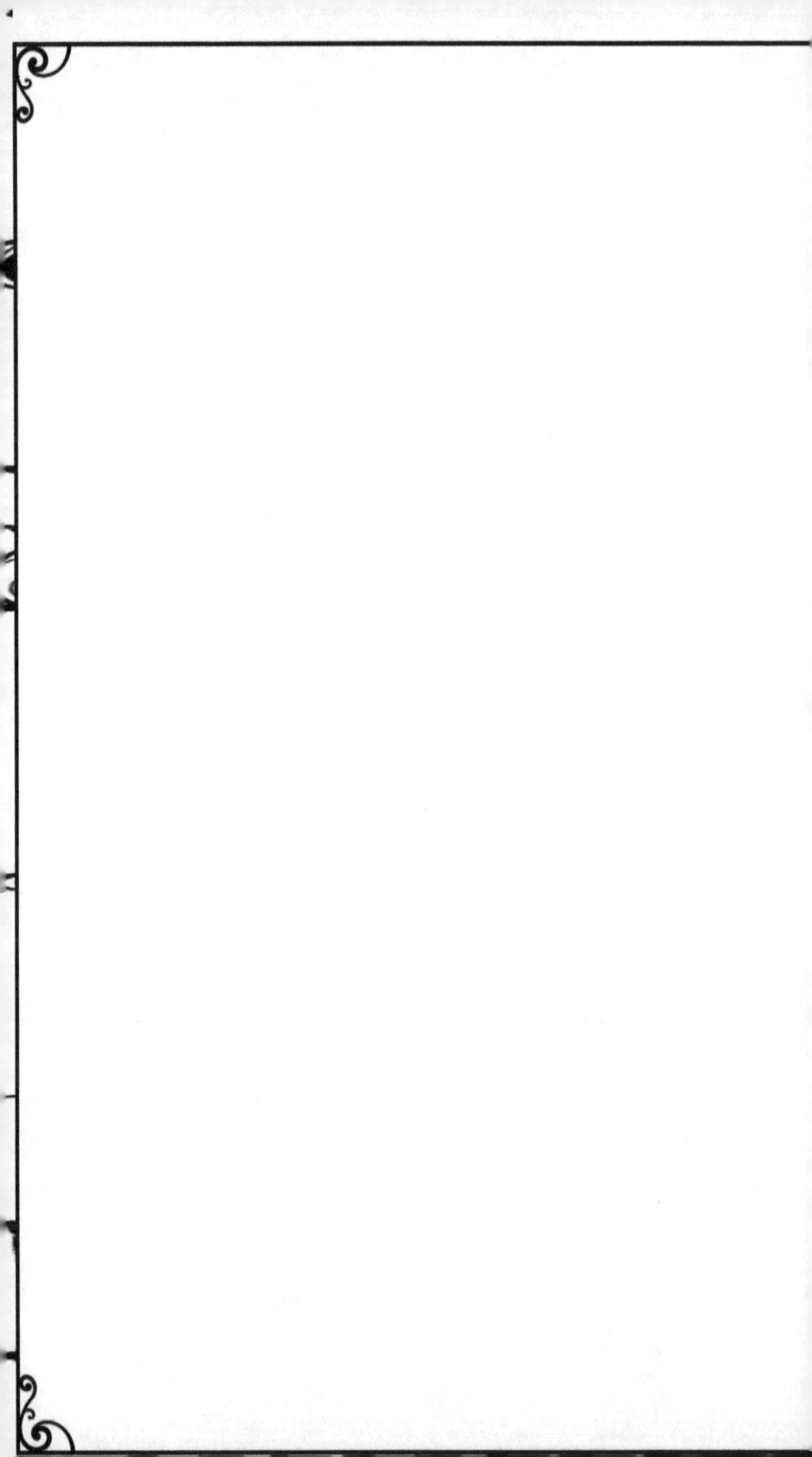

More Books by Selina A Fenech

Shadow Dragon Saga

Into a haunted realm a creature unlike any is born, and
must be protected. Diverse young adult epic fantasy
with dragons and magic

Memory's Wake Trilogy

A modern girl lost in and hunted in a fairy tale world.
An illustrated young adult portal fantasy with
Arthurian and Victorian themes.

Empath Chronicles

Teenagers with superpowers fueled by emotions ... what
could go wrong? A young adult superhero romance.

Fairy Tale Wishes

Romantic fairy tale retellings with a twist.
Young adult, standalone paranormal romance in
urban and epic fantasy settings

About the Author

Professional daydreamer, Selina A. Fenech writes "adorably dark" Epic and Urban Fantasy for teens and adults. Filled with sweet and quirky characters, laugh out loud moments, and perilous adventures, her magical worlds are perfect for readers who love daring twists and happily ever afters.

A cancer survivor determined to live life to the fullest, she is an escape room enthusiast, avid gardener, foodie and self-proclaimed geek, residing in Australia.

In addition to literature, Selina applies her unique take on the dichotomy of light and dark as a professional fantasy artist working under the name Selina Fenech and has published many illustrated books, oracle decks, and colouring books.

Find Out more About Selina

OFFICIAL WEBSITE:www.selinafenech.com